SOPHIE LARK

WHERE TO START

romantic suspense

BRUTAL BIRTHRIGHT
1. BRUTAL PRINCE
2. STOLEN HEIR

dark romance

SINNERS DUET
1. THERE ARE NO SAINTS
2. THERE IS NO DEVIL

fantasy

ANASTASIA

MY WEBSITE   AMAZON   PATREON

INTERIOR ART: LINE MARIA ERIKSEN
INSTAGRAM: @LINEMERIKSEN

COVER DESIGN: EMILY WITTIG
INSTAGRAM: @EMILY_WITTIG_DESIGNS

MINX

SOPHIE LARK

This is for everyone who's been all the way to the bottom.
Keep climbing, the sun is up there waiting for you.

Xoxo

Sophie Lark

1. Go To Town - Doja Cat
2. WHOLE LOTTA MONEY - BIA
3. Kream (feat. Tyga) - Iggy Azalea
4. 7 rings - Ariana Grande
5. Weekend (feat. Miguel) - Mac Miller
6. Chemical - Post Malone
7. So Pretty - Reyanna Maria
8. Turn Up - S3nsi Molly
9. Freak - Doja Cat
10. Power - G-Eazy
11. Woman - Emmit Fenn
12. Like Real People Do - Hozier
13. LOVE. FEAT. ZACARI. - Kendrick Lamar
14. Wait 2.0 - NoMBe

Music is a big part of my writing process. If you start a song when you see a 🎶 while reading, the song matches the scene like a movie score.

Spotify

Apple Music

Whoever said money can't solve your problems
Must not have had enough money to solve 'em

— Ariana Grande

Bocca baciate non perda ventura; anzi rinnova come fa la luna

The mouth that has been kissed loses not its freshness;
still it renews itself even as does the moon

— Giovanni Boccaccio, *Decameron*

1

RAMSES HOWELL

Today's my favorite day of the year, and it's already ruined because Anthony Keller just walked in with the most stunning woman I've ever seen on his arm.

The Belmont Stakes are one of the only things that get me excited anymore. Last night it rained just enough for the grass to smell like a rainforest and the dirt to turn over like velvet. I'm in the presidential suite, best seats in the house, the finish line right under my nose.

And here comes Keller, strolling in with the one and only thing that could make me give a shit what he's doing next door.

My head turns. The way a racehorse looks running—how the muscles flex and flow under the coat—that's how her body looks inside her dress. It's a modest dress otherwise, up to the neck, long sleeves. Only the curves make it outrageous.

Her face isn't what I expected. Beautiful, yes, but the word that pops into my head is "serious." She's focused, unsmiling, until she catches me looking. Then her mouth quirks with something I can't read—amusement? Disdain?

She steps into Keller's suite.

I'm left with a cold drink and the heat of being caught like an amateur. I know how to glance at a pretty girl and then turn away to examine the image in my mind. It was that goddamn body in motion that kept me staring so long.

"Every dog has his day." Briggs takes a pull of his beer, watching Keller whoop it up next door with disgust. "I fucking hate seeing that mutt happy though."

Some people Briggs hates just because I hate them. Some, he has his own reasons. Keller's both.

He was your classic balding tech nerd with a start-up. Now he's got hair plugs and a personal trainer and he's strutting around like King Shit 'cause his company goes public tomorrow.

I want to ask Briggs about the girl, but that's admitting out loud Keller did something good. Right now, I wouldn't say I liked the color of his socks.

Instead, I tell Briggs, "Next year I want both suites and I want them connected."

Briggs makes that grunting nod that means he's filing away some task I've asked him to do. He doesn't write it down, but he always gets it done. No questions, no excuses, Briggs delivers.

That's why he's my right hand, and I mean that about as literal as it gets. He does all the work I'd do if I had an extra hand. I trust him to act as me, for me. He's the only person I trust like that. If Briggs were to die or retire, there wouldn't be another hand. I'd just have everybody else who works for me.

"Here comes Bosch," Briggs mutters.

John Bosch is sitting in my box, but I've heard he's got his eye on Keller's company. I want to know if a deal is struck.

I want to know everything that happens at Belmont Park today when the air's thick with money. Everybody has chips on the table, amped on the adrenaline of knowing someone's going home a winner. Alcohol and loose lips...whether they leave thrilled or disappointed, they're less in control, and that's an opportunity for me.

I'm in the main suite, full spread on the table, every single beer made in Germany laid out on ice. All these busy little bees should be buzzing around me, information flowing in...

Instead, my own traders are sneaking next door.

"Where the fuck did Pennywise just go?" Briggs says.

He answers his own question by watching Penn duck through the doorway into Keller's suite.

"Ah."

Briggs says that syllable like he already knows exactly what's going on.

I finally crack.

"Who's the girl?"

Briggs grins. "Blake Abbot."

"Who's Blake Abbot?"

"Probably the highest paid escort in Manhattan."

My face relaxes a little. It takes the sting out of Keller bringing a girl that hot, knowing he had to pay for her. Now I'm curious instead.

"What's a night with her cost?"

Briggs grins. "There is no night with her. You have to get on her roster. It's like a country club membership."

A hooker with a business model. I kind of fucking love it.

"Can't be that exclusive if she let Keller in."

Briggs shrugs. "Vickers tried to get a seat. Offered $50k— didn't even get a phone call."

I snort. "Is her pussy gold-plated?"

Briggs picks up a prawn the size of his fist, dunks it in cocktail sauce, takes an enormous bite, and talks while still chewing.

"Fuck if I know. She makes 'em sign an NDA. But Lukas Larsen says she'll change your fucking life. Look at Keller—a year ago he could barely get a deal done. Now he's man of the hour."

"Keller ain't shit," I say with more venom than I intended.

He offered us a stake in VizTech. We turned it down after looking at his books. A week later somebody filed a complaint against us with the SEC. Took Briggs about an hour to confirm it was that spiteful little weasel.

I've got no problem with a man who swings a hatchet at my face. Business is war. But if you stab me in the back, I better never find out whose hand was on the knife.

"Who else is she seeing?"

"Zak Simmons." Briggs has the answer at the ready. He's my fixer and my attack dog, but his number one job is keeping his eye on everyone who matters.

"Larsen's having a great year. Simmons even better."

"Yeah. Well, that's what they say—date her and you run hot."

I bet they do. Finance guys are superstitious as fuck. Our whole job is numbers, but there's nothing more subject to hysteria than the stock market.

"Desmond Lowe used to see her, too—said the sex was insane, wouldn't shut up about it," Briggs smirks. "'Till she cut him loose."

Lowe's an arrogant piece of shit. The idea of him getting dumped by an escort makes me smile.

"I like her already."

"Well, don't." Briggs frowns.

"Why not?"

"Because I know how competitive you get."

I give him a sideways look. "Not over some girl."

"Right," Briggs snorts. "Just everything else."

I crane my neck, trying to peek into Keller's box. I spy a tantalizing slice of the girl's back, her shoulder, and the edge of her ear.

I don't believe in "running hot." But I am intrigued by the idea of country club sex.

Eyes on the curve of that hip, I say, "I have the best of everything else...why not that?"

"Fuck no." Briggs shakes his head.

"Why not?"

"Because what if it's really that good? And it never feels that good again? Nah, pass. I'll stick with sloppy, drunken last-call sex —the kind I can get any time I want."

Yeah. That definitely settles it.

I cross the room to grab a Reissdorf I won't be drinking. From here I can see unobstructed into the junior suite.

Keller really does look different—head up, shoulders back, tanned and almost stylish. But it's Blake Abbot who's the magnet in the room. The most important people have clustered around her. She's talking to Freidman, who runs the sixth-largest hedge fund in the city. I don't think I've seen that cold coffee-drinking vulture so much as crack a smile. Now he's got all his dentures on display, bony shoulders shaking with laughter.

If she's not careful, she'll give a coronary to a future client.

I'm revolted at my own thought.

The idea of Freidman's wrinkled old claws touching that lush body makes me want to puke.

Besides, that's dismissive. Freidman isn't hanging on her every word because he wants to fuck her—she genuinely made him laugh.

I want to know what she said.

I head out into the hallway, passing the door to the junior suite. There are no discerning words from the babble of conversation within—just the smell of too many men, threaded with a hint of her perfume. My feet lurch like I missed a step.

I watch the way she stands, how she positions her body, rests a fingertip against her jaw. The slow smile, the eye contact. She's good at what she does, really fucking good.

She's not the only woman in the room—Miriam Castro, head trader at Bridgewater, moves through the crowd like an assassin. What *really* impresses me is how Blake chats her up just as easily.

She's so natural that I almost miss the moment where she slips. Keller interrupts her conversation with Castro, placing his hand possessively on the small of her back and whispering something in her ear. Her upper lip curls, a flash of irritation she hides with a smile.

She's alluring. I don't want to be allured, I'm actively annoyed. Yet I find myself wanting to abandon my own suite to squeeze in next to Keller.

Somehow I've wandered all the way into the doorway.

Her eyes flick up. Catch mine. Hold there exactly one full second.

"Do you need anything, Mr. Howell?" An alarmed attendant appears at my elbow.

"No." I brush past him, heading back out to the bank of monitors along the wall. I've got monitors in my own suite, but I like these better all of a sudden.

I take my time scrolling the names on the screen. Asteroid, Goldfinder, Handsome Chap... I've been following them all closer than usual this year, thinking I might finally buy a racehorse of my own.

The last name on the list is a new arrival. Flightline was added this morning after Cobwebs failed the piss test. I heard about it an hour before the bookies and gave the colt worse odds in my head than they did. He's only won a single race.

I place my bet for Asteroid, the second favorite.

Heels click against tile. I smell her again, smoky, musky, barely sweet. Her perfume is spiced like tea, the skin beneath warm as honey, mellow sweet. I'd pay a lot to bottle that scent and spritz it around my house. But then I'd never get any work done.

I turn, thinking she came to talk to me. Instead, she takes a position three monitors down and places a bet.

I'm still certain she came out here for me.

I wait for her to print her ticket and turn around.

When the moment comes, it feels like a rush of air against my face.

She looked good from behind, even better straight-on. I can't tell if her eyes are blue or green.

Nobody's talking. We're sizing each other up.

I nod at her shoes, sleek and pointy and dangerous.

"I'm surprised you didn't get one of those saps to make the walk for you."

She smiles. A dimple appears and disappears like a wink. "I didn't think they could be trusted."

Her voice runs down my spine. She's holding her ticket so I can't see which horse she picked.

She's tall, I'm taller. Her breath slows the closer I get.

I step right inside her space so we're sharing the same air, so she has to tilt up her chin.

Her eyes are definitely green.

I snatch the ticket out of her hand.

That flash of anger again—I'm impressed how quickly she hides it. Even when I'm irritating her on purpose.

I say, "Flightline's forty to one. What do you know that I don't?"

"Lots of things." She snatches her ticket back. "The capital of Morocco. How to poach a perfect egg."

"What makes you think I can't poach an egg?"

"I didn't say you couldn't poach one. I said you can't do it as perfectly as me."

I pretend to be offended. "Don't underestimate me."

She smiles up at me, unflinching. "I would never."

We're standing so close there's only an inch of space between my hand and her thigh. I want to brush against her accidentally-on-purpose. I think she wants me to try. I know it's her job to act like she wants it—but like the anger, this feels real. A heat seeping out from underneath that still, smooth calm.

We haven't introduced ourselves. I know who she is, and I'd be insulted if she didn't know me.

She crosses her arms, tilts her head, lets her eyes roam from my face down to my chest and back up again. "I'm glad to see you here."

I smile. "Why's that?"

"Well, as you know, all billionaires must buy a racehorse, a race-car, or a rocket to Mars."

"I haven't bought any of those yet."

She holds up a finger, "But you will...", then drops the finger as she casts judgment, "...and I like the horse billionaires best."

It amuses me that she has preferences in billionaires.

"What's the difference?"

I have my own theory. I want to hear hers.

She ticks them off on her fingers. "Space billionaires: megalomaniacs. Nobody's too good for Earth. Formula I: that's a particular kind of psychopath, sharpening the pencil sharper, sharper, sharper by an eighth of a second 'till you go insane. But horse owners..."

I wait to be judged, wondering if she'll get me right.

"Horse owners are dreamers. Forty-four thousand foals registered every year—only sixteen make it to Belmont."

I like her theory but it's much too generous.

"They're not dreamers, they're gamblers. You crash a race-car, you write a fifteen million-dollar check and buy another one. Here you put your entire business on the line. That horse tumbles and breaks its leg, you didn't just lose your race, you lost your farm. The favorite today has a million-dollar stud fee. His owner just put a million-dollar-a-day stud fee on the track because he has to, to keep it."

"Oh, okay." Blake nods her head like she's chastened. Then quirks a smile at me. "So *you'd* never buy a horse..."

I smile back. "I didn't say that."

The pause that follows is different than the one before—this is more like uncorking a bottle of wine and letting it breathe.

I ask her, "What are you here for? And don't tell me Keller."

A secretive little smile flits across her face. "I'm here for the same thing as everyone else...to catch a rising star."

I gently mock her. "You think Flightline is the next American Pharoah?"

Her laugh doesn't give a damn what I think. "Probably not. But what's the fun of winning three to one?"

"You little minx—you looked at my screen."

"Subtler than stealing your ticket."

Keller pokes his head out of the junior suite. He sees Blake talking to me and hustles over.

"Race is about to start."

"I know," Blake says without moving.

Keller gives me a nod. "Ramses."

"Why don't you come watch from my box?" I have to extend the invitation to both of them to make sure Blake accepts. "It's got a better view of the finish."

This isn't what Keller wants at all.

"They're pretty similar," he mutters.

"Close only counts in horseshoes," I say with a wink at Blake.

I'm not always this big an asshole. But it feels good when I am.

Keller casts a look inside the suite and sees Bosch over by the buffet. Abruptly he changes his mind.

"Yeah, why not."

Fine by me. If those two want to make a deal, they're gonna have to do it sitting right next to me. Well...two seats down. I put Blake in the seat next to mine.

Briggs stands by the beer tub, giving me a slow shake of his head.

I ignore him, which is easy to do because Blake is a much more pleasant view.

Her hair is long and black and soft, but not shiny. It's so un-shiny that it almost looks like a void, like a hole you could fall into. When it brushes the back of my hand, my whole arm shiv-ers. Her nails are unpainted, filed sharp. I want them scratching down my back.

When she moves, the side of her knee presses against mine. Only one thin layer of wool separates us.

My cock is getting hard. Hard enough that in a minute people are going to notice—most especially Blake. It's hanging down the trouser leg closest to her. Every time she presses her knee against me, it throbs and swells a little more. I don't think this has happened to me since high school. It would be comical—except I really can't seem to stop it.

I guess I could get up and move away from her. But I'm not going to do that.

She's got her eyes fixed on the gates where the twelve colts have lined up. Flightline has the outside berth, the worst position.

The gates drop and the horses surge forward, two stumbling and falling behind from the start. Flightline cuts a sharp angle, moving to the inside track. His jockey is aggressive, weaving through the pack. Once the colt reaches the rail, he rides it like a freight train, hooves thundering, kicking up clods of dirt.

Asteroid got a strong start. He's fighting for the lead against Goldfinder, the favorite. I should be watching my own horse, but I can't keep my eyes off Flightline slowly moving up the rail.

Or off Blake. She's leaned forward in her seat, barely breathing, hands at her mouth.

The colts are starting to flag. They call the Belmont Stakes the "test of a champion". It's the longest dirt track in North America, a one-and-a-half mile loop. Sometimes horses sprint so hard at the start, they have to walk across the finish line.

Flightline isn't slowing down—that motherfucker's speeding up. He's a big fucker. Broad chested. If I'd seen a pic of him before the race, I might have revised my odds.

Asteroid and Goldfinder are still in the lead, a full length ahead of any other horse.

Flightline shoulders through the pack into third place. He closes the gap behind the lead horses, coming even with their heels.

"What the fuuuuuck..." Briggs groans.

The box is full of shouts and cheers, wild threats and encouragement. From Blake, not a whisper. I don't know if she's taken a breath this whole time.

Flightline's jockey leans all the way forward, almost whispering in his ear. He barrels ahead, charging straight through the gap between Asteroid and Goldfinder's surging necks.

He crosses the finish line almost a full length ahead. Blake just made $800k.

Now I expect screams or maybe for her to faint dead away.

What I see isn't shock. It isn't even excitement.

Her face glows with pure satisfaction.

Now I'm both aroused and extremely suspicious.

When the jockey pulls off her helmet, I realize she's a woman. They're all so tiny and muscled, it's hard to tell. Her grin is half her face as the officials throw the blanket of white carnations over the back of her horse.

Briggs is pissed. He put $100k down on Goldfinder but only to place, not show.

"Missing it by one's worse than coming in last."

"No, it isn't," Pennywise says glumly. His horse actually did come in last.

I can't stop watching Blake, trying to figure out what the fuck is going on. She smiles serenely while everyone congratulates her.

"How much did you bet?" Keller asks.

"Two thousand." She lies easily.

There's a lot of reasons not to tell your client you just made $800k. I have a feeling Blake's reasons aren't the ones I'm guessing.

If someone asks what I do, I say investment, but that's not really accurate. What I *do* is gather information and decide what it means.

I've been watching Blake all night.

The numbers aren't adding up.

Keller puts his hand on her waist again, reasserting his claim. She lets him do it.

Seeing them together again now isn't just irritating, it's intolerable.

"Thanks for the view," Keller says to me, looking a little too happy.

Blake puts out her hand. Mine swallows hers whole.

It's the first time our skin has actually touched. She feels exactly how she looks, like some kind of tawny animal. Soft, soft, soft with the lightest dusting of golden hair on the backs of her arms.

"It was nice meeting you," Blake says, like that's all we did.

"We'll talk later," Keller says to Bosch, like they already did.

I paid zero attention to their conversation, not even using half an ear.

That's the slap to the face I need. I don't make mistakes.

I turn my back on Blake and do *not* watch her leave, which may be the most self-sacrificing thing I've ever done.

Instead, I intercept Bosch. In ten minutes, I've got him singing about his deal with Keller, and in twenty more, he's agreed to scrap it.

Keller isn't getting his payout. Not if I can help it.

"What's that gonna cost us?" Briggs asks after Bosch leaves.

"Less than we'll make shorting the stock."

"That's aggressive. And spiteful."

"Your two favorite things."

Briggs grins. "Glad to have your head back in the game."

"It is. One hundred percent. Except..."

Briggs groans, swiping his hand down over his face.

I say, "You ever seen someone celebrate like that winning forty to one?"

Briggs shrugs. "Desmond calls her the Lucky Whore."

Heat flares in the pit of my stomach.

I don't like that. I don't even like that I called her a hooker in my head earlier. That word didn't suit her at all when we spoke.

"Lucky?" I snort. "She had a fix. I want you to find out everything you can about her."

Briggs looks like he's slowly swallowing down every single annoyance he's ever had with me. It takes a long time.

At last, he gives his little grunt.

"Sure thing, boss."

2

BLAKE ABBOT

The best way to hunt big game is to lure it.

Ramses Howell is the biggest game in town. His investment firm isn't the largest, but it's had the highest returns the last four years running. Once is lucky. Twice is impressive. Four times...fucking unheard of.

I'd had my eye on him for a while. This was my first time in a room with him.

Technically I was supposed to be in the room next door. I made sure he saw me on the way in and it didn't take long to tempt him out of his box. He was aggressive, rude. Exactly what I expected. Until he wasn't.

I'd heard he was persuasive. Nobody mentioned that he can persuade you before he opens his mouth. They say he's big, but that doesn't give you the sense of hands that could eat you and shoulders that block out the sun.

He was charming and intimidating. The charm was for me, the intimidation for Keller. Or maybe they were both for me. All I know is it was slightly terrifying watching him bully Keller into abandoning his own suite party.

Talking with him is like boxing a bear. I didn't know if I was going to get cuddled or mauled.

And goddamn him for snatching my ticket! He's faster than he looks.

I'd planned to tell everybody I bet the favorite. Now Ramses knows how much I won. I'm sure he's suspicious. I should have behaved differently—fake cried or something.

You can practice and prepare for so many things. Never everything.

I sure as hell didn't expect to log into my brokerage account this morning and find myself three million dollars richer.

Somebody made a wire transfer last night around midnight.

The transfer is anonymous, but the memo line reads: *I want all three seats.*

I knew Ramses was going to be trouble. It's why I've never taken a shot at him before.

You know what happens to the guy in the movie who thinks he's ready to hunt the T-Rex? It never ends well.

On the other hand...I love a man who knows how to tempt me.

Ramses calls as I'm sitting down to tea and toast. A strange number pops up and my stomach drops. The couple of seconds I'm staring at the screen feel like an eternity.

I thought I wanted this. I did everything I could to get it.

Now that it's here, I'm fucking terrified.

I pick up, praying my voice sounds steady.

"That was fast."

I hear him on the other end of the line—the deep sound of his breathing, the weight of this man that somehow comes all the way through the phone.

"It doesn't take me long to decide when I see something I want."

"I'm flattered."

Actually, I'm a little bit pissed. How in the fuck did he find my brokerage account?

With an edge of impatience, Ramses says, "But are you accepting?"

I take a sip of my tea and set down the mug.

"I don't have any openings at the moment. I only see three clients at a time."

Even more impatient, like a judge dropping a gavel: "Cut them loose. I don't share."

This is a man who hasn't heard the word 'no' in a very long time.

The pleasure of denying him is almost sweeter than all those zeroes in my account.

"That's not how this works. There's a waitlist. And I *never* see clients exclusively."

Rule number one. The one you don't break.

The heat in Ramses' voice is nowhere near as contained as he'd like to believe.

"Don't use the word *never* in a negotiation."

Don't tell me what to do.

I swallow my anger and force a smile, hoping Ramses can hear it in my voice as I say, "This isn't a negotiation. If you don't follow my rules, I'm not interested in doing business with you."

Then I hang up the phone.

My hands are sweating and my heart could punch a hole through my chest.

I'm not actually confident. Not even a little bit.

But I'm a damn good actress.

I TAKE the subway back to Belmont Park. Sadie is exercising Flightline on one of the smaller tracks, taking him around at barely more than a walk to work out the lactic acid from the race. She spots me in the stands and trots over.

Her nose is sunburned and peeling, bits of blonde hair poking out of her stubby braids like straw. Her smile makes Times Square look dim.

I lean over the railing to hug her.

"You fucking savage. The way you shouldered through the two in the lead—"

"It was a risk splittin' the biscuit." She grins. "But I could feel Flighty was just getting going."

"Heart of a champion," I say, patting him on the nose.

"Heart of a blue whale," Sadie laughs. "I think he could've run the track twice over."

"Buy him a melon on me." I try to pass Sadie an envelope. Watermelons are Flightline's favorite.

She shakes her head vigorously, shoving the money right back.

"I won the big purse, I don't need that."

"I don't care." I stuff it down the front of her shirt. "I always pay for good information."

"You don't have to pay *me*." Sadie is offended.

"Of course I'm gonna pay you. You think I'd stiff my own sister?"

I knew that would work.

Sadie takes the envelope out of her shirt, folds it in half, stows it carefully in her pocket. Her face is deeply pink and she's blinking hard. "I like when you call me that."

Sometimes I can still see Sadie's childish face inside her adult one. She'll make a certain expression and the way she looked at six or eleven will rise to the surface before disappearing again. It makes my chest hurt in the strangest way because all those other Sadies are still there inside her, but they're also gone forever.

"You *are* my sister," I tell her, "and I'm so fucking proud of you."

"Ah," Sadie makes a flapping motion with her hands that means if I say anything else she's gonna lose it. Sadie is deeply uncomfortable with compliments. "What about you up in the main box!"

"Oh, you saw that?" I pretend to examine my nails.

"'Course I did. Who's the big guy?"

I smile to myself, remembering the thrill of hanging up on the most dangerous man in the city.

"He's..." *Devious. Vindictive. A huge mistake.* "A new acquaintance."

"Client?"

"Possibly."

"Rich?"

"Extremely."

"Well...let me know if he's got any hot friends." Sadie's smile goes watery.

"Joel didn't—"

"Yeah." She wipes her nose on the back of her hand. "Dumped me this morning."

"BASTARD!" That was louder than I intended. Several trainers turn their heads. Ten percent quieter, I add, "He's fucking jealous, you know that, right?"

Sadie sighs. "They all think it's fun to date another jockey 'till I steal a purse."

"You didn't steal it. You earned it."

"Either way...single again," Sadie says dully.

I'm beyond pissed that Joel tarnished the win for her—he couldn't have waited a couple of days to split up?

"We'll get you back on the horse." That's a pun and I don't care. "A better horse. Not some finance douche—I'll find you somebody nice."

"I don't need 'nice' for a rebound." Sadie's grin is already resurfacing. "I just need them to have a big cock."

"Well...that's why we don't date jockeys."

Sadie laughs, giving Flightline a little nudge with her heels. "You'd be surprised."

I would love for a man to surprise me in a good way for once.

And don't tell me Ramses did this morning...whether anything *good* comes from Ramses remains to be seen.

I'M STILL AMPED to the ten thousandth degree on my date with Zak Simmons. He's been talking nonstop from the moment I got in his car, and I haven't heard a word of it because I keep replaying Ramses' phone call over and over in my head.

What he meant...what I could have said...and why in the fuck I ever thought it was a good idea to attract his attention.

I got greedy. High on my own success.

Simmons ordered the appetizers without asking what I wanted. I don't give a shit, I'm not even hungry, but my brain is a calculator and it always keeps score.

He's been a client of mine for about a year now. He pays the most. He's also the most boring, which is why I charge him the highest fee. Call it a Tedious Tax. I wish I could raise it every time he mentions his ex-wife's boyfriend.

Aiden came in the picture last month. He's got long hair and a motorcycle. I wish I could compliment Simmons' ex for finding such a perfect way of getting under his skin. He must have told me twenty times how much he doesn't care and how it doesn't bother him at all.

"He's taking *my* kid to a Mets game using *my* season tickets!"

"Parker doesn't like baseball," I remind him. "You should take him to see *Hamilton*."

"I hate Broadway," Simmons says, not giving a shit that his kid feels the exact opposite.

I haven't met said kid, but I keep files on all my clients. After each date I make notes of anything they tell me, so I probably have a better idea of what Simmons' son is into these days than he does.

My phone vibrates in my lap with a notification. I glance down and see that Keller's stock has dropped another ten points. His IPO's in a nosedive. VizTech is worth half as much as when it went live this morning.

"Why are you smiling?" Simmons asks.

"Because today was your big lunch meeting."

"You remembered." Simmons looks gratified.

No, I just wrote it down. Now we can talk about what actually interests me.

"How did it go?"

"Knocked it out of the park." Simmons happily spears a prawn from the plate between us. "Should close the deal by the end of the week."

I've got a source that says otherwise.

Before I can press for details, a shadow falls across my plate. A very large shadow.

"Blake." The exact tone of his voice seems to melt everything inside me. "We didn't finish our conversation."

I turn slowly to give myself time to think.

Ramses stands behind me in an all-black suit, looking like he's here to carry out a hit on me. They say he grew up rough in Bushwick, and I think he cultivates that image on purpose—hands of a boxer, permanent five o'clock shadow.

It's working on Simmons. He sets his prawn down uneaten and gulps his wine instead. "I didn't know you two knew each other."

"I'm at dinner," I inform Ramses coldly.

"I'll join you."

He grabs a chair from the next table and drags it over, dropping all that mass onto four spindly legs. The maître d' watches him do it and says absolutely nothing. It takes a year for a pleb to get a reservation at this place, but they'd probably let Ramses stroll into the kitchen and cook himself a grilled cheese.

Power is doing whatever you want and nobody dares tell you no.

Pleasure is looking a powerful man in the face and telling him to fuck off.

"Ramses," I say sweetly. "Fuck off. I'm on a date."

Hanging up on him felt good.

Cursing at him is positively erotic.

My whole body throbs, all the hair standing up on my arms, the smell of the orchids in the vase between us like a punch in the face. He's huge, he's fucking scary, and he's six inches away, changing the temperature in the room—my left arm is warmer than my right.

Simmons glances between us, trying to figure out what's going on.

Ramses isn't pissed that I told him to fuck off. Actually, I'm one hundred percent sure he liked it. He hasn't broken eye contact for a second. Even when he dragged the chair over, he stared me down the whole time.

His voice is a bass speaker set flush against my spine. "We haven't finished negotiating."

"We haven't started. And we're not going to—I'm busy."

"That's fine." Ramses leans back in his chair. It makes a cracking sound beneath him. Not a little creak—an actual snap. He doesn't seem worried. I'm waiting for the whole thing to collapse.

He rests one heavy arm on the table, his fingertip just barely touching the tine of Simmons' fork. He's got huge hands but they're not clumsy like you'd expect; they're nicely shaped, just really fucking big. Each movement is intentional, including the touching of the fork. Ramses is a line-crosser and an instigator. Everything he does is to set you on edge.

"I'm not here to talk to you," he tells me. "Yet."

He swings around and stares down my dinner date instead.

"You've been looking for somebody to save you on that Allscape deal...my firm will do it and we'll set the price at $90 a share if you get up and leave right now."

Simmons is no pushover. He's a shark who kills and eats in the blood-red waters of Manhattan every single day.

I expect him to bite back. Or at least put up a fight.

"Sorry, Blake," he mutters as he vacates his seat.

Just like that, the asset I spent a *year* cultivating evaporates into thin air.

All that's left is the man taking up the other half of the table.

Ramses picks up Simmons' wine and finishes it. "Where were we?"

I'm fucking furious. I'd like to take my merlot and throw it in his face.

He sees how angry I am. He quits grinning and sits up in his chair, holding up his hands like he thinks I might take a pop at him. "Alright, that was a little heavy."

"You rolled right in with the tanks."

Each word that comes out of my mouth is a stick of dynamite. If Ramses lights one more spark...

He keeps his voice carefully neutral.

"I had to create an opening on your roster." A hint of amusement creeps through. "Though maybe I should have waited for Keller's spot...I don't think he's going to be able to afford you much longer. Hope he wasn't paying you in stock."

"I hope you don't think I'd hold it."

The words are out before I can stop myself. Ramses pauses half a second to file that away.

Fuck, fuck, FUCK! He's so goddamn infuriating. I'm making mistakes.

"I overstepped," Ramses says. "Can we start over?"

His hair is so dark I expected brown eyes, but actually they're blue. Blue like the sky at night—deep indigo with glittering pinpricks like distant stars.

I think I'm experiencing the exact sensation of a person who just strapped themselves to a rocket and lit the fuse.

I say, "I'm keeping the three million."

"And what does that get me?"

"It gets you a first date."

That wicked smile is already spreading across his face again. I lean across the table and look him right in the eye.

"Let me make myself clear—you fuck around like that again, you try to intimidate my other clients, and the closest you'll get to me is a glance across a crowded room. I do NOT work with people who don't respect my boundaries."

"Understood." Ramses' smile is better hidden now but I see it lurking at the edges of his eyes, the corners of his mouth. "What are your rules?"

I'm starting to suspect he only wants to know so he can trample them.

"Three rules," I tell him. "Clear as glass, hard as iron. I'm not exclusive, I don't sleep over, and 'red' means 'stop,' no matter where we are or what we're doing."

Ramses gives the kind of nod that's more acknowledgement than agreement. "What if I want to take you on a trip?"

"Separate rooms. I sleep alone at the end of the night."

"Suits me fine. There's never much extra room in the bed."

The thought of Ramses sprawled across a king-sized mattress makes my thighs clench.

He picks up the wine bottle, pouring the remainder into my glass. Then he presses the stem into my hand, his fingers trapping mine.

"How often can I have you?"

I take a heavy swallow, trying to obliterate the throbbing sensation low in my guts.

I'm a professional. A goddamn professional.

"As often as I pick up."

"Do you see your favorite clients more?"

Now it's my turn to smile. "Of course."

"Good." Ramses leans all the way back in his chair, arms folded comfortably over his chest. "If I'm not your only client, I'm damn sure gonna be your favorite."

I look at him sprawled out in his seat, his ego filling half the restaurant.

"I'm not sure you'll last a week."

Ramses laughs. "And what about me? What if I'm not happy?"

I toss back the rest of my wine, setting down the empty glass. "The only men I've disappointed are the ones I've dropped as clients."

Low and soft, he says, "I'm nothing like them."

"That's what all men say."

"Try me." Ramses leans forward, his chair groaning beneath him. "I don't go once. I don't go twice. I go until I'm satisfied."

The images flooding through my head would get a nun excommunicated.

"I can't wait to see that."

Ramses' gaze is a bath and I'm a sponge soaking up water, heavy and warm from my head to my toes.

"Blake...I think you and I are going to be friends for a long time."

I thought he'd say, *I think you and I are going to have a lot of fun together.* The actual end of that sentence puts a stupid surprised look on my face.

The waiter arrives with my carbonara and the porterhouse ordered by Simmons. He stares confusedly at the empty seat across from me and the massive form of Ramses that has materialized instead.

"We don't need that." Ramses passes him a credit card.

"I needed mine," I remark as the waiter carries away the food.

"No, you don't."

"'Cause you have a sandwich stuffed in your pocket?"

Ramses stands up from the table, shoving back his chair. "Because we're going somewhere better."

"Don't let the chef hear you say that."

"He'd probably agree—if he was being honest."

Now I'm all the way curious and up on my feet.

"Where are we going?"

Ramses takes my hand and tucks it into the crook of his arm in a gesture that should be chivalrous but feels captive instead.

"We're going on our first date."

3

RAMSES

"You drive yourself around?" Blake says when she sees the Lincoln pulled up to the curb.

"Mostly." *Always.*

I hold the door open for her so I can watch her climb inside and also 'cause you have to slam it shut pretty hard.

When I slide in behind the wheel, she's looking around the interior at the dials, gearshift, oxblood seats. It's the same way she swept the room on her way into the Belmont Stakes. What's she looking for?

I already know the answer because it's the same thing I look for when I enter a room: she's gathering information.

"What's your verdict?"

Her eyes flick over to me quick like she knows she got caught. Without apology, she smiles and says, "Do you really want to know?"

"Hit me, I can take it."

She watches my hands as I start the car, shift gears, and pull into traffic. "I'm starting to think you love it."

I give her a stern look. "Don't even think about it. You won't be walking all over me in pointy shoes like Lukas Larsen—you're not getting off that easy."

A slight raise of an eyebrow is all that earns me. Her reactions are subtle; I have to watch close.

"I have no idea what you're talking about."

"It's okay, he told me himself. Well, he told Briggs and that's the same thing."

Her laugh makes me want to do very bad things.

"Does the information flow the other way? Will you tell Briggs all my secrets?"

No, but he told me yours.

"Don't change the subject."

She turns her head so instead of her profile I'm viewing her straight on. The way she uses eye contact is maddening—she doesn't look at me as often as I'd like.

"I would never discuss what I do with my other clients."

Not, *I don't discuss.* She says, *I would NEVER,* like it's a matter of deepest honor.

She's a tiger attacking me every time I approach her boundaries.

I haven't kissed her yet and I'm wondering how long I should wait.

"No problem." I lay my arm across the back of the bench seat. When I'm done switching lanes, I leave it there. Her hair hangs over one shoulder. My fingertips brush the bare nape of her neck. "We've got better things to talk about."

"Like you," she says.

"That's right." I smile.

She casts one more look around the car. This one is theatrical, to make me sweat. She touches the tiny St. Christopher's medallion on the rear-view mirror. It feels like she pressed her finger against my breastbone where it used to sit.

"I guess the easy answer is that you don't want people to think you became just another rich douchebag. A vintage car's less flashy than a McLaren."

"But you'd never go with the easy answer."

"Not this time." She rests her hand on the fifty-year-old dash. "It could be sentimental—your grandpa's old car..." She shakes her head sadly. "But I'm afraid it's so much worse than that."

"Diagnose me, doctor."

Softly, softly, like fingers stroking down my spine, she murmurs, "It's all about control. No one can drive this car but you."

I don't know if she's right, but the idea excites me. I shift through ancient gears that only answer to my touch, then I rest the full weight of my hand against the base of her neck.

"I like to be in charge."

"In the boardroom and the bedroom?"

"*Especially* in the bedroom."

Her knees are turned toward me, her elbow resting on the door. The car seals us off from the rest of the world like an isolation chamber.

We've already agreed to fuck—somehow that only makes the tension between us ten times higher. Now I'm obsessing over exactly when and how I want to do it. I'm not gonna tear the wrapping off this gift—I want to open it up nice and slow.

Blake's smile rarely shows her teeth. "I can't say I'm surprised."

"What would I have to do to surprise you?"

"I don't know yet. I haven't finished my analysis."

"We're not going to make it to dinner if you keep talking dirty to me."

Blake laughs, watching the rows of brownstones spooling past her window. "You keep promising food, but I feel like we're driving away from it..."

I pull up in front of what is very clearly a house and not a restaurant.

"You don't trust me?"

"Not really."

"Smart girl."

She doesn't wait for me to come around the car and open her door, stepping out onto the sidewalk and gazing up at the sandstone facade with its overflowing window boxes of herbs.

"Please tell me you're not taking me to meet your mother."

"You'll never meet my mother."

"I know," Blake says coolly. "That was a joke."

"I didn't mean—" I stop, trying to still the churning in my guts. "It has nothing to do with you."

"Okay." Blake accepts that without comment. "So what are we here for?"

I shove the thought of my mother back where it belongs and force a smile. "It's a poached egg competition."

Excitement flickers in Blake's face. "Oh, you're in so much trouble..."

She hurries up the steps.

The door pops open before we reach the top.

"Ramses!" April Izard bursts onto the stoop, already dressed in her black chef's coat, candy-colored tattoos visible beneath the rolled-up cuffs. "And this must be Blake."

Blake has stopped dead three steps down, mouth hanging open.

"Oh my god."

April grins. She's used to it. "Get inside before Nina escapes."

She shoves her Bobtail back inside with her foot. The cat leaps neatly over April's sneaker and bolts down the steps. Blake scoops her up and passes her back.

"Thanks." April kisses the top of Nina's head. "She's an escape artist."

Blake still looks stunned. More stunned than I was hoping, actually. She follows April inside a townhouse overflowing with plants and the smell of spices.

April takes us to the kitchen. Her counters are butcher block, her appliances the size of a small spaceship.

Faintly, Blake says, "I watched your show every day."

"You're an OG." April sets Nina down by the window. Nina promptly disappears behind the curtains.

"What show?" I'm surprised I don't know what they're talking about.

"It was just on YouTube," April says, pulling supplies out of her pantry and arranging them neatly on the spotless kitchen island.

"It was my comfort hour," Blake says. "I missed it when you stopped."

"Got too busy at Tankers."

Tankers was the first gastropub in New York. Or as April likes to say, the start of her first ulcer.

"April's opening a new place in Midtown," I tell Blake.

"*We're* opening it," April corrects me.

Blake gives me a look like she's finally impressed. "What kind of food?"

"Asian-inspired small plates."

She gives a low sound of anticipation that makes my balls go tight. "I'll be your first customer."

April has finished laying out all the supplies we'll need for our dinner. She passes us each an apron and tells us to wash our hands.

Blake and I stand side-by-side at the double sink, dutifully lathering. When she bends her head, I spot a tattoo behind her left ear. I can't tell what it is—from this angle, it just looks like a squiggly line.

"I can't believe you know April Izard," she mutters.

I can't believe my good luck that Blake is apparently a massive stan. For the first time, she's completely discomposed, cheeks flushed, hands shaking.

"Should I be jealous?" I growl.

Blake laughs softly. "No. Her show just...meant a lot to me."

"Hurry up, slowpokes!" April calls. "If you were my line cooks, you'd be demoted to dishwashers already."

Blake hustles over to the island and takes her place in front of her cutting board, hair tied back, apron neatly knotted. She's wearing the dress she put on for Zak Simmons, soft, black, and clinging. I'm wondering if she would have worn the same thing for me. The material looks velvety. I want to run my hand down her back.

"Ramses!" April raps my knuckles with a wooden spoon. "Cut your shallots!"

Blake laughs. Hers are already half finished, a uniform pile of transparent slivers. I don't even know what we're making.

"Thai basil has a bolder flavor than Italian basil," April says, rolling up the herbs plucked fresh from her window box and shaving off curling ribbons of the dark green leaves. "We'll use day-old rice because it'll soak up more of the sauce and won't clump together as much."

By the time we're sautéing shrimp, I've figured out that we're cooking Thai fried rice. April demonstrates each step. Blake and I imitate with varying levels of success.

I'm trying to copy exactly what April does, down to the way she deseeds the chilis. Blake is less precise, throwing an extra chili and a handful of diced red pepper into her pan.

"Bad girl. You're not following instructions."

She raises an eyebrow. "I'm surprised you are."

"I know when to take the experts' advice."

"Spoken like a titan of industry."

Even her compliments sound like mockery.

I keep thinking about the file Briggs dropped on my desk—everything he found out about Blake in twenty-four hours. There was less information than he usually digs up, but still several nuggets I doubt she'd want me to know.

Now I'm in a dilemma because I have questions and I can't ask them without giving myself away.

I start with a few soft pitches to see if she'll answer honestly.

"You from New York?"

"I grew up in Coney Island."

"Is your family still there?"

Blake's knife goes still above her basil. Quietly she says, "I don't have much family. I was raised in foster care. But I think you already know that."

My stomach gives a guilty roll.

"I run background checks on everyone. It's nothing personal."

Blake resumes cutting her basil, still not looking at me. "I assumed you would."

But she didn't expect that to come up.

April's over by the sink scrubbing out the shrimp pan.

Quickly, I say, "Don't worry, it was clean enough."

Minus your juvie record.

Blake sets down her knife, turning to face me. Her anger charges the air around our heads.

"I don't care what you found. You don't know anything about me."

"I know you're self-made. I knew it the moment we met."

That disarms her, or at least takes the edge off. She picks up the knife again without seeming like she wants to stab me with it. "That matters to you?"

"I respect it. I know what it takes to go from where we started to this zip code."

"You know what it took for *you*," Blake says.

She cuts her basil into tinier and tinier pieces until it's green confetti.

"Hey," I say, and I wait until she looks at me. "I'm sorry. It was shitty to ask like that when I already knew the answer."

Blake sighs, deflating like a balloon. "It's okay."

She glances at April's back. April is taking a very long time with the shrimp pan, probably on purpose.

"Thank you," Blake says quietly. "For bringing me here. I used to watch her videos, watch her wrangling all these exotic ingredients I'd never heard of. April was so good at describing them, what they smell like, what they taste like.... I'd never tried avocado or cilantro. I think I was twenty the first time I had steak."

Her eyes are huge and hungry in her heart-shaped face.

An image flashes in my head of the seventh-grade lunch lady informing me that my account balance was -$22 and I couldn't take anything else until it was paid. Shame lighting my face on fire while I walked all the way back down the line to return my empty tray...

"I used to imagine I'd have a kitchen like this someday," Blake gazes around at the double fridge, the stainless-steel exhaust hood, the dangling rows of copper pots. "Where I could cook anything I wanted."

"What's your kitchen like now?"

"Nice. Not as nice as this."

"What's your dream kitchen?"

"I want a castle," she says at once. "An actual castle, falling down on the outside, modern on the inside."

I laugh. "No one will accuse you of thinking small."

"You said my *dream* kitchen." Blake is unperturbed. "If I'm gonna dream, I'm gonna dream big."

April shuts off the water, drying her hands on a towel.

"The moment of truth," she announces.

She's got two pots of water gently boiling on the stove.She shows us how to swirl the water with a spoon, then drop a cracked egg directly into the bubbling whirlpool.

Blake does it perfectly, first try.

"Told you." She winks.

I'm determined to make the best goddamn poached egg this kitchen has ever seen. I swirl the water into a boiling tornado and drop in my egg. It immediately breaks apart.

"Well, fuck."

"Try again," April says. "With a little less vigor."

My second egg is acceptable enough to take its place atop my pile of fried rice.

Blake plates her food next to mine, sprinkling her basil confetti around the rim.

"Garnish won't save you," I warn.

"Neither will your bankroll," Blake retorts. "You've already invested in April's restaurant."

April chortles. "That's right, Ramses—completely impartial judge over here."

We watch wide-eyed while she samples our dishes. April knows exactly how to do it since she herself has been a contestant on Iron Chef no less than four times.

She cuts into Blake's egg. The yolk oozes out over the rice, rich as liquid gold. My egg falls into two halves, solid all the way through.

"Not a good sign," Blake remarks.

"It's not over yet."

April takes a bite of my rice without any overcooked egg. She chews slowly.

"Well?"

"Hold on." She takes a forkful of Blake's rice.

I've never waited so long for someone to swallow.

"Sorry Ramses," she says. "Not even close."

Blake laughs way too hard. She and April give each other the kind of handshake fist-bump that makes it seem like *they're* the ones who've been friends all along. What the hell is going on?

I snatch up a fork, take a bite of Blake's rice and then mine. *Fuck.* It's better.

I turn on April instead. "I did exactly what you said!"

"You've got to taste it while you're seasoning," April informs me for the very first time.

I eat another bite of Blake's rice, then a couple more. It's sweeter and spicier and saltier than mine. The egg's better, too.

Blake snatches back her plate. "Loser eats his own shitty food."

"Was that the bet?" April looks disappointed. "I was hoping he was going to have to run naked through the stock exchange."

Blake laughs. "Where were you when we were setting terms?"

"This was a bet of honor," I say. "And sadly, I'm disgraced."

"Don't worry," Blake smiles. "I'll give you a chance to redeem yourself."

REDEMPTION TAKES the form of a Bombe Alaska that involves so much sampling of the rum that our flambé becomes a bonfire. April gives me the win since mine is slightly less burnt than Blake's. She's probably just sucking up—I may have already invested in her restaurant, but she's still trying to hit me up for top-of-the-line ranges.

"Time for *your* dinner, grumpy," April says, scooping up Nina and carrying her into the pantry to be fed.

Blake and I stand side by side at the sink washing dishes.

"Do you always go all out on dates?"

She says it light and easy, but there's a note of vulnerability beneath. Tonight feels special—she's wondering if it actually was.

"This is the only one I've had in a year."

She snorts. "I don't believe you."

"I'm not saying I don't fuck around. I'm saying I don't date."

"Why not?"

"I don't have time."

She flicks that away like the nonsense it is. "Everyone has the same number of hours in the day."

"I don't prioritize it, then."

"Neither do I." Blake rinses a plate and sets it in the rack to dry.

"Why not?"

She shrugs. "They never like what I do for a job, and anyway, I like my space. As soon as I got my own apartment, I told myself I'd never live with someone else again."

I hadn't considered that she might have an actual real-life boyfriend. He's lucky he doesn't exist.

"What was your longest relationship?"

"A year," she says. "Yours?"

"Three years."

"Wow."

"It was in high school." I brush that aside, much more interested in talking about Blake. I probably shouldn't ask the next question, but I have to. "Have you ever dated a client? I mean, really dated them."

"Once."

The kitchen gets hot, the last of the rum burning in the back of my throat.

"What happened?"

Blake dries the blade of a chef's knife carefully, the edge glinting against the towel.

"I learned my lesson."

I want to ask who it was, but I think I already know.

The only men I've disappointed are the ones I've dropped as clients...

Desmond calls her the Lucky Whore...

The fact that Blake might have actually had feelings for that dickbag puts a ball of heat down low in my guts.

I want to take her home with me. I want it so bad that every tick of the clock on the kitchen wall is a delicious kind of torture.

I could take her to a hotel this minute, but the problem is, I haven't entirely figured out what I want to do to her.

I don't just want to fuck Blake. Fucking is easy. Fucking is meaningless.

I want to open her up like an engine. Put her through her paces like a pony.

I want to make her break her own rules and then punish her for setting them in the first place.

Blake was right about me: I crave control.

The more she fights, the more she resists, the more I want it.

A woman's body isn't half the mystery of her mind. I see the emotions flickering like firelight behind her eyes—spite, amusement, desire—and I know the fantasies locked inside her brain can only be darker.

How do I break in?

Blake acts like her key is money, but I spotted that lie the day we met. She didn't get hot for that $800k. Not even for three million.

What is it, then? What will it take?

Whatever it is, I'll find it.

I'll creep inside the darkest part of her mind and find that one desperate need that will put her completely in my power.

And that's exactly what she *doesn't* want to give me.

So I'll have to trick her.

Blake tucks her hair behind her ear with soapy fingers. I can see her tattoo better now—a simple line drawing, ears and a tail, the slope of a back. A tiny cat.

An idea begins to form in the most devious part of my brain.

"Are you free Friday night?"

Blake gives me a cautious look. "I could be."

"I'll send a car to pick you up at seven."

She sets the last of the plates in the rack, neatly folding her dishtowel. "What should I bring?"

"Just yourself."

Something in my tone makes her suspicious. She slowly unties the strings of her apron. "Am I coming over to your place?"

"Nervous?" I tease.

"Not nervous. Curious."

"About what?"

"Your fantasies." She slips the apron over her head and hangs it over the back of a chair. "What does Ramses want that he doesn't already have..."

I laugh. "Nothing."

Blake smiles. "If that were true, you wouldn't have hired me."

I'M NOT PLANNING to kiss Blake when I drop her off.

I'm enjoying the anticipation. Knowing I can kiss her, touch her, undress her at my leisure, creates a heady sense of omnipotence. I have two whole days to devise exactly what I'm going to do to her.

She lives in the flower district in Chelsea, in an ugly brick building that I assume looks better on the inside. The scent of fresh blooms is thick in the air, though the shops have shuttered for the night.

"Which one's yours?" I look up at the windows.

"I'm on the top floor." She doesn't point out which one.

I want to see inside.

Blake is so fundamentally secretive, I want to walk into her bedroom, pull back the comforter, inhale the scent of her sheets. I want to flip through all the clothes in her closet, read the spines of the books on her shelves, see if she has actual food in her fridge. Does she have a pet? Does she leave wet towels on the floor? Does stepping inside feel like stepping into her skin, walking through the hallways of her mind, all her attachments, all her preferences laid bare...

"Seven o'clock Friday?" Blake says, as if she read my thoughts, as if she's already erecting barricades before I can even ask to come up.

I let her halfway open her car door, then I seize her by the nape of the neck and yank her back.

Our mouths smash together. My grip is so tight she can't pull away, can't even turn her head. Her mouth gives way, her soft tongue, full lips, crushed beneath the onslaught. I delve my tongue deep into her mouth and taste her.

Blake is a riot of flavors, fevered, dizzying. She tastes like late nights and bad decisions, like temptation made flesh.

I press her tight against my body, but Blake is impossible to contain. She resists by not resisting at all, by sinking in... She flows like mercury, impossible to grasp, liquid in my arms but never absorbing.

She lets me do what I want, even responds to me, but I'm kissing her with hunger and she's holding back. Her nipples press through the soft material of her dress, nudging against my chest, while her eyes remain clear and focused.

I'm not the only one who likes to keep my hand on the wheel.

I kiss her harder, rougher, until her cheeks flush and the scent of arousal rises off her skin.

When I release her, she's breathing heavy. Her lips are swollen, her hair disarrayed.

"Ramses..."

I interrupt by kissing her again. The feel of her body beneath my hands is so luscious that I let out a groan directly into her mouth. Blake stiffens and now she's kissing me back in an entirely different way, wetter, messier, ravenous...

When I pull back, I keep my hand locked on the nape of her neck.

"*That's* how I want you to kiss me."

4

BLAKE

I don't know if I've ever been more nervous getting dressed for a date.

Usually the sex is the least of my worries. Most men aren't that hard to please.

A surprising number want to be dommed. The person *most* surprised to discover this is usually the man himself. He calls me up thinking he wants to tie me to the bed and do all the things his ex-wife never let him do...three sessions later, I've got him on his knees with my dirty underwear stuffed in his mouth.

Powerful men are in charge all day at work, barking orders, carrying the pressure of their business on their shoulders. When they discover the relief of letting someone else take control, it's like a switch flips in their brain. Soon it's the only way they can unwind.

Making pointillism out of Lukas Larsen's back with my stilettos is the least fucked up thing I've done to him, but I'd never tell Ramses that. What I do with my clients is as sacred to me as a priest in a confessional. I know how badly they need it and I'd never betray that trust.

The second most common kink is a foot fetish. I don't know how the wiring of the mind works, but I know for certain that the cosmic creator of circuit boards was having a laugh when he soldered in men's perception of feet.

The third group are what I like to call the horny teenage boys. They're the easiest because they tell me all the dirty things they're gonna do to me, but what actually happens is they blow in six minutes, order room service, and fall asleep on the couch.

Ramses isn't going to fit in the usual categories.

Men come to me for a service, a convenience—they don't have time to date, they're in the middle of a messy divorce, they want to do some freaky shit without worrying it's gonna get blabbed all over town.

With Ramses it feels...personal.

I don't think he's in love with me, I'm not an idiot.

But I do think he views me as a challenge, and that's a dangerous position to be in with a man who doesn't just play to win—he plays to annihilate.

He's going to push me. Test me. Try to fuck with me in some way.

Well...

Let's see how bad you really are, Ramses.

I learned a long time ago how to separate my mind from my body. It doesn't matter what happens to my body when my mind's far away. That's how I can fuck men who are ugly, men who bore me, men whose morals I despise. I can use them the way they use me because no matter what my body's doing, my mind is in control.

Ramses won't take it easy on me.

There's a reason he put three million in my account—and it wasn't to stroke my ego.

He put in a number too big to say no to.

That's how these men operate, no different than the gangsters in the Godfather—they make you an offer you can't refuse.

There's nothing polite about Wall Street. Nothing fair, nothing civilized. Players date the way they do business—hostile takeovers, backdoor deals, threats, bribes, extortion...

No matter how many adorable "poached egg competitions" Ramses concocts, he doesn't fool me for a second. Everything he does is pointed at his end goal. And whatever that objective may be, it's for *his* benefit, not mine.

I tell myself that over and over while I'm shaving my legs, blow-drying my hair, painting my face. I'm trying to drown the eager little twist of anticipation squirming in my guts.

I want to see Ramses naked.

I've wanted it since the moment I saw his hands. I want to see the cock that matches those hands.

I saw it swelling down his trouser leg at the Belmont Stakes, coming alive like it could sense me, like it had a life of its own. I could barely breathe trying to sneak glances without Ramses noticing...

My attraction to him is a big fucking problem.

Attraction clouds judgement. It's supposed to be *my* weapon against *him,* not his against me.

That kiss...

Those starless eyes staring into my soul, hand locked around the base of my neck...

That's how I want you to kiss me...

My panties soaked like my water broke.

Fuck, fuck, fuck, fuck, *fuck.*

I'm in so much trouble.

On impulse, I send Ramses a text:

I don't need a ride, I'll be at your place at 7:00

I TAKE the train to Tabitha's apartment. She lives in a walk-up in Queens. The walk-up part is pretty shit for her these days—she's got arthrosis in her hips, knees, ankles. The price of dancing fourteen hours a day for the Bolshoi Ballet.

On a visit to New York City in the eighties, she defected to become mistress to a Vanderbilt. He set her up with a Beaux-Arts mansion that became her brothel. By the time I met her, she'd been operating the most successful escort agency in the city for thirty years.

Tabitha taught me more than any parent ever did.

She's nothing like a mother. But very occasionally, she's been something like a father to me. A harsh and demanding father, never satisfied with his son. Which my clients have taught me is the perfect recipe for success.

I knock on her door.

Tabitha takes a long time to answer.

"You could text."

She only opens the door halfway, shuffling back into the dim apartment. Tabitha didn't used to shuffle. She used to walk like she hung from a string out the top of her skull, all of gravity pulling down in a straight line.

Visiting her reminds me how long I've been doing this job.

If Tabitha was a swan in her ingenue days, she's become lean and hard as a bird of prey. She looks me up and down. I wish she were senile instead of arthritic.

"Why are you so fancy?"

"I'm on my way to a date."

"*Obviously.*" Her sarcasm is Chernobyl-grade caustic. "I'm asking why you went to so much trouble."

I spent an hour ironing my hair to a glossy sheet. I cut the tags off my dress *and* my underwear. My pussy is manicured like the

White House lawn. Tabitha can't see that part, but she fucking knows it just by looking at the rest of me.

"I'm seeing Ramses Howell."

Tabitha's out of the game but she ain't dead. She knows who Ramses is.

"Hm." That's Russian Prima Ballerina for *"I'm impressed."* They're never actually impressed, but sometimes they're slightly less disappointed. "First date?"

"Second date. First hookup."

"Ah." That means, *Acceptable performance so far, let's explore how you're about to fuck this up.* "You know what he likes?"

She hasn't sat down but stands by the piano, back straight, hands clasped loosely in front of her. She's the examiner, me the student.

Like I forgot to do my homework, I mutter, "He doesn't date anyone I know."

Tabitha raises an eyebrow. It takes about a hundred years and destroys my soul.

"That sounds like an excuse."

I soak in all the sweet, sweet mentorship.

"That's not the issue, I promise."

Tabitha crosses to the window and raises the sash before lighting a cigarette. She opens the window to spare her cage full of finches, so her apartment smells more like paper and violets than like smoke.

She breathes in deep, exhaling out into the alleyway. "What's the problem?"

"I'm attracted to him."

The smoke threads around her dark, polished nails. Her lips are painted the same color. She didn't know anyone was coming over today. Who do performers perform for when they're alone? Are they ever alone in their heads?

She takes another puff, releasing the smoke in spiraling curls. "You've made this mistake before."

I'm aware. It set me back two years and still costs me clients.

I'd like to tell Tabitha, *I'm not going to make the same mistake twice,* but that's what everyone says before they make the same mistake twice.

Instead I say, "I've grown up since then."

She snorts. "Then why'd you come bouncing in here like a sixteen-year-old on her way to prom?"

I smile at her. "Can't it just be because I was excited to see you?"

"Don't kid a kidder."

Tabitha stubs out her cigarette and sets it in the lip of her ashtray like she might smoke the rest of it later. I wish I knew if she's broke or just cheap.

The escort business moved online and a fire gutted Tabitha's gorgeous old mansion. I could have cried for the mulberry wallpaper, the rosewood and Venetian glass gone up in flames, all of Tabitha's old ballet costumes and her cabinet of jewelry gifted by decades of lovers.

When you love an object, you put a tiny piece of your soul inside it. Then it feels alive in your hands, holding your memories and your joy, reflecting it back at you.

But if you ever lose the thing you love, if it's stolen or burns away...a little bit of you goes with it.

Tabitha lost too much of herself. She's not doing well.

She sits on the windowsill looking out into the alleyway. The front windows offer a pretty view of her tree-lined street, but she only opens this one to smoke, staring out at bare brick walls.

Tabitha turns her lighter over in her hands, silver, engraved with someone else's initials. "These men will take everything from you. Only give them what they pay for."

"Don't worry. I still keep the rules."

Tabitha gave me a list of rules the day I signed my contract. I don't keep them all, I never did. But the last one is burned in my brain:

Never believe it's real.

That's the mistake I won't make again.

5

BLAKE

Ramses owns the penthouse of the Skyline Tower over Central Park.

His building is prettier than all the glass pencils on Billionaire's Row, gray stone with gothic towers and a green patina copper roof.

Ramses hasn't responded to my text. He's probably annoyed that I took an Uber to his place instead of letting his driver pick me up.

I didn't do it on purpose but I'm not sorry either. Everything is part of the game, and that includes not letting Ramses get too comfortable giving orders.

The doorman directs me to Ramses' personal elevator.

Sometimes I love stealing the experiences of the super-rich. Other times I hate walking around in their world, acting like one of them.

You can make money, but you can't ever stop being poor in your head.

Poor isn't a number in a bank account. It's every part of your day blowing up in your face because you lack the basics of life—

the bus pass to get to school, the shoes for gym class, the food that isn't waiting in your empty backpack. It's a feeling that you're deeply unlucky, hated by the universe, unloved by anyone else. You're unworthy and you can see that in the faces of everyone who avoids you because your clothes don't fit, your hair is messy, you smell.

I haven't been that person for ten years. But the ghost lingers.

I don't know if I'll ever feel like I belong in a place this beautiful.

The elevator rises through a tube of glass, the park unwinding below. The peachy sunlight of golden hour shimmers on the Hudson. The mirrors behind me are a wall of clouds, numbers whirring past as I climb fifty floors.

The elevator slows and stops. With a gentle chime, the doors open directly into the penthouse suite.

This isn't an apartment at all—it's a mansion up in the sky. All the walls are windows, and the windows go all the way around, a glass zoetrope of the city.

I expected to see Ramses. The deep silence tells me I'm the only one here.

I can smell his cologne, the wool of his suits, the leather of his shoes. I see the place on the couch where he sits, the cushions dented from his weight.

I'm Jack in the giant's castle. Everything in Ramses' house is made to his scale—soaring ceilings, galley-sized furniture, art that covers the whole wall. The colors are rich, moody, masculine, his kitchen black walnut and glossy dark tile.

I'm alone in his private space. I can look at anything, touch anything, go anywhere I like. He might be watching on a camera, but he can't stop me.

I'd *never* let someone wander around my place without me there. Probably not even if I were standing right next to them.

Ramses threw the door open and invited me in.

In fact, he even left a gift for me.

A large box sits on the stone slab that functions as a coffee table, elegantly wrapped in champagne and gold.

I open the envelope, reading Ramses' dense scrawl:

This is what I want you to wear tonight.
If you're as good as you say you are, you'll know
how to behave.

I hear the words like he spoke them in my ear.

The tissue sparks against my fingertips as I tear it apart.

I have no idea what I'm about to find in the box. Even when I pull the garment free of its wrappings, I'm still not entirely sure. It's so thin that I could crumple it up in a ball in my hand, light as a stocking, nearly transparent.

I carry the box into the closest bedroom, a guest suite with raw suede on the walls and bedding the color of a rain cloud. I strip naked, scattering my clothes across the bed and pulling on the suit instead.

It's all one piece, a bodystocking that leaves my feet bare. The hands end in a kind of fingerless glove, only my nails protruding.

I zip up the back of the suit. Even though I'm covered neck to ankle, I'm cool and comfortable, the material so thin I feel almost naked.

Digging through the tissue, I find a pair of ears, soft black fur set on a headband studded with tiny teeth. I set the band in place, the teeth catching my bangs and pulling all my hair straight back off my face. When I shake my head, tiny silver bells jingle behind the ears.

I slip in front of the full-length mirror.

A sleek black cat stares back at me.

In the shadowed light, the suit doesn't appear a suit at all — it looks like living skin. When I turn, the curve of my ass seems naked flesh painted black. The suit shifts along with me, every movement, every breath.

The headband changes everything else. My face is naked without my bangs, eyebrows black and ferocious. The ears add height.

The suit holds my body tight, nothing jiggling, all sinuous curves. I take a few steps. My thighs swish against each other, arms gliding at my sides. The points of my fingernails glint at the end of the gloves.

I fucking love this suit.

And I love prowling around Ramses' house without him here. Ramses is best enjoyed at a distance...sneaking into his office, spinning around in his chair, smelling his aftershave, reading the headlines framed on his wall. *WaMu Seized, Sold Off in Largest Failure in US Banking History...*

That's the kind of shit that gets these guys hard—transfers of billions of dollars.

Me too.

Poor is knowing that money *absolutely* fucking matters.

Rich is knowing it's also just a bunch of ones and zeros flying around in air for anyone to grab.

I'm listening for the chime of the elevator, for Ramses returning home. How long does he plan to make me wait?

I tiptoe out of his office, pausing at the junction between living space and the hallway beyond. Do I dare enter his bedroom?

Before I can decide, I spy a smaller package on a table in the hallway. This one is flat like a jewelry box, an envelope tucked beneath the ribbon.

Giddy with the sense of a treasure hunt, I slip out Ramses' second note.

Put this on and present yourself to me in the den.

My eyes flick up to the doorway, startled, like Ramses might be here after all.

He's not. I know what an empty house feels like.

I pull the ribbon. The silk runs through my fingers, cool as water. This is what you learn first—money makes everything feel good.

Inside the box is a collar made of pearls, three layered strands, rich and smooth as cream. I lay it around my neck, fastening the clasp. A flat gold tag glimmers against my breastbone:

Minx

A flush creeps up my neck. I've never had a nickname before. I would have said I didn't want one.

My smile surprises me in the mirror.

Minx suits me.

This outfit suits me even more. It's so fucking comfortable I want to live in it, but I don't feel like lounging. I want to prowl.

Ramses is a showman, he's going all-out.

I want to go all-out, too.

But something's missing...

I run back to the purse I abandoned, retrieve my eyeliner, and make a few improvements. When I'm finished, I've got a cat eye that would make Michelle Pfeiffer jealous.

Perfect.

I can't stop touching myself in this suit.

I've got a closet full of lingerie, but I've never dressed as an animal before.

Maybe I should feel degraded by Ramses. Maybe I would've if he'd left me a puppy suit.

Cats are different.

Cats are sexy. Cats are powerful.

I descend the three steps into the sunken den, letting my hips sway back and forth, crossing my feet one over the other. I tiptoe through the last patches of sunshine, the room bathed in rich red light.

Ramses isn't there. A camera sits in his place, mounted on a tripod, already recording. I meet its blank black eye, certain that somewhere, Ramses is watching.

I pad past its gaze, turn, and stalk back again. Sometimes I look at Ramses. Sometimes I ignore him completely.

I flop down on the couch, hanging my head backward off the cushions, putting my feet up in the air. Ramses' couch is an acre long, the cushions so plush I sink all the way in.

I point my toes, flex, point again. Then roll over on my tummy and sit back on my heels, stretching out my back.

Lolling around like this is ridiculous and silly, but I can't believe how much it's turning me on. The room is sun drenched, my body heavy and warm. It's easy to let go of my inhibitions, alone in the clouds.

The eye of the camera burns on my skin, its red light pulsing like a heartbeat.

I'm alone but not alone. Ramses can see me, but I can't see him.

I roll onto my back, letting my legs fall open.

My skin glows through the transparent suit, nipples pointing at the ceiling. I run my palms down silken curves...

Adrenaline bumps through my veins like Ramses is right here next to me, but my mind tells me I'm as free as in my own bedroom at home, free to slide my hands down my waist, to cup my palm over my pussy, soaking up the heat radiating through the suit...

I pretend it's Ramses' heavy hand cupping my cunt. I imagine his thick fingers grazing the nub of my clit, sliding back and forth, teasing, pressing...

My hips bump upward, the sunshine making my hand so much warmer than it normally is, warm like a man's hand, warm like a mouth, wet and melting...

The softest of climaxes rolls over me, raindrops pattering down my skin. I shiver against the cushions, lips parted, a moan sighing out.

I roll over, letting one leg hang down off the couch, all my weight pressed against the thick, soft pad between my thighs.

My body is saturated with sun. The pleasure comes over me in slow waves as I rock my hips against the cushions. I'm warm and lazy and completely relaxed.

The elevator chimes.

My hand freezes between my thighs.

The doors slide open. A heavy tread crosses the hall.

Ramses' shadow precedes him into the den, crawling across the floor and surging up the wall until the head nearly touches the ceiling line. The man himself steps into the doorway.

His face is flushed, eyes glittering. When he sees me, a slow smile spreads across his face.

"There you are—I missed you."

He crosses the room in three strides, towering over me. His heavy hand lands on my head and slides all the way down my spine.

He's petting me. Fucking petting me.

His hand covers my back, the weight loosening my muscles, the warmth making me calm. Ramses looks down at me, his expression playful and affectionate.

"Did you miss me too, Minxie girl?"

He's talking to me like a cat. Looking at me like a cat, touching me like a cat.

This is way past role-play—it's like a completely different personality.

Why are you so good at this, you psychopath?

This is not what I expected. It's kind of freaking me out.

At the same time...

I like the way Ramses is looking at me, like he hurried home just to see me. I like the way his fingers knead down my back. I can't be stressed with those big, warm hands all over me.

He didn't give me any instructions. Does he want me to answer? Am I even allowed to talk?

This is part of the test, part of the challenge.

I said I was the goddamn best at this, he expects me to figure it out.

Well, I *am* the goddamn best.

I turn my cheek against Ramses' thigh, nuzzling my face against his leg, making a deep purring sound in my throat.

His thigh goes hard like oak.

His hand slides up under my hair, gripping me at the base of the neck. He stoops and says right in my ear, "Good girl. I like when you purr for me."

I melt all the way down.

Maybe it's the way he's holding me, maybe it's the expression on his face, maybe it's how I'm gazing up at him, curled up on the couch—when Ramses calls me a good girl, my brain floods.

I want to be a good girl.

I want him to smile at me like that.

But quick as he came, Ramses turns and leaves, abandoning me in the den.

His heavy steps disappear down the hallway.

I wait, thinking he'll come back.

Five minutes pass.

Ramses reemerges from the bedroom, striding past the den. I hear ice cubes in a glass, then the creak of his body settling down on the other couch.

What the fuck?

I wait a little longer.

No, he's definitely staying out there.

I stand up, confused and annoyed.

Here's another dilemma: am I supposed to crawl around on all fours? That's awkward.

Cats aren't awkward. Cats are graceful and confident.

I walk out of the den the way I came in, slinky and slow.

Ramses sits in the main living room, briefcase open, papers spread out. He's reading some kind of report and doesn't even glance up as I come in.

He changed clothes. The suit is gone, replaced by gray sweatpants and a baseball shirt so faded it's hard to tell the sleeves were ever blue. His forearms are bare beneath, covered in dark hair.

Ramses takes a sip of his drink, still indifferent even as I walk across his line of sight.

I'm starting to get irritated.

Did he bring me here, make me put on this suit, just to ignore me?

I lean against a pillar, arms folded, watching him.

Ramses turns another page of his endless and tedious-looking report.

Yes, that's exactly what he did.

It's all part of the game. Part of the power struggle.

Smiling to myself, I prowl across the room again. But this time, slower, rolling my hips. I pause in front of Ramses to stretch, arching my back, thrusting out my tits, flexing my ass in the suit as transparent as stockings. Then I make another circuit.

By the third time around, Ramses has stopped turning pages.

I get down on the rug in front of him and roll around in the dense pile.

The rugs in Ramses' house are thick and fluffy, gray as a baby rabbit. They're probably made of baby rabbits, sewed together by orphans. Ramses seems the type.

Whatever they are, it feels spectacular against my skin. I lay on my side, running my bare toes through the softness.

Ramses glances my way, then pulls his eyes back to the page, not fast enough.

Ha.

I roll on my back, maneuvering so I'm laying across his foot now, one of my legs up on his lap. My toes slide across the bulge in his sweatpants.

Ramses pushes my foot away carelessly, like you'd do to an animal getting in your way. His cock only grows harder.

I move up to the couch instead, flopping down on his papers, deliberately wrinkling them.

Sternly, he puts his hand on my back and presses down, holding me still.

"Relax."

I'm not gonna relax—I have his number now.

I wait a few moments, then start encroaching on his space again, laying my head in his lap, letting my fingers dance and up and down the back of his calf.

I'm not quite laying across his cock, but its warmth is close to my cheek, his sweatpants stretched tight. Heat radiates out of his thighs, thick and solid beneath me, each as big as my whole body. Wrapping my arms around his leg is like hugging a redwood.

I look up into Ramses' face.

He's trying not to smile, trying to keep his eyes glued to his report.

I like looking at him when he can't look at me.

Black stubble outlines his features, making his jaw sharper

but his lips softer. Ramses has a long, lean face, a nose that ought to be unattractive but isn't, and eyebrows that add all the ferocity his mouth is trying to give away.

His hair needs cutting. It's soft against all the hard shapes and lines. His clothes are soft on the firmness of his body.

His penthouse is the same—moody, masculine, but with textures that suck you in like quicksand. It's a midnight dream in here.

This game isn't what I expected.

Ramses looks like a brute, but he's brilliant; I've been tracking his trades for months.

Neither of us quite matches what we look like on the outside.

I'd like to see more of his outsides.

It's what I've been thinking about all day. Obsessing over, even.

He's just so...big.

And I'm a curious cat.

I curl on my side. Ramses' cock is right in front of my face. He's not fully hard yet, just swollen and warm.

I sneak up my hand in its kitten glove, black to the knuckles. Lightly, I scratch my nails down the length of his cock, over the ridge of the head. It heaves under my palm.

Ramses clamps his hand over mine, trapping it.

He looks down at me.

"You want attention?"

I smile up at him.

Yeah. Right fucking now.

I could get into being a cat. Cats are assholes.

Ramses sweeps up the papers, throws them in his briefcase, and sets it aside. He takes a sip of his drink, then picks up a remote and uses it to play music.

♪♫ *Weekend — Mac Miller*

He settles back against the couch, arms spread wide across its frame. I loll across his lap, heart racing because I know we're about to kick it up a gear.

I try to take his cock out of his pants. He stops me again.

Now I'm getting frustrated.

The first time in forever I've been attracted to a client, and he won't let me touch him? That sounds just about fucking right.

What does he want, then?

I watch Ramses' face.

There's what he *thinks* he wants and what he *actually* wants. They might be the same—or they might not be.

Ramses takes another sip of his drink. The ice clinks in the glass. I can smell the lime on the rim. Am I going to keep up this no talking thing? I kinda want a drink.

Ramses dips his finger in the gin and holds it over my lips.

The liquor drops on my tongue, cool and delicious.

He dips again. This time I lap it right off his fingertip.

The way I'm only getting the smallest drip at a time makes me want more, desperately.

Ramses dips two fingers. The droplets patter down. I lick them off my lips, then grab his fingers between my teeth and suck them clean.

I'm not an eating-out-of-other-people's-hands kind of person. I don't even share forks.

But right now, I'm not Blake.

Right now, I'm an animal, and animals don't have the same scruples.

Ramses plays the game so hard I'm sinking into it, losing myself in the challenge.

I don't just lick his fingers. I lick them like a beast, hungry, frantic. I even make little whimpering sounds.

Ramses stops breathing. When I look up into his face, it's stunned and blank like he's a robot and I just wiped his programming. The grin that bursts through is so effortless and real that, for a second, I break too and grin back.

He grabs my face and kisses me.

I kiss him like I licked his fingers, wild and crazy, tasting as much of him as possible with my tongue.

That turns his engine all the way up. He thrusts his hands in my hair and kisses me *deep*.

Ramses' lips are full and firm. His mouth tastes slightly of gin but much more of him. His kiss overwhelms me—there's so much of him, so much of his scent, his heat, his hands covering my body.

I'm kissing him back like he asked me to the other night, messy, wet, uninhibited. I grab his face and lick my tongue up his cheek.

It feels outrageous and makes me want to laugh, but it's fucking sexy too, the way his stubble rasps against my tongue. Every part of him tastes good, feels good. The scent of his skin drives me nuts. When I lick his neck, it's saltier than his lips.

I'm grinding on his lap, rubbing against the hardness I so badly want to uncover. His hands grip my waist, then slide up my back. I try to put my hand down his pants where it's humid and throbbing. This time when he stops me, I growl and bite his lip.

Ramses grabs me by the throat and lays me across his lap, his arm pressed against my chest, pinning me with its weight. He leans over, looking right in my face.

"Knock it off."

It's disorienting how easily he can move me. I'm not small, but I'm tiny compared to him. It makes me feel like I've shrunk.

The sun is all the way gone, the walls a glossy vista of city lights.

I feel different in this suit, in this place. Ramses isn't what I expected. Everything I pictured happening has disappeared; I'm wandering blind.

He strokes his hand down my body, looking deep in my eyes.

"Are you here for me?"

I gaze up at him, giving the smallest of nods.

"You want to please me?"

Yes.

"You want to make me happy?"

Yes.

"Then I want you to come for me as many times as you can."

He watches my face to see if I understand.

It's an order, a clear objective.

I get that thrill that comes when I know exactly what to do.

I close my eyes, letting the pressure of Ramses' palm saturate my body, waves of pleasure rolling through. My lips part and I start to float away...

Ramses slaps my cheek lightly, jolting me out of the ride.

"Look at *me*. You come for *me*."

I can't hide my irritation. I don't want to look at him. I don't want to look at anything—I want to close my eyes, focus on the feeling.

Ramses only grins, a flash of white in all that black stubble. "That's right—you stay here with me."

His eyes are deep water, no waves. At first it's hard to hold his stare. Soon I can't look away.

A flush spreads from my belly up to my neck.

Ramses' strokes are slow and measured, down my thighs, over my breasts. My nipples are hard enough to hurt, poking through the suit. Ramses' palm drags across their tips. I arch my back, groaning.

He touches my breasts, letting his thick fingers circle lightly around the nipples as if he's drawing on my skin.

I squirm in his lap, thighs squeezing together.

He pinches my nipple, rolling it gently. Each tug sends waves of pleasure down my legs.

It's hard to focus on the feeling when my eyes are open, when I'm looking up at him. It's so many things at once, distracting me, pulling at me like birds.

I don't think I've ever looked in someone's eyes for so long. It feels like the rules change the longer it goes on. Looking away means something. Holding on means more.

His hand moves down to my thighs, kneading gently at the long muscles of the quads, the tight places around my knees. The pressure makes me go loose. He moves me like a marionette, his thumb working out the tension points. The blood flows smooth like an unblocked dam, and I tingle down to my toes.

My thighs fall open.

Ramses knows what I want. He lets his warm palm pass across my mound, amused when I groan and try to press against his hand. He trails his fingers up and down the cleft between my pussy lips, feeling the wetness soaking through the suit.

"Good kitty...you like to be touched."

Like doesn't begin to cover it. I'm fucking rabid for it. The material is thin, but it blocks sensation. I roll my hips against his hand, his fingertips sliding across my clit, maddeningly close but unable to make full contact.

I make desperate sounds, panting.

Ramses smiles.

His fingers are light and teasing. The waves of pleasure build and build but can't quite crest.

He presses one finger against my entrance. The material gives way enough to push an inch inside. I moan and spread my legs wider, trying to drive down on his finger. The suit stretches a little more.

I hump against his palm, dying for the orgasm to break. I can't believe I'm letting him see me like this, looking right in his face while I do it. That's how crazy I've gotten hanging on the edge too long.

Ramses tears the suit open at the crotch. It takes him no effort at all, like the material is spiderweb. Cool air hits wet skin, exposed, opened up like a flower.

He moistens two fingers in his mouth and presses them against my clit.

I start to come instantly. The intensity of those fingers against my bare button is a live wire. I've never been touched until this moment.

My pussy melts against his hand, his fingers sinking in. He rubs slow circles while the orgasm drags on and on.

The sounds I make are inhuman. My eyes roll back. My whole body shakes. I'm draped across his lap like the Pieta.

He smiles and slowly rubs until the last spark extinguishes.

"Good girl. *That's* what I want."

I'm limp in his lap, flushed with chemicals, the tide gone out, all my nerves exposed.

But Ramses isn't stopping.

His hand stays right where it is, rubbing deep, slow circles around my clit.

I'm soft and swollen like a bruise. Throbbing with a feeling too good mixed with too much.

Ramses looks down at me, dark glee spread across his face. He's not lying, he's getting some kind of deep pleasure out of watching me come. In a slightly disturbing way, like a scientist observing an experiment.

I'm the Manhattan Project. Ramses is the doppelgänger Oppenheimer.

The waves are building again, surging back faster than I could have guessed.

I already feel a sick kind of dread like this isn't going to be the last time or even close to the last time.

I can't catch my breath, can't hold back for a second. Ramses has control of my pussy. He's figuring out the cheat codes faster than I can process, his fingers testing, his eyes watching my face.

My skin is silk and oil, the folds swollen and aching. Ramses delves a finger inside me, uses the wetness to tease my clit until it's stiff and throbbing, until I dig my nails into his arm, clinging to him, whimpering.

He pushes one thick finger inside. I'm so sensitive all the way around, that one single finger feels like the whole world. He moves it in and out a few millimeters. I clench around him, making a sound like a sob.

He fucks me with his fingers, slow and deep.

I'm floating, sinking, floating, trapped under his arm, completely in his power.

His voice is hypnotic. It echoes through my brain.

"I planned to make you wait at least an hour. But the moment I saw you in that suit..."

He looks down at me, his smile sunshine on my skin.

"I have *never* seen anything so tempting. I had to get here. I fucking *ran*."

I think of Ramses rushing into the doorway, flushed and sweating, and I come hard and fast, clenched around his fingers.

He seizes me by the chin, forcing me to look at him. "You stay right here with me."

I drown in his eyes while the world breaks apart and washes away.

Ramses is the only thing that stays steady, the black hole that swallows everything else.

His fingers creep into parts of me that have never been touched. He finds the spot I can't resist and presses like he'll make me come until it kills me.

It's some kind of fucked up torture where every time I try to drift away, try to dissolve into the feeling, Ramses slaps my cheek and jolts me back again. He locks me in his gaze while he makes me feel exactly what he wants me to feel.

"Don't you dare hold back on me. I want you to give it all to me. *All* of it. Show me how bad you want it. Show me how happy you are to be here with me."

He shoves his fingers in deep like a hook and hits that button again, again, again, while I stare into his eyes, shaking, twitching, begging.

"Is that the hardest you can come? I thought you were the best—you can come harder than that. Yes, you can. Give it to me, I fucking want it. Show me how badly you want me. Show me what you'll do to please me. Fucking *come.*"

That hits the bullseye.

My belly contracts to a single point, then explodes. This isn't a climax—it's a detonation, blasting through my pussy like I might have ripped something. It ricochets through my brain, obliterating everything in its path. Everything I think, everything I want, everything I am, disappears.

The only things left are Ramses' eyes looking into mine, watching me exit this world, then dragging me back again.

His smile spreads, wicked and pleased.

"Good girl. *Now* I'm satisfied."

Relief washes through me.

I take a breath...

And burst into tears.

I'm so shocked at myself that I clamp my hands over my face, trying to hide like a kid.

I don't cry. Ever.

Especially not around other people.

Especially not in front of *him.*

Ramses stiffens but catches me with his hands, laying me down on his chest. He cradles the back of my head like it's fragile. His arms wrap all the way around.

I turn my face into his chest, so fucking embarrassed that I cry harder. I have no more control over this than I had over what came before. The sobs shake through me just like the pleasure did, liquid and loose.

I curl up in the cave of his arms, glad now that I feel small and shrunken because that makes it easy to hide.

Ramses rests his palm in the middle of my back. He makes long, slow strokes down my spine.

"*Shh,*" he murmurs in my ear. "You did so well, I'm so proud of you."

6

RAMSES

I drive Blake back home, which I wasn't planning to do. I have a chauffeur. This arrangement would have been the perfect opportunity for Tony to finally do his job. But Blake refused a ride over, probably out of pure stubbornness, and now I want to drive her home myself.

She's quiet in the passenger seat.

I wish there was a way to tell her not to be embarrassed.

I get it. The last thing in the world I'd want to do is cry in front of somebody else. I'm guessing she feels the same.

But that moment was nothing short of incredible.

The sense of power I felt with her body under my control, her eyes locked on mine...and then the complete release. It was like I conquered Everest and base jumped off the peak.

It doesn't take a mentalist to see that Blake's self-control is her armor. It's how she walked into the Belmont Stakes and worked that room like a warrior, safe in the role she's played a hundred times.

Tonight, I put her in a new role.

One she doesn't control.

I do.

I'm still so fucking turned on I can barely sit still in my seat. It's like I can feel her on my fingertips, melting, dissolving under my hands.

I roll down the window to let fresh air into the car.

Blake does the same, leaning her head against the sill, closing her eyes, breathing deep.

I think of her weight in my arms, heavy and warm. How she relaxed against me when I stroked her back. The wetness of her face soaking through my shirt.

"Sorry," Blake says.

"Don't apologize. I got exactly what I wanted."

She turns and looks at me, amused though her eyes are still red.

"Are you going to pretend that's how you wanted to end your night? Somebody blubbering all over you?"

"Not somebody," I say. "You."

Color seeps into her face. She chews the edge of her lip, frowning slightly.

"You like making me uncomfortable."

I smile. "You didn't look so uncomfortable earlier."

Her flush deepens.

"Have you done that before? Is that your kink?"

I shake my head, coming to a gentle stop at a red light. "I've never even thought to try it."

"What made you pick it, then?"

I lean across the bench seat and tuck a strand of hair behind her ear, letting my fingers glide across the hidden cat.

"Your tattoo. I thought it suited you."

She shivers slightly, holding my gaze. She's looking at me longer now.

Humans can be trained just like animals. Punishment and reward control us all.

"The way you were touching me..." She lets out a soft sigh. "I've never felt anything like it."

Neither have I.

I say, "I want to see you again tomorrow."

"I can't tomorrow."

"Why not?"

"I'm busy."

"With what?"

"Don't start," she says warningly.

I switch angles, still on attack.

"When can I see you then?"

"Tuesday."

"What's wrong with Sunday or Monday?"

She lets the silence drag out between us, unsmiling.

I wait just as patiently.

At last, she says, "I could do Sunday."

Every battle matters to the overall war.

"Two o'clock," I say. "And this time, *I'm* picking you up."

WHEN THE ELEVATOR doors open into my apartment, I smell Blake's perfume. The torn suit lays limp across the bed in the guest room, Blake's collar safely back in its box.

I stand in the shower letting the boiling water roll down my back, clouds of steam erasing the rest of the bathroom from view.

My cock is heavy and swollen. It's been like this almost twelve hours now. It burns like a fever in my hand.

I stroke it slowly, running through the night from the moment my little kitten stepped in front of the camera.

She stunned me. Fucking stunned me.

I'd planned to leave her there at least an hour or two, to soften her up.

But the way she moved, glancing back over her shoulder, teasing, flirting...She slipped into the role and played it like she was possessed.

I think of how she touched herself, filing away exactly how her hands moved across her body. I think of how *I* touched *her*, looking down into her face the entire time, watching every gasp, every sigh.

I try to remember the moments when her body jolted, when she completely lost control. What was I saying? What was I doing?

I've never seen anything so tempting...

Show me how bad you want me...

Show me what you'll do to please me...

I remember how she looked up at me, eager, anxious...

And how she gave it all to me.

My cock erupts, lava flow pumping hot down my hand.

I let the water run, washing it all down the drain.

My shoulders sink, tension releasing from my back. My head clears and my mood floats.

I work for a couple of hours, able to concentrate better than I have in weeks.

I haven't been sleeping well. I wake up at two a.m., then four... the silence isn't silence, it blares in my ears.

Tonight the bed feels soft, the sheets cool. I turn out the light without flipping on the TV.

Sleep comes faster than I dared hope, red and warm and sensual. I rest my hand on my cock, feeling it ebb and swell with each half-remembered dream.

Late in the night, I wake just once.

Sleep hasn't abandoned me, it's close like the blankets, I can pull it right back over my head.

I sift through the images floating in my mind—Blake smiling up at me in her black cat ears. The shape of her pussy lips through the suit. Her sharp little nails scratching across my cock...

But the memory that carries me back to sleep is the feeling of Blake in my arms, heavy and calm. My breath slowed to match hers. She was a gravity that pulled me in until I felt a peace so whole and complete, it seemed like the whole world had finally come into balance.

I sink deep and don't wake until morning.

As soon as I roll out of bed, I call Carl Contigo, my contact at Goldman Sachs.

I had to check six banks before I found Blake's account to wire my bid. Even though I had an inkling that my little Minx was rolling deep, I was pretty fucking surprised to hear that her balance was $12.7M.

Not bad for a foster kid eight years out of juvie. Actually, it was goddamn impressive. That's why I deposited $3M, as a sign of respect. And 'cause I thought that's what it would take to get her attention.

Apparently, I was wrong.

Or at least, not as grandiose as I expected.

"Pull up Blake Abbot's account."

Carl groans.

"Ramses, I told you—"

"Just do it."

I keep $450M in assets at Goldman Sachs. Carl would put a lampshade on his head and dance the conga if I made him. His beach house in Montauk was bought solely off my commissions.

I hear the sound of him tapping away on his laptop. It's 6:20 a.m. His wife is probably glaring daggers right next to him in bed.

He says, "Okay, got it."

"What's the current balance?"

"Twenty-four point two million."

I get a rush like I just sniffed a line.

I fucking knew it.

"What were the last three transfers?"

"They can see if I access that," Carl whines. "It's all tracked."

"No one's gonna see 'cause no one's gonna look. Pull it up."

More clicking. After a moment, Carl says, "There was your deposit of three million last week. Before that, a transfer of... twenty-eight point five from a brokerage account—"

"Which day?" I say quickly.

"June twelve. And then, the same day...a transfer out...of twenty million even."

"Out to where?"

Click, click, clack...and the sound of Carl's wet breathing, his phone probably clamped between ear and shoulder, too close to his mouth...

"A Swiss account."

My whole body throbs. The morning light makes the surfaces in my kitchen sparkle.

"And how much is in the brokerage account?"

"I can't see, it's at IBKR."

I'm elated, grinning to myself as I say, "Keep an eye on her; let me know any time she makes a transfer."

Carl makes a grumbling sound that means he'll do it, but he's gonna be a sulky bitch about it.

I set the phone down, the kitchen awash in watercolor light.

I knew it. I knew it the moment she didn't lose her mind over that $800k.

And then at dinner, when I needled her about Anthony Keller, *I hope he's not paying you in stock...*

Blake snapped right back at me, *I hope you don't think I'd hold it.*

She's trading. And not in small amounts.

The day Keller's company crashed, she made $28.5M.

She knew the IPO was going to fail. She shorted his stock.

My sneaky little kitty is insider trading, using what she learns from her clients and the parties she attends to make plays.

How much does she actually have? I want to see the balance of that Swiss account.

I don't know if I've ever been so attracted to someone.

No, strike that—I definitely haven't.

I like women and I love sex, but they've never been the priority. Money was the priority. Success.

I'm starting to run out of boxes to check. The things that used to motivate me don't glitter as bright.

Blake is a puzzle. Clicking the pieces into place is a thrill I haven't felt in a long time—I hadn't realized how long.

I have a full schedule booked out for the day, regardless of the fact that it's a Saturday. Briggs is meeting me at the office in thirty minutes. I haven't even started getting ready.

My mind is full of schemes of what I'll do to Blake tomorrow.

7

RAMSES

I wait at the curb outside Blake's building, watching the windows overhead.

At 1:55 I text her:

> Waiting downstairs.

A moment later, the blinds twitch on the third-floor corner window.

I smile to myself. *Found you.*

Blake texts back:

> I'll be down in 5.

She descends the steps precisely five minutes later, wearing a crisp white blouse, shorts, and flats, her hair pulled back in an Audrey Hepburn ponytail, a straw tote over her arm. She looks like a sunny Sunday afternoon.

I get out of the car.

She flashes a grin as she heads for the passenger side, her dimple winking.

I grab her by the arm, pulling her tight against my body.

"Don't walk by without kissing me."

She tilts up her mouth obediently, kissing me deep how I like. I hold her at the base of her neck and the small of her back. Her body fits against mine like it was made to do it, though we have completely opposite shapes.

"Where are we going?" she says when we break apart. "Did I dress right?"

"I've never seen you dress wrong."

She laughs. "Plenty of people would disagree."

"What people?"

Her eyes slide away from mine. "Oh, you know...teachers, bosses...people you live with."

People you live with...is that how she views her foster family? Was it one family or many?

I want to know everything about Blake, but I have a sense how royally pissed she'll be if she knows I've been snooping around again.

"It's me we're gonna dress today," I tell her as we pull away from the curb. "I saw the makeover you gave Keller. Thought you could help me pick out some new suits."

Blake chuckles, low and intoxicating. Making her laugh is becoming an obsession of mine.

She admits, "I did give him some advice."

"Was that for his benefit or to make it easier to look at him?"

She shakes her head at me. "You just can't help yourself."

"No, I can't." I sling my arm across the back of her seat. "I'm jealous."

She snorts. "You're not jealous of Anthony."

"Not anymore. Have you cut him loose yet?"

She gives a sideways glance. "Why would I do that?"

"Because you got what you wanted."

The calm in the car is dangerous. Blake's finger taps the windowsill.

"What do you think I wanted?"

She's a goddamn CIA operative probing for intel.

Hook me up to a lie detector—you won't see me sweat. And it ain't 'cause I'm honest.

"You told me yourself—you said you'd never hold his stock. You knew he was gonna flame out. You shorted VizTech."

Blake's chest rises and falls, nice and steady. I'm not stupid enough to think that means she's relaxed. She's forcing herself to breathe slowly—so she doesn't bite my head off.

"You looked at my account."

I dodge: "I already looked at your account the day I deposited the three million."

Her face is turning red. Her hands twist in her lap.

It seems like she considers many possible sentences before she finally says, "You're the only other person who knows about that account."

"It impressed me."

She turns to look at me, flame in her face.

"That's peanuts to you."

"That's not true at all. The first million I made was the hardest work I ever did. You've got a fuck of a lot more than that."

Her hand flies up to her mouth like she wants to bite her nails. Just as quickly, she pulls it back down again.

"I'd appreciate if you'd keep that piece of information between the two of us."

I bet you would.

"I haven't even told Briggs."

That makes her smile.

I push just a little more. "What's your number?"

I'm not asking how much she has—I'm asking what number she's trying to hit.

Every player knows their number.

And Blake is a motherfucking player.

I don't think she's going to answer. I'm sure she won't. Then, low and quiet, she says, "A hundred."

A hundred million. Just the sound of it on her lips makes me throb.

I'd planned to stop there—but now I have to know.

"How close are you?"

Two impulses battle on her face: the need to keep her secret against the temptation to dazzle me.

At last, she whispers, "Sixty-seven."

A thrill runs down my spine. I remember that chase, that hunt.

"The first hundred is *grueling*. It's easy to make a few hundred K on a deal. But to grow to nine figures...you have to put your nuts on the table."

"So to speak." Blake smiles. "I've definitely taken some haircuts."

Now that I've found a crack in her armor, I'm wedging in relentlessly.

"How old were you when you hit your first million?"

"Twenty-two."

"Fucking hell." I whistle. "You beat me. I was twenty-four."

She grins. "But right when I was up to ten, I got knocked back down to six."

I shake my head, grinning right back at her. "Happened to me so many times."

She's feverish, finally telling someone this monumental thing, the words spilling from her lips:

"I won a stock-picking competition. That's how I got into Columbia—the prize was a scholarship. But..." Blake pauses, a strange dullness settling over her eyes. "I didn't graduate. Dropped out in my second year. When I needed money...I started doing this."

This is why she drives me crazy. Each answer only spawns a dozen more questions. I ask the one I think she might actually answer:

"How soon did you realize you were picking up useful information?"

Blake's smile creeps back. "Immediately. The first time somebody bought me a purse, I sold it and invested in Paysign. Made a four hundred percent return."

I don't ask why she *keeps* doing it. I know better than anyone how hard it is to get good information. Information is the edge— the only weapon that matters.

"How did you find your first clients?"

"Through a friend," she says, without offering anything else.

I turn the wheel, extremely pleased. That was more than I hoped to get out of her so soon.

I ask one last question, one I hope isn't out of bounds:

"What will you do when you hit your number?"

Blake peeks up at me from under her bangs, looking younger than her years. "Get my castle, of course. I want the most beautiful place imaginable, garden like a fairytale. And I want it to be all mine."

There's a strange tightness in my chest. Blake sees some hint of it on my face.

"What's wrong?"

"Nothing's wrong." Lying comes too easy. Truth is green on the lips—-words that come out alive and grow into something else. "...I used to have a fantasy like that."

Blake sits up in interest. "You wanted a castle?"

"I wanted a house." It flashes into my head the way it used to flash past the bus window—roses blooming in the garden, fresh paint on the steps. "This house I used to see on my way to school. I'd imagine buying it, and picture how perfect my life would be if I lived there."

Blake gives a sad kind of smile. The kind that shows that she knows exactly what I'm talking about—that I didn't just fantasize about that house once or twice, but every fucking day.

"What was special about it?"

"Nothing." The word comes out harsh. "I'd never want to live there now."

Blake frowns slightly, eyes searching my face.

I pretend like I have to look both ways for the next turn.

My mother once told me she'd love a house like that. In fact, the one she lives in now is similar in style. Much larger, of course, and nowhere near the neighborhood where I grew up.

"What are you going to do in your castle?" I say to Blake.

"I dunno. Read all day, probably."

"Then you need one with a library."

"What good would a castle be without a library?"

We pull up at Porter & Robb. Franklin Robb has been cutting my suits since my first custom fit. He doesn't do the measuring for anyone but me.

That's what wealth actually buys you: access. To people, to experiences, to opportunities.

Success is a snowball; it builds as it rolls.

Failure is an avalanche, barely a warning before it all comes crashing down.

Robb has a close beard, a thin face, and round tortoiseshell glasses. His hands look like driftwood, but they cut the cloth with machine precision.

I can tell he likes Blake because she asks the right questions as we examine the fabrics.

"What mill is this from?" She fingers a bolt of Zegna wool.

"The one in Piedmont."

"You go there often?"

"Six times a year." Robb smiles proudly.

"Prettiest place I ever visited."

"You've been?"

"Twice."

I feel the funniest twinge of jealousy. *I* want to take Blake to the prettiest place.

This crush on her is building. Maybe I should get out while I can.

Blake slips her hand in the crook of my arm and that thought pops like a soap bubble. I rest my hand on top of hers, holding it there.

She says, "Are you going to try anything on?"

"I loathe trying on clothes. That's why I come here."

"They have some ready-to-wear." Blake examines the neat rows of summer jackets and light linen shirts along the wall.

I scoff. "Those aren't going to fit me."

"They might."

Robb glances up, mouth full of pins. He's laying out the Zegna wool. "I can whip up one of those shirts for you in a week."

"Try one on for me," I say to Blake. "I'll see if I like the color."

I like giving her orders. She flicks that cool green gaze at me and smiles. It's like a whip-crack—the quick dart of her eyes and then the slow glint of teeth. She moves to do what I asked, hips swaying lazily, fingertips trailing down the clothes. This is what a tiger-tamer feels when he thinks he's in control.

She pulls not one but many shirts and jackets down from the wall. Even some twill trousers.

The dressing rooms are the size of a phone booth. Robb is old school, his shop all dark mahogany, brass fixtures, and forest-green couches.

He disappears into the back room to give us privacy.

I relax on one of his chaises while Blake slips in and out of the mahogany phone booth, trying on the clothes for me.

A woman in a man's shirt is a universal turn-on.

Watching Blake parade a succession of sport coats while topless underneath, a pair of suspenders barely covering her nipples, is a whole new level of gender-bending arousal.

My favorite outfit is the pinstriped vest and trousers, a pocket-square in the breast. She even slips on a pair of Robb's Italian loafers.

"You should wear pants more often."

Blake smiles. "I thought you liked me best with no pants."

I pull her down on my lap, slipping my hand inside the pinstripe vest. Her breast is soft as sun-warmed fruit. I pass my thumb over her nipple.

She presses her mouth against mine, her fingers twining through my hair. I *love* the way she's kissing me now, lips parted, her tongue eager and wet like she wants to be fucked.

The men's pants are loose on her. It's easy to slip my hand down the waistband and find the heat of her cunt. Her silken panties cling to her pussy lips. I hook my finger in the gusset, pulling gently on the thin material, rubbing it lightly across her clit. Blake groans and her mouth opens a little more.

I dip my middle finger inside her. It slips right in. She's soaking.

I push my tongue in her mouth as I press my finger deeper. She sucks gently on my tongue like it's a cock. I push it in and out of her mouth at the same pace as my finger. Her inside walls squeeze while her tongue massages mine.

Her hips rock and she grips tight all the way around. My cock is dying to replace that finger. I pull it out of her and bring her wetness to my lips. Her pussy is fragrant as coffee, a thousand layers of rich and heady scent. I kiss her so she can taste it, too.

"Find anything you like?" Robb has reemerged at last.

Blake slides off my lap, saying, "Plenty of things."

Her hair is witchy and her face is flushed. I'm probably worse, if I could see myself. Robb pretends not to notice, brandishing his notepad and pen.

Blake rattles off everything I liked, with a few additions.

"What was that last one?" I demand.

She shows me the material she chose, a deep burgundy.

"I've never worn a red suit."

"It's *vermillion*," Robb says in a scandalized tone.

"With bone buttons," Blake helpfully adds.

I curl my hand around her waist and hook her against my side. "I hope you know what you're doing."

She smiles. "Me too—'cause it's not gonna be cheap."

I TAKE her for dinner at Harry's, a steakhouse in Hanover Square that's a favorite spot for finance types. On our way to our table, Blake nods to two people I know.

"Former clients?"

"Richard was a client three years ago," Blake says. "Graham is just an acquaintance—I was waving to the girl he's with."

I take a closer look at the blonde seated across from Graham Garcia, who is not actually a finance type, but *does* happen to be a Senator married to somebody who is definitely not said blonde. The girl has a frail, almost consumptive look, pink around the nose and eyes. Still pretty but scrawny, like a mild wind could knock her sideways.

"Not my type."

Blake laughs. "Magda's a model."

"I don't give a shit. I'm not attracted to that."

Blake takes a sip of her wine, tilting her head, watching me. "What are you attracted to?"

"Strength."

I don't know if that answer pleases her, not entirely. A small line appears between her eyebrows.

"What's wrong?"

"Nothing," she says.

"You're frowning."

"How do you know Magda isn't strong?"

"Look at her."

"You always judge a book by its cover?"

"Everyone does—when's the last time you picked up a book with a shitty cover?"

She won't give me a smile. Only her eyes flashing up, bright and annoyed.

"How do you know *I'm* strong?"

"Because you're here with me and not in Coney Island still."

A muscle jumps in her throat.

"Well, you're wrong about Magda. And probably me, too. I'm not strong. Not all the time."

I wonder what memory just put weight on her shoulders, sadness pulling her down.

Emotions flash across her face like streetlights, but streetlights from another dimension—I see them clearly without knowing what they mean.

Her next expression is plain: pure panic.

I turn to see Desmond Lowe strolling up to our table.

"Hello, Blake." He smiles, showing straight white teeth.

Desmond is good-looking, I can admit that—tall, fit, tanned, slightly resembles Bradley Cooper, but more British and also more of an asshole.

I barely give him a glance—it's Blake's face I'm watching.

Searching for any hint of how she feels toward the one and only client she "actually dated."

Fuck, I wish it were anyone but him. Anybody else I'd brush off like crumbs, but Desmond isn't so easily dismissed.

He runs the only fund in the city bigger than mine, and he's actually pretty good at his job—despite the fact that he was born with a silver spoon the size of Manchester in his mouth. But he started five feet from the finish line and acts like he ran a marathon, which really pisses me off.

Blake has gone so still she hardly looks like she's breathing. Is she nervous what he'll think? Or what *I* will?

"I'm on a date," she says, which is almost exactly what she said to me.

"I can see that." Desmond smirks. "Ramses. I didn't think you were the type to share."

I *am* the type to put a fist in the middle of that smarmy face, but I'd prefer not to get banned from one of my favorite restaurants.

Instead, I smile right back at him.

"I don't mind sharing at all. You looking for some stock tips? Rough quarter for MaxCap—you barely beat the market."

It's too easy. Desmond goes stiff and angry, which means he's already lost. I lock eyes with Blake to make sure she sees it, too, catching the smile she tries to tuck away. Oh yeah, she likes me sticking it to her ex.

Desmond recovers with the kind of laugh only the son of a viscount knows how to give—a pompous "a-ha."

"What a new money thing to say. We don't keep score on annual returns, we keep score on volume. It's not hard to make moves when you have the amount of a small day trader under management. Come back to me in a decade or so and we'll talk about performance."

Blake's calm voice cuts across me.

"Based on my experience, Desmond, in another ten years, you won't be able to perform at all."

Desmond's mouth puckers up like an anus.

My laugh is a hell of a lot more genuine than his. "That true, Des? They gonna have to add ED to your family crest?"

He's furious but he hasn't taken his eyes off Blake, even when I'm mocking him right to his face.

"Very amusing." He steps closer to her. "Let's ask my neighbors how much you enjoyed our time together—they heard it all."

I'm up from my chair, standing right in front of him before Blake can answer, blocking every inch of Desmond's view of her in her adorable Sunday afternoon outfit.

Heads are turning. I don't give a fuck.

It takes everything to keep my hands out of fists.

"I don't know what it is with you Brits never knowing when to quit. You're not wanted here—get it?"

Desmond's lip curls. "You're making a fool of yourself, Ramses."

"I'm not the one crashing someone else's date."

I turn to give Blake a wink, to let her know I'm well aware what a raging hypocrite I'm being in this moment. Blake's dimple winks back as she bites her lip, trying not to smile.

Desmond's eyes dart between us. His mouth makes bitter shapes.

"You'll find out what she's really like."

He leaves, stalking out of the restaurant entirely.

Blake watches him go. She looks pale and slightly nauseated as I take my seat across from her once more.

To break the ice, I say, "I hope he's right."

She laughs nervously. "What do you mean?"

"I *want* to find out what you're really like. I want to know everything about you."

That doesn't exactly set her at ease. She takes several swallows of her Shiraz.

I wait until she sets down her glass.

"What happened between you two?"

She shakes her head, gaze fixed on the tablecloth. "I don't want to talk about Desmond."

That's a problem because I have about a thousand questions after that brief encounter.

I start with the one that bothers me most:

"Did you love him?"

Her eyes meet mine. Blake's eyes are the kind of green that contain many shades—green like new leaves, like emerald, like olive—all jumbled together in a starburst pattern.

"I thought I did."

I can't tell if that makes me more jealous or less.

"Did you—"

"Why do you care?" She interrupts. "What does it matter what happened with Desmond?"

"I told you," I smile. "I want to be your favorite."

"Well, consider that spot secured. I'd prefer never to see Desmond again as long as I live." Her smile sneaks back across her face, her eyebrow rising in the way it does when she's about to say something naughty. "And it's been a long time since I was as excited for a date as I am right now..."

I let my knee press hers beneath the table. "What are you excited for?"

Her lips part, her breathing deepens.

She whispers, "I want to get lost with you."

Something warm expands inside my chest. All day yesterday while every need and opportunity and setback were clamoring in my brain, I kept returning to the two hours Blake wore that cat suit, when I didn't think about work at all.

I *always* have work on my mind.

Except when I'm with her.

I reach under the table to slide my hand up her thigh. "What are we waiting for?"

"Our food," Blake laughs.

"Let's take it to go."

8

RAMSES

Back at the penthouse, without discussion, we put our to-go boxes in the fridge.

Blake slips off to the guest room where I've already laid out a brand new catsuit on the bed.

"Do you have a whole closet of these stashed away somewhere?" she calls out.

"I can definitely get more, so fuck 'em up as much as you like."

Actually, it's me who's gonna rip that thing off her, but I want to see it *on* her first. Making Blake dress up as a cat might be the smartest idea I ever had—she looked so fucking hot I almost rear-ended a cop speeding back to my apartment.

♪♪ *So Pretty — Reyanna Maria*

She reemerges, stunning me all over again. The hints of her body through that transparent suit are so much sexier than simple nudity. Each turn and flex reveals something new.

The pearl collar glints in the ghostly grotto of her long, dark hair. Just reading the name *Minx* on her tag sends a rush of heat to my head.

She's already put on the character like she put on the suit, taking slow, sensual steps on the balls of her feet, swaying her hips. The way she moves, the way she stands, the way she sneaks glances at me, become furtive and feline.

When she wears that suit, she *is* my little Minx.

She leans against the kitchen counter, resting her chin on her hand, her sharp nails poking through the ends of her fingerless gloves.

I say, "You look hungry."

She smiles, her eyes sliding down my body to the zipper of my pants.

I like that she doesn't talk when she has the collar on. I like trying to guess what she's thinking.

Right now, it's not hard to guess. Minx is hungry. And she's about to get fed.

I open the fridge door, pulling out a carton of cream. Her little pink tongue pokes out, running across her lips.

I pour the cream into a saucer and carry it one handed. With my other arm, I scoop her up and carry her like a cat, elbow hooked under her ass, her legs tucked against my body.

"Come on, Minxie girl."

It shocks her how easily I pick her up. She stiffens but then sinks in, head nuzzled against my chest, her adorable fuzzy ears tickling my chin.

Carrying her gives me the same sense of peace as before, though she's not crying now, just rubbing her nose against my neck. It's something in the way her body fits against mine, like she belongs to me.

I set her down on the rug.

Minx kneels, palms resting flat on her thighs, looking up at me expectantly.

I dip my fingers in the cream.

She licks it off my fingertips, cold and rich and thick.

The feel of her tongue makes my cock swell. I dip my middle finger in the cream and slide it across her lower lip. She closes her mouth around my fingertip and sucks gently, her tongue flicking.

"Greedy girl."

She smiles, licking her lips.

I dip my finger and touch it to my own tongue, tasting what she's tasting. I lean forward to kiss her. She licks and laps at my lips like a little kitten, then sneaks her tongue into my mouth to steal more.

My cock tents the front of my pants. Minx gives it a hungry look.

"Sit back," I order.

She sits neatly on her heels. Her pose is obedient, but her eyes watch my zipper like a cat at a mouse hole. Whatever comes out is about to get devoured.

My cock leaps into my hand, rising like warm bread. I grip it beneath the head and dip the tip in the saucer. Minx's eyes widen and her lips part as she gazes up at my cock, dripping with cream.

A fat white droplet hangs suspended from the head. It falls in slow motion, landing on the flat of her tongue. Minx closes her eyes and swallows.

I touch my cream-soaked cock to her lips. She mouths the head, sucking it softly like a popsicle.

The warmth of her mouth after the chill of the cream is like snowbank to sauna. I melt on her tongue.

She massages under the head of my cock, licking, lapping. She tries to stroke my shaft with her hand, but the glove of the suit gets in the way.

"Here..."

I find a pair of scissors and pull the gloves off her hands, stretching the suit so I can cut it at the wrist. Now her hands are completely bare.

Minx pounces on my cock, seizing the shaft and sliding her hand down *hard* until it catches under the head. There she squeezes as tight as she can, pulling until my cock points straight down.

It feels like all the blood in my body is being forced down into my cock until it throbs like a drum, her fingers locked in a vise-grip beneath the head. Her other hand slips into my pants to cup my balls.

"*Jesus.*" My knees begin to shake, heels stuttering against the floor.

Minx grins. She clamps her mouth around my cock, moving her hand up and down the shaft while gently jostling my balls. The effect is a bit like chucking Mentos in a bottle of Diet Coke. My cum starts boiling.

She slides my cock deeper into her mouth, coating the head with thick saliva from the back of her throat. Her hand stays under my balls, fingertips stroking.

Fuck. She's not just good—she's a magician at making that cock disappear.

I've never been sucked in quite this position, pulled down relentlessly. Each bob of her head makes me hotter, harder, throbbing like I'll burst.

I dip my fingers in the cream and dribble it down the shaft of my cock. She opens her mouth, letting it drip onto her tongue. She licks in long swipes, catching every bit she missed.

She grabs my cock, dunking it deep in the saucer and sucking the cream off the head, licking the long, slow drips off her fingers. A droplet slides down her wrist. She runs her tongue all the way up the back of her hand, lapping it up.

I grab a handful of her hair and push her mouth back onto

my cock, tilting her head, finding the right angle to thrust deep into her throat.

Throats warm up just like pussies do, turning soft and swollen and receptive. The longer I fuck her mouth, the more her saliva thickens. The head of my cock slides deeper.

The milk-fat makes her tongue slippery. Warmth spurts from my cock, mixing with the cream.

Minx kneels between my knees, her head bobbing, hands working. She's not just a pro, she's a fucking all-star. I've never had a blowjob so wild and relentless. It's all I can do to keep from exploding.

"Wait." I stop her to give myself a minute to breathe.

She grins up at me, licking the cream from her lips.

I stoop to rip open the crotch of her new suit, exposing her bare, wet pussy, shocking pink against the dark material.

"Rub your pussy while you suck my cock."

Minx sits back on her heels, knees butterflied apart to expose the little nub of her clit. She knows how to put herself on display, how to show me what I need to see. She rubs her clit with her left hand, stroking my cock with her right. I watch how she touches herself, sometimes sliding her fingers up and down across her clit, sometimes pressing and rubbing in circles.

At first she's doing it for me, touching herself light and pretty, the way she thinks I like. But it feels too good—soon her pace quickens, she presses harder, and her eyes roll back.

She makes eager little sounds, lifting her hips, fucking against her fingers. Her right hand jerks on the shaft of my cock.

I grab her by the back of the head and feed my cock deep into her mouth. The head hits the back of her throat, pounding into the pocket just like a pussy. Her throat is warm and spongy. Her eyelids flutter as she moans around each stroke.

She's rubbing her slit hard enough to start a fire. Her grip around my shaft is still so tight that even though my cock throbs like a volcano, my cum is trapped in my balls, raging, boiling. The load inches up the shaft through flesh so engorged it can barely pass.

Minx strokes my cock mercilessly. Her arm works like a piston, her fingers flowing sensually and smoothly.

I've got pretty good control; I can count the number of times I've blown early on one hand. But in this moment, I'm as much in charge as a bull in a stall being milked into a cup. Minx pumps my cock ruthlessly. When she can see I'm close, she opens her mouth, tongue extended, looking right in my eyes like she's begging me to blow.

I spurt into her mouth, hot and molten. She locks her lips around the head, sucking until black sparks drown the wall of windows, until all I can see is the explosion in my brain.

She lifts her head, cream running down her chin. My cock stands up like an exclamation point.

I grab her and pull her down onto my lap, impaling her on my cock before it can go soft. I spasm inside her, thrusting upward into a pussy even warmer and wetter than her mouth.

I can't feel enough of her skin. I tear the suit down off her shoulders, running my hands down the long curve of her back, gripping her by the hips, pulling her down harder, harder.

In her ear, I growl, "You're a bad girl pulling down on that cock…"

Minx rides me, gasping and panting, her eyes rolling back.

My right hand is wrapped tightly in her hair, fist locked in place against the base of her neck so her head tilts back, my lips pressed against her ear. I speak directly into her brain.

"I want you to show me what a good girl you can be…"

She's grunting with each stroke; she barely seems to hear me. But I know every word is echoing around in her brain.

"Show me how much you want to please me by coming as hard as you can."

The effect is instant.

Her back arches. Her hips thrust forward, pussy clamped around me like a hand. Her breasts point at the ceiling, head thrown back. She lets out a long cry with my cock rammed deep inside her, the head pressed tight against her back wall.

"Ah...ah...AHHHHHHHH!"

She came because I told her to.

I might be a god.

She falls backward in slow motion, lying on my thighs, head hanging off my knees. Her legs hug my waist, my softening cock still inside her.

I press my thumb against her clit, watching her face.

She lets out a shuddering groan. Her cheeks are tinted pink like cherry blossoms, the flush running down across her breasts. Her stiff nipples point straight up. I tug one gently and her cunt twitches around my cock.

I press her clit like a button, rubbing slow circles with my thumb.

"You're the most beautiful kitty I've ever seen. You're so pretty, you're so soft..."

Minx groans, eyelids fluttering as her head lolls against my knees. Her body is warm and limp. My cock is halfway hard inside her, soaking in my own melting cum.

Her clit is the most delicate thing I've ever touched. It's soft and springy beneath the ball of my thumb.

Pleasure rolls over her in shivering waves.

Low and coaxing, I say, "I know you like to roam, little kitty...I don't ask where you go...but only *I* can touch you like this. You're never gonna have a better time than here with me..."

I massage her clit in slow, sensual strokes. Her eyes glaze over, lips parted.

My hands on her body are just as relaxing to me as to her—

maybe even more so. Touch has always been my strongest sense. I'm learning every inch of her and everything she likes.

Her weight is warm and heavy, pressing down on my thighs. Her breathing deepens. The sky outside the windows is black and star-speckled, with wisps of ghostly gray clouds.

Quietly, I say, "I was attracted to you from the moment I saw you. You're so powerful...every time I talk to you, I feel like I'm on fire. I can't stop thinking about you..."

I'm not usually this honest. The other night, I had no intention of telling her how I hurried home to see her. But I've become as relaxed and dreamlike as my little Minx.

"The first time I called you and you hung up on me, I went and jerked off."

She raises her head, eyes glinting with starlight. My cock is getting thicker inside her. I move it a fraction and her pussy clenches tight.

"You're so clever, always working the room. I can't keep my eyes off you. Even when I know you're manipulating me, I want you to do it..."

Her pussy quivers, convulsing around my cock. My thumb rubs sweeping circles on her clit. She lets out a low cry.

"I love what a good girl you're being. Every time you come, I'm so happy..."

Her body shakes, back bent like a bow. How many times can she do this? More than she thinks...

She goes limp against my thighs, head lolling back. Slowly, I release the pressure of my thumb against her clit. She shudders.

I lift her off my cock and wrap her in a blanket, laying her down on the couch so her head rests in my lap. Gently, I stroke my fingers through her hair, starting a movie first so I can pet her as long as I like.

My fingertips tickle through the roots of her hair. I massage the tight muscles at the base of her neck, then at the top of her shoulders, sliding my palm all the way down her spine.

It's a job to get all the lumps out. She shows up here in knots —I have to knead her like dough.

Petting her soothes me.

I've never actually owned a pet. Growing up, I would have killed for a dog but my mom was allergic, and now I travel too much.

I never considered a cat.

This game I'm playing with Blake is feeding me in a way I don't quite understand. I've been charged up all week, my brain alight with a thousand new ideas. Maybe it's just the novelty, but god I hope it lasts. I hadn't realized how bored I'd gotten of everything else.

My father named me Ramses because he wanted me to be a conqueror of worlds. For a long time, that's exactly what I was.

But there's a point of diminishing returns, where you've achieved what you set out to achieve. You keep setting goals, finding new mountains to climb, but the new mountains start to look a lot like the old ones. And sometimes you wonder why you climb mountains at all.

Does Blake like our game?

I know I'm making her feel good. But does she crave it the way I crave it? Does she obsess over it like I do?

It's like we discovered a new continent. One I'm desperate to explore. One that's nothing like the places I've visited before...

I rest my palm on her head, wishing I could read her thoughts with my hands the way I can read her body—wishing they were tattooed across her skin in braille.

I ask her, "Do you like this?"

She raises her head off my lap, looking up at me. "Am I allowed to talk?"

I unclasp her collar and take it off, laying it flat on the stone coffee table. "Now you can."

She grins. "I fucking love it."

I laugh, warmth in my chest. "What do you like about it?"

She considers.

"Wearing the suit makes me feel everything so much more. When I'm acting like a cat, I feel things like a cat... The sun feels extra warm, the couch is extra soft. You seem bigger, stronger, like an ogre almost. It's so intense. Your hands on my body..." She shivers. "It takes me over."

"An ogre?" I pretend to be offended, though I'm not at all.

I *want* to seem strong and powerful to her. Intimidating, even. Because Blake intimidates the fuck out of me sometimes. She's so self-possessed. It's like nothing can touch her—not even me.

"Maybe not an ogre..." Blake dances her fingers up and down the back of my calf with her head in my lap. She likes to touch me the way I like to touch her—for the fun of it. Creating sensation for her own enjoyment as much as for mine.

I wonder if she can feel my cock swelling beneath her. It never went entirely soft and now it's acting like it didn't just explode.

She looks up at me, her dimple appearing. "It feels like you're a different species—bigger, stronger, in control of everything around me. It makes me want to impress you."

There's no way she can't feel the way my cock just jumped.

My voice comes out in a growl. "That makes me *very* happy with you."

"Why?" Blake's genuinely curious. She wants to understand this like I do—like we're scientists of sex.

I answer like we're gonna solve the theorem.

"It gets me off hard when you show me that you want to please me. It's not what you do—it's the look on your face while you do it."

Blake grins. She likes that answer.

I stroke my hand down her back, wanting to keep her in this half-glazed state of honesty. "What else did you like?"

"The cream..." Her tongue darts out, touching her lips. "It was like I *had* to have it. The way it tasted...and the way *you* tasted mixed with it...salty-sweet..."

Her eyes close exactly the way they did at April's house when she was tasting the seasoning on her rice.

For me, it was all about the visual: the look of that cream spilling out of her mouth, mixed with my cum...

I stroke her hair to calm myself down.

"That's so relaxing..." Blake mumbles against my thigh.

Her weight seems to increase with each stroke. We're quiet, the light from the TV flickering on our skin.

I picked one of the Marvel movies, almost at random. It's the one with Ultron. We get to the part where he's trying to buy vibranium from a mercenary and he transfers a billion dollars using his robot plug-in to the world's banking system.

"It's all in your dummy holdings," Ultron says. "Finance is so weird."

For some reason, this strikes both Blake and me as hilarious. We both start laughing.

I took the collar off, but I haven't stopped petting her hair. Blake's hair is long and straight, blue-black in the light of the TV. She's still wearing the cat ears. I scratch around them, making her laugh softly and snuggle against me.

Her breathing deepens. She stops reacting to the movie. I keep stroking her hair, gentle and slow...

She falls asleep on my lap, curled up in the blanket. I watch the rest of the movie, petting her the whole time.

When the credits roll, I'm tempted to cover Blake with another blanket and let her sleep on the couch, or better yet, carry her into my bed. She's so deeply asleep, I doubt she'd wake.

I absolutely plan to make her break her "no sleepovers" rule. "Red means stop" I can respect, but the rest of the list has to go— starting with her other clients.

I want her all to myself.

But I'm not going to trick her into sleeping over. Not yet.

Gently, I wake her.

She sits up, startled that she fell asleep.

"What time is it?"

"Close to one."

"I should go."

I woke her up to drive her home. But as she rubs the sleep from her eyes, I say, "We never ate our dinner. Aren't you hungry?"

Her stomach gurgles as soon as she thinks about it.

"Don't lie," I laugh. "You already gave yourself away."

I heat up our food and put it on fresh plates, carrying it into the living room. Blake starts the next Avengers movie while we eat.

Sometimes we watch and sometimes we talk. About halfway through the film, we rip off the rest of Blake's suit and fuck on the couch. By the time I drive her home, it's four o'clock in the morning and we've watched one and a half movies and had sex twice more.

When I drop her off, I say, "What are you doing next weekend?"

"Why?"

"I want to take you to Bali."

Blake hesitates, biting her lip. Without meeting my eye, she says. "I can't."

"Why not?"

"I'm already booked."

She gives me a quick kiss on the mouth and exits the car so I can't argue with her.

I don't know if she's actually busy or she's just trying to reestablish boundaries because she fell asleep at my house. Either way, I don't like it.

I watch her climb the steps and disappear inside her building, waiting to confirm that the light switches on inside the third-floor corner unit.

This isn't the moment to argue.

But it's definitely time to clear her roster.

9

BLAKE

What the fuck am I doing?

That's the last thought in my head when it hits my pillow and the first thing I think when I wake up around ten.

I can't believe I fell asleep on his couch.

Breaking my own rules is pouring gasoline on the brushfire that is Ramses. He's going to blaze either way—it's up to me to set barricades so he doesn't burn down my house.

What I said in his car was a lie. I don't have anything booked this weekend. And I'd fucking *love* to see Bali, especially flying private.

But this thing with Ramses is strapped to a rocket and I need to slow the fuck down.

Ramses is a boundary pusher and a line crosser.

I'm the actual problem.

I fell asleep at his house because I was way too comfortable. When I woke up, I should have gone home. Instead, I stayed another three hours because I wanted to. Because I was having a fucking blast.

This isn't supposed to be a blast. It's supposed to be my job.

Never believe it's real.

I've done this before.

I swore, I swore, I swore I was never going to do it again.

There is no Pretty Woman. Men who hire sex workers aren't looking for love.

When you learn something the hard way, you shouldn't have to learn it twice.

That would make me an idiot. Am I a fucking idiot?

I'm sure acting like one.

I let Ramses scare off Zak Simmons, and I didn't even try to get him back. I dropped Anthony Keller myself when his IPO went toe-up. That was always the plan, but I haven't replaced him. My only remaining client is Lukas Larsen, and he's always been the client I see the least because we have a very specific arrangement. He won't work to balance Ramses.

I need clients so my business doesn't wither and to keep Ramses in check. Giving him his way in this would be lying down and begging him to run a bulldozer over me any time he pleases.

Plus, I fucking promised myself.

If you can't trust yourself, then you really can't trust anyone.

I'm getting another client—today. I can pick off the wait list.

And I'm not going to Bali with Ramses, not this weekend. His games are brain-bending enough right here in New York.

It's already fucking with me. Minx is so seductive. I love being her. Everything is pleasure, everything is release. Doing what Ramses wants comes too easily, it feels too good.

I see what he's doing, and worse, I see it working.

He's invaded my head, corrupted my thought processes. He colors my thoughts like Ultron infesting the internet.

I smile to myself, thinking how much I enjoyed that ridiculous movie. I'd seen it before and found it utterly forgettable.

Now the scenes glint in my mind, linked to Ramses' jokes, his comments, the moments we appreciated together.

He's not your fucking boyfriend.

I shake that thought out of my head and open my laptop instead.

I'm sitting at my kitchen table, drinking tea. For the first time, I think how empty my apartment can feel.

Usually, that's exactly what I love about it. I keep my counters bare, the whole space spotless so nothing leaps out at me, nothing glares with its ugliness, its messiness. Everything stays exactly where I put it, nothing gets broken or fucked with.

I lived in a lot of ugly places, and I loathed every minute. The screams and thuds of the other kids, the shouting of the parents, the stink of dirty dishes, full diapers, overflowing garbage bins. Ratty carpets, mangy dogs, art that's just words on plaques shouting values you don't share. What I would have given for a bare white room of my own.

Now I think...I should get a plant. Why am I the only thing alive in here?

Maybe even a cat.

I think how calm and peaceful Ramses becomes when he strokes his hand down my back.

I could have a cat on my lap right now, keeping me company while I work.

I never wanted a pet because I hated being forced to care for the kids and animals I didn't even want to live with, let alone work to maintain.

But I like cats. I've always liked cats. The one behind my ear is one specific cat, Luna. She didn't belong to me, but she used to come and sleep in my bed. She picked me over anyone else in the house, even Sadie, and animals always love Sadie best.

That was the worst house I lived in. I hate to think about that time—years that are just a black blur in my brain. The memories are there, but I keep them in the dark.

Some of those days, the only good thing I felt was the moment when Luna slipped under my covers and curled up next to me. That's why I keep her behind my ear.

But I don't want to think about that, either.

I want to do what I always do, which is lose myself in work.

I crank my music and start scrolling through earnings reports, company analytics, and the Relative Strength Index. The numbers flow across my screen and my brain does the thing it does best, where it starts to find the connections, the patterns, the things that stand out.

How do people compose music? How do they write books? I have no fucking clue, that's a foreign language to me. I speak numbers. In fact, you could say it's my native tongue.

I analyze data through the rest of the morning, and then I spend the afternoon building my options strategies for the companies on my watchlist that are about to have an earnings release.

I don't think about Ramses at all. Except for the three or four times he pops into my head.

Maybe it was six. But who's counting?

RAMSES DOESN'T CALL or text all day, which strikes me as a somewhat ominous silence. He could be bugged that I turned him down about Bali, but I don't think so. I think he's regrouping, planning his next attack.

Or fuck, maybe he's just busy. His life doesn't revolve around me.

I meet my friend Magda for dinner. She texted me when I saw her at Harry's last night: *Heads up, Desmond's here too.*

I didn't actually see the text until later, so it wasn't much good as a warning, but it was an excellent reminder that Magda has my back.

We haven't met up one-on-one in a couple of weeks. She fills me in on how her pottery class is going and how her mom's doing —she has MS and lives with Magda.

"Everybody thinks people in wheelchairs are saints, but she was a bitch before she got sick and she's worse now. And fuck, I can't blame her. She's fifty-four years old and some days she can't hold a spoon. But don't yell at me, I'm the one here helping you."

"I'm sorry." I wish there was something better to say than that. There probably is, but I can't think of it. So I add, "She's lucky she has you."

Magda snorts. "Tell her she's lucky about anything and she'll run over your foot."

"Does everybody get mean when they get old?"

"They definitely give less of a fuck about being nice."

"I saw Tabitha."

Magda laughs, "Speak of the devil."

Magda is one of Tabitha's favorites just like me, but that sure as hell didn't mean she gave us preferential treatment.

I say, "She's not looking good."

Magda sighs. "Sometimes I wonder if she's the best friend I ever had or my worst enemy. And that makes me wonder if I did *you* a favor."

Magda's talking about how she hooked me up with my first escort job when I was a broke-ass drop-out too depressed to put pants on in the morning.

I tell her, "You saved my life."

"Oh, shut up, that's not true."

"Yes, it is."

When I was lost in the dark, with no hope and no options, Magda opened a door. Not everything through that door has to be ponies and roses because it's all better than what I was planning to do.

Magda puts her hand over mine and squeezes once, hard, before letting go.

"Anyway," she grins. "I want to hear about your date with the Pharaoh."

"Oh god," I roll my eyes. "Please don't call him that."

"Why not?"

"Because it would make him so happy."

Magda laughs. "What if I *want* to make him happy..."

I give her a naughty look. "Then you'd be richly rewarded."

She sits up straight, pressing both palms flat on the table. "Tell me everything."

Priests keep their secrets. But not from other priests.

"It's good," I tell her. "Way too fucking good."

Magda makes a face that's part grimace, part nodding. "It's dangerous when the sex is too good."

Magda has her own Desmond—his name is Kyle, and he's a client-turned boyfriend-turned raging coke addict who ruined her life for about three years. But before that, she used to tell me stories of the outrageous ways he made her scream.

Maybe we all have to learn the hard way.

"Ramses' hot." Magda acknowledges. "Looks like he'd eat a baby on a sandwich, though."

That's what I thought at first.

Now I think of all the other expressions I've seen on his face that were anything but brutal.

I think of how he looks when he touches me. I think of how he held me as I cried and how he didn't make me feel bad about it afterward. But I also consider my constant suspicion that everything he does is to fuck with my head.

"He's...complicated."

Magda bites her knuckle, giving me a sneaky look. "What's he into? Can I guess?"

"You can try."

"Ooo, that sounds nasty...he wants you to pee on him, doesn't he?"

"Not yet."

"Not *yet!*" Magda crows. "That's a clue...give me a hint...does it involve...leather?"

"Surprisingly, no."

"But it could!"

I laugh. "You're never gonna guess."

I'm not worried someone will overhear us. When Magda and I go out together, we avoid the fancy Michelin star places by the Financial District where we're sure to bump into clients. Ramses took me to Harry's on purpose—he wanted to be seen with me.

Magda and I are safe and sound in a tiny shawarma shop completely devoid of Wall Street bros, so I give her a brief description of the game and its makeshift rules.

"You kinky bitch!" She laughs. "You like that shit?"

"I'm addicted."

Ramses hasn't called me all day, which was exactly what I wanted—to calm things down, slow the pace. But already I'm dreaming of riding that elevator back up to his apartment in the clouds, to slip inside my cat suit.

"They never get enough of bossing people around, do they?" Magda says.

"Mm...it's more than that, though."

"How so?"

I'm trying to think how to say this.

If Ramses just wanted to dominate me, he'd stick to whips and chains.

I think of how long he spent petting me. How he wrapped me up in the blanket. How carefully he plated my food.

And I remember how lifeless my apartment felt this morning.

"It's almost like...he really just needs a pet."

Magda snorts. "One he can legally fuck."

"He's efficient."

Now we're both giggling.

"That's what they're really paying us for," Magda says. "So they don't feel alone. But *we* still are."

My laugh stops when she hits me with that little nugget.

I used to dream of the gorgeous solitude of a castle in the middle of nowhere.

But now I'm wondering if it will just feel like being alone in my apartment.

10

BLAKE

I'm standing in the middle of Lukas Larsen's living room, wearing a leather corset and a pair of platform stilettos that put me over six feet. Lukas huddles on the carpet, completely naked, forehead pressed against the floor.

"May I kiss your foot, mistress?"

"You can *lick* my foot, starting with my toes."

"Yes, mistress," Lukas cries, face bright with delight. He grabs my stiletto in both hands, licking and sucking on my freshly pedicured toes, moaning with pleasure like he's devouring a twelve-course meal.

I've been the one licking feet. It doesn't matter. I can do anything with my body when I disappear inside my head. It's my greatest strength. My only strength sometimes.

Ramses does NOT let me escape. He demands eye contact the whole time. Real orgasms. He forces me to be present with him.

That was hard for me at first. I don't have sex that way, on or off the clock.

But I'm learning. Ramses only had to remind me once the last time we fucked.

Lukas is drenching my foot with his tongue, his cock leaking cum in a long, thin strand like a spider's thread.

Resting my riding crop lightly on his shoulder, I say, "Work your way up my leg. *Slowly.*"

Lukas inches up my foot, licking the ankle strap of my shoe, gradually advancing up my shin. His wet tongue bathes every inch along the way.

He's an obedient slave. If he forgets to be obedient, I'll remind him. His back is already striped from minor mistakes.

Lukas loves correction. Sometimes he fucks up on purpose so I'll smack him again.

When he gets to my knee, he misses a spot. I crack him right on the ass, making him yelp.

"Every inch."

"Yes, mistress!"

When he reaches my thigh, I say, "Get my phone."

Lukas scrambles to retrieve my cell phone from the neat pile of clothes I left on his couch.

An idea occurs. I point the crop at him.

"Ah ah! Bring it in your mouth."

Eagerly, Lukas clamps the phone between his lips and crawls over to drop it in my hand. He looks just like a puppy fetching a stick. He peeks up at me in just the same way, checking for approval.

I can see why Ramses gets off on this.

I sit back on the couch, spreading my legs.

"Eat my pussy while I shop for clothes."

Lukas pants with excitement. This is his favorite, favorite thing.

He kneels between my legs, licking my pussy while I scroll through my favorite stores.

I'm shopping with Lukas' credit card. He loves when I run up his bill. And he loves it even more when I model what I bought.

I pick out $2k of silky lingerie from Fleur du Mal, then switch to the next site. The most I've spent in one go is $12k, but honestly, it's hard to keep it up for long because Lukas isn't very good at oral. Right now it feels like he's trying to sand my clit off with his tongue.

"Gentle!" I snap, whipping him smartly with the riding crop.

"Sorry, mistress," Lukas mumbles into my pussy.

He calms down for a minute, but not for long. He really is like a dog, humping and slobbering.

While I'm scrolling, a call comes through from Ramses.

Usually, I would never answer a call while I'm with a client. Especially not from another client.

But it's been three whole days since I talked to Ramses. If I ignore him, he'll think I'm angry.

Plus...I want to hear his voice.

And when I'm the mistress, I get to do whatever the fuck I want. That's the whole point.

I answer the call.

"Finally stopped sulking?"

Ramses' deep chuckle makes me wetter than anything Lukas has accomplished between my legs.

"I think you know me better than that."

Terror and excitement sweep me from head to foot. The little hairs on my arms look electrocuted.

"So you've been plotting your next move?"

"Not plotting," Ramses says. "Setting in motion."

"Are you going to tell me what it is?"

"You'll know when it happens."

That doesn't sound good. And yet, I'm so curious to know what horrible thing Ramses has planned for me, I'm almost excited to see. What the fuck is wrong with me, seriously?

"What are you doing right now?" Ramses says.

I look at Lukas Larsen's blond head between my thighs and a chuckle sneaks out.

"Do you really want to know?"

Ramses' voice drops another octave, rumbling in my ear. "Are you doing something that would make me jealous?"

"Extremely."

"Bad girl. It's like you want to be punished."

I laugh quietly. I'm just like Lukas. Maybe we all are.

"Is that you trying to set up our next date?"

I can hear his smile. "Are you free tomorrow night?"

"I could be."

When I end the call, Lukas lifts his wet, messy face. Eagerly, he says, "Was that Ramses?"

Jesus, word's already gotten around.

"Back to work," I say, shoving his head down.

MY SESSION with Lukas lasts two hours.

When I'm finished, he's a quivering, sweaty mess. I run a bath for him and set out a fresh, fluffy towel before I leave.

I change my shoes in the elevator. The stilettos go back in my duffle bag so I can walk the rest of the way home in sneakers.

It's almost midnight.

I'm exhausted.

It's a fuck of a lot of work being the dom. I have to plan these sessions ahead of time, pack my tools, spend an hour and a half on hair, makeup, nails, and wardrobe.

The two-hour session is stage performance for an audience of one, who has to be whipped, teased, taunted, and beguiled through an escalating sequence of titillations, all leading to the final climax.

BDSM is an art.

That's why I was so impressed with Ramses.

He created an experience. And at the end, he made me bawl like a fucking baby. It was powerful.

No less powerful because I know what he's doing. Actually, that just impresses me more—it's a fuck of a lot harder to work sleight-of-hand on a fellow magician.

I laugh, remembering what he whispered to me as I lay across his lap:

Even when I can see you manipulating me, I want you to do it...

I could say the same to him.

What I like most about Ramses are the things we have in common.

I'd fucking kill to look through his watchlist, to see what companies he's tracking and ask for his numbers.

A fantasy flashes through my head where I can ask Ramses anything I want and he has to tell me everything, all his strategies and secrets. In one afternoon, I could learn everything I've ever wondered about Ramses Howell and Obelisk.

The idea of sitting inside his office, having that kind of intimate, honest conversation, is so strangely and suddenly erotic that my face goes hot and I realize I've taken a wrong turn.

I'm walking through a shabby neighborhood, paint peeling off the buildings like eucalyptus bark, trash overflowing the bins. It's still nicer than plenty of places I've lived.

A couple of sex workers share a coffee outside a bodega. One is younger than me and blonde, the other wears a blue furry coat and fishnets, nothing else beneath. She has a pretty, crooked smile and she's making her friend laugh. They gulp down the rest of their coffee, then totter back to the street on sky-high heels.

Sex work is sex work. But private clients aren't the same as working a corner, like growing up poor on Coney Island ain't the same as growing up poor in Mumbai. Even escorts have privilege, I guess.

I've had some shit experiences, especially when I started. I bet these girls have had worse. I'm lucky and I'm unlucky. Successful and fucked in the head.

I pass the girls, wondering if they feel any connection to me. Can they tell we're all doing the same thing tonight? Or do I look like just another rich bitch in a $1600 coat?

I once read a book called *Pimp*, written by an actual pimp.

He said he could only work his girls for so long before they'd go crazy. He called it "mileage on a ho".

As I turn the corner, I think, *I've got a lot of miles on me.*

I can feel it. Things that used to be easy aren't so easy anymore.

God, I'm weird this week.

It's Ramses' fault.

I can't believe I cried in front of him.

And what's he planning to do? He's had three entire days to sulk and scheme.

I picked a new client off the list, but I haven't called him yet. Ramses has me amped up and distracted.

And yet the only thing I'm looking forward to this week is seeing him again.

I press my palms against my cheeks, face still on fire.

I wish I were walking to his house right now...

Five minutes with his hands down the front of my pants and my heart wouldn't be racing like this. I'd get what I need and I could go to sleep...

I wish I could hire Ramses to do what I want for an hour...

I laugh, really picturing that. My sneakers pound the pavement, the duffle bag bouncing against my ass. The night smells like outdoor beer gardens and gardenias. I'm getting close to my house.

It's me who needs an escort. One with Ramses' exact hands...'cause I don't want to be alone right now, either.

That thought flashes through my brain like a joke, but when my key touches the lock, it rings in my ears like a bell:

I don't want to be alone right now.

My apartment is quiet as a tomb.

My brain's still zinging from the session. I didn't come—not once. Most clients aren't like Ramses. They don't give a shit if I get off.

I have a vibrator, several in fact. I could take care of this nagging itch and send myself off to sleep.

Instead, I find myself pulling out my phone.

I text Ramses:

> I'm scared to see you tomorrow. What are you planning?

His reply comes with pleasing speed:

> Don't be scared.

That's an order more than an assurance. I'm grinning anyway. I send back:

> Why are you still up?

So fast he must be at a keyboard, he responds,

> I'm always up this late.

He only waits a breath before adding:

> Are you home now?

It's hard to tell tone from a text, but that feels like an invitation, not more jealousy.

I type back:

> Just getting undressed.

I slide off my shoes and start unbuttoning my coat to make it true.

I'm hoping Ramses will take the bait.

Undressing for the camera and touching myself while Ramses watches would be a fuck of a lot more fun than doing it alone.

His answer is even better:

> It's tomorrow.

> Come do that over here.

Laughing like an idiot, I snatch up my shoes.

I'm at his place by 12:49.

11

RAMSES

I'm doing the morning run-down with Briggs, and I can't stop grinning.

This is a problem because the run-down is not going well and grinning is suspicious.

After the third or fourth piece of bad news, Briggs says, "What is going *on* with you?"

"What do you mean?"

I know exactly what he means, but Briggs is fun to gaslight.

I'm smiling so hard my cheeks are aching. They're not used to this type of exercise.

It's making Briggs very uncomfortable.

"Why are you so happy?"

Because last night Blake mewed like a kitten while she rode my cock, and it made me explode like Vesuvius.

Out loud, I say, "It's a nice morning."

"A *nice morning*?" Briggs stares like I'm speaking Swahili. "Are you fucking with me? Did I forget something? Are you actually pissed?"

"You seem uptight," I remark, opening all the blinds. It really is a gorgeous day. My office has the best view in the building—why do I keep these closed?

My assistant comes in and starts listing off my messages. This is perfect because it makes Briggs shut up so I can mentally examine the highlights from the night before in blissful detail.

She wore some strappy black leather thing that didn't cover her tits. She gave herself a bath for the first ten minutes, licking her arms, washing her face...I was so hard my cock could have punched through my pants...Her eyes were glittering like there was no Blake, only Minx. She—

Briggs is barking at Melanie about something. I should stop letting other people into my office.

"What's the problem?"

"It's not a problem, it's an invitation." Melanie stuffs some embossed piece of nonsense into my hands.

"Tell him to fuck off!" Briggs shouts.

I finally decipher the copperplate. *MaxCap Investments is proud to announce its fourth annual...*

"Nope, I'll be there."

"*What?*" Briggs turns around to goggle at me.

"And tell him I'm bringing a date."

Briggs waits until Melanie leaves then wheels around and starts squawking.

"Are you serious right now? You actually want to go to that thing?"

I toss Desmond Lowe's invitation onto my desk. "You're coming, too."

Briggs is both stunned and dismayed.

"Why do we want to spend three days watching that fucker publicly jerk off all over his own—"

I've gone back to thinking about how wild my little Minx was last night, like she was possessed. She was the one pushing boundaries, begging for more...

"Please tell me this isn't about Blake," Briggs says.

Already, he knows better than to call her anything but her name.

I wouldn't say it's *about* Blake, exactly…

But I realized something last night.

Knowing she came straight from another man's house was a hell of a turn-on. When she was done with him, she wanted *me*.

I grin and slap Briggs hard on the shoulder.

"It's about having fun. When's the last time we had fun?"

Briggs looks about as festive as malaria. "If you're bringing a date, then I have to find one, too."

"Yup. And your own ride."

"My own *ride?*" It's like I told him he was going to have to hitchhike to the Hamptons naked. "What about the jet?"

Briggs loves taking the jet. He'd take it from Manhattan to Queens if I let him.

"No jet," I say firmly. "Blake and I are driving."

I've got plans for that drive. And they definitely don't involve Briggs.

I PICK Blake up at seven o'clock. She's as punctual as ever, though she looks a little nervous as she climbs in the car.

"Are you going to tell me where we're going?"

"Don't worry," I say. "You'll like it."

As we drive, I let my arm rest across the back of her seat. She leans into me, her head on my shoulder. Her body melts against mine. I like that she's substantial, tall and curvy. Some of the girls I've dated were so much smaller than me, it felt like they'd snap from an enthusiastic hug.

We pull up in front of the Billionaire Traders Club. Blake perks up immediately, recognizing the building.

"You ever been to one of these?"

I already know she hasn't—you have to have a billion under management just to be considered.

The meeting's already in full swing. Traders, brokers, and angel investors mill around, eating expensive catering and drinking way too much.

Pennywise and Briggs are here. Pennywise is one of my most successful traders. I poached him from Oakmont, and he's doubled his book since then.

He hustles over as soon as he sees us, giving Blake a curious up and down.

"If it isn't Lady Luck...has Ramses got you picking stocks as well as ponies?"

"Yup," Blake says without missing a beat. "He says a couple more winners and I can have your office."

"You don't want Penn's office," I say. "He sleeps in there when his wife's mad at him and it smells like Takis."

"Breakfast of champions," Pennywise says, unashamed. It's almost impossible to embarrass Penn because he's as thick-skinned as a rhino and has very little morals—two of my favorite traits in a trader.

I take Blake around the room, introducing her to everyone else. She already met Briggs, but he comes over anyway to fuck up my day.

"Blake! You got any hot friends I can hire for Desmond's party? I was seeing this waitress from Staten Island, but it's been like a month so she's expecting me to come over to her place sometimes, and I made a solemn vow to never take that ferry again."

Blake's smile comes a half-second late. "I might, but you're going to have to tell me what you did to boycott Staten Island."

Briggs shakes his head stubbornly. "It's just a rule. When you do a walk of shame, there can't be ferries involved."

Blake's laugh sounds natural, but I see how she angles herself to watch my face as well as Briggs. "What's your type?"

"Blonde, tall, huge tits, super filthy, Catholic."

"But you're not Catholic," I remind Briggs.

"That's to make sure she doesn't miss the 'super filthy' part. Ain't no one dirtier than a girl who went to Catholic school."

Blake nods in agreement. "All that hot, hot religious repression. I get it."

"I need her for the whole weekend," Briggs says. "That's the only way I'm gonna make it through three whole days with that limey fucker."

That little line appears between Blake's eyebrows. It's hard to see beneath her bangs, but I'm getting better at catching her signals. Her eyes flick over to mine, then back to Briggs.

"I might know someone."

I slip my arm through hers, pulling her away from Briggs and resisting the urge to pop him on the way past. I wasn't planning to mention Desmond's party just yet.

Blake doesn't say anything about it, which probably isn't a good sign.

I weave her through the crowd, my arm still linked with hers.

Low and calm, she says, "I'm surprised you brought me here."

"Why?"

"Because there's a difference between being seen at Harry's and being seen together here."

"Educate me."

"People will think we're actually dating."

"They'll think that for sure when they see us together at Desmond's."

She lets go of my arm, turning to look at me.

"I'm not going to that."

"We can talk about it."

"We don't need to."

We're interrupted by an acquaintance of mine, then one of Blake's. This is why we came, so there's no keeping them away.

Blake knows a few people but not as many as me. The Billionaire Trader's Club is as exclusive as it gets. Just the annual dues are $150k. I paid Blake's already.

When I tell her that, she's not as elated as I expected. In fact, she kind of looks pissed.

"Why did you do that?"

"Because it's the best investment club in the city. You'll make connections and pick up a ton of information."

She only scowls harder. "That's what I thought."

Now I'm annoyed. "What's the problem?"

"The *problem*," Blake hisses, pulling me away from the group and closer to the windows, "is that I don't want anyone to know I'm investing. And joining an investor's club isn't exactly subtle."

"Maybe it's time to graduate from that."

She tosses her head, cheeks full of color. "It's not your choice when I *graduate* from anything. And by the way, that's condescending as fuck."

"I'm doing you a favor—"

"You're doing *yourself* a favor," Blake snaps. "You're trying to replace my other clients with this club."

When she can see right through me, I feel cheap as glass.

And this wasn't fucking cheap.

I step close, looming over her.

"I had to call in a fuck of a lot of favors to get you in here."

Blake folds her arms over her chest, eyes narrowed. "Are you a member?"

I pause half a second. "No, but—"

She scoffs and turns away from me. I grab her arm and pull her right back.

"So what if I'm not? You could learn a lot here."

"*I* could. But not you," she says scornfully.

"Traders would give an arm to get in here."

"Yeah," Blake drips sarcasm. "Pennywise, Briggs, the rest of your stooges...but not you. And not anyone else on your level. You think I belong here? I think I belong where you go."

I stare at her, lost for words.

Blake...kind of has a point.

I don't waste my time in clubs. Not even this one.

But Blake isn't me. She's still got a lot to learn. Including, don't spit in someone's face when they offer you a gift.

Coldly, I say, "You're not on my level. Not even close. I've got ten years of experience on you, and you don't know everything you think you know."

"Fine." Blake is even icier. "I'll take the membership. But I'm not dropping my other clients."

"*Client*," I say. "You've only got Lukas."

"Actually, I'm back up to three."

The rest of the room seems to burn away until all I see is Blake's stubborn face. I'd like to turn her over my knee and spank her.

"Who?"

"None of your business." She pulls free of my grip.

She's lying.

Is she lying?

Who the fuck did she take?

I'm scanning her face but I can't fucking read her. All I see are those green eyes burning up at me, that smoky skin, that set mouth. When she isn't wearing her charming mask, she's angry underneath.

That I can understand.

I'm angry, too.

I grab her hand, linking my fingers roughly through hers.

"Where are we going?" she says as I pull her from the room.

I punch the elevator button. "Out of here."

"You can't act like this," Blake says, still with that steady calm. "I told you from the beginning—"

"I know!" I bark.

The elevator doors open.

The moment we're inside, I'm all over her. Hands on her face, her breasts, down her dress. I scoop her up and slam her against the metal wall, her legs around my waist. The elevator rocks on its cable.

"Take all the clients you want," I snarl. "You're mine tonight. And this is what *I* want to do."

I pull on her skirt. The material tears. Blake rips it to the thigh so we can yank it all the way up. The elevator sinks like a submarine.

Blake unbuttons my trousers and I tug her underwear to the side. I'm inside her before we've dropped four floors.

She cries out at the first thrust. I fuck her with each floor we pass: 29, 28, 27, 26, 25, 24…

She bites the side of my neck, licking and sucking hard. Her teeth nip beneath the collar of my shirt, her stilettos scratch the backs of my thighs.

Her scent overwhelms me when I'm buried in her hair, my nose against her scalp. Nothing smells quite like her. I noticed it the moment I stood in that doorway searching for her.

Now I'm bathed in Blake, in this little metal box plunging down. Her hair and breath, the heat from her skin, the wetness of her pussy around my cock…that's the perfume that brings me alive, that charges me like a stimulant. I breathe her in over and over while I thrust deep inside her, nuzzling and snuffling against her neck.

Blake's cries echo in the box as we drop. She's always loud, she can't hold back. I remember Desmond's taunt, *Ask my neighbors what you thought, they heard everything…*and I know there must be truth in it. My jealousy ignites and I fuck her harder,

harder, harder against the wall, rocking the elevator on its cable, trying to obliterate any flesh memory of anybody who wasn't me. Trying to prove that no one's ever made her feel like *this*.

15, 14, 13, 12...

Her fingers dig into my back, my dress shirt shredding like paper beneath those nails. The cuts spark like salt on the deep, meaty pleasure I feel in fucking her as hard as I can.

Her pussy locks around my cock and I know this is it. The elevator slows, the last numbers inching by: 4, 3...2...

Sweat rolls down my back, flaming in the cuts. My legs are pistons, driving in deep. I fuck her rabid, raging, wanting to take every bit of her and leave nothing for anyone else.

She screams and I make a sound I've definitely never made before. Call it a war cry—because I know what I want and I'll do whatever I have to do to get it. The hot, flooding pleasure confirms it. I've tasted this now, and I'm not fucking sharing it.

I let Blake down, supporting her while I tuck myself away and button my pants.

The elevator doors open, letting out a rush of warm air and the scent of sex directly into Halston Reeve's face.

I've got a lot of enemies in this city, but there's only one person I hate.

I can't be alone in a room with Reeves because I'll fucking kill him.

He observes Blake's torn dress, our wild hair, and the subtropical humidity. His hard face twists.

"You really are just an animal, aren't you, Ramses?"

For once, the rage doesn't come. I laugh, grabbing Blake's hand and pulling her past him.

"You got that right, motherfucker."

12

BLAKE

I didn't actually have a third client when I lied to Ramses last night.

Now it's time to get one. No more fucking around.

I call up Sean Martin, an executive in his fifties who works in medical devices, not finance. I tell myself that I'm not intentionally picking the person least likely to piss Ramses off.

For his part, Ramses lays low the rest of the week. I see him a couple more times, meeting for a quick lunch on Thursday then a full Minx session Saturday night. He doesn't push about Desmond's party, and I don't bring it up again either.

After Desmond saw me with Ramses, he texted me twice and sent a hundred pink roses to my house. I ignored the texts and threw the flowers in the trash. I'm not going to be the chew toy they fight over.

I have to admit, though...

During my lunch date with Ramses, when I saw he was heading back to the office and didn't have time for sex...I got a warm flush realizing he called me there just to see me.

I like spending time with him. I don't know how to say it more plainly than that. His conversation ignites my brain and it's the best sex I've ever had.

But he's not my boyfriend. And I'm a fool to think he ever could be.

Johns don't love you. They can't because they're trying to buy you. And they're trying to buy you because they don't want to actually love you. It's not a line to a destination—it's a circle that goes around and around.

Ramses tried to buy me all over again with the membership to the BTC. He'll keep trying because that's his nature. He wants to own everything, control everything, and above all, get what he wants.

I'm not a stock.

I'm a player.

And what's best for *me* is to keep my client list full and keep playing the game.

That's what I tell myself when I check my phone again to see if Ramses texted.

He'll use you and throw you away when he's done. That's what they do.

THE NEXT WEEK, my newest client asks me to accompany him to some big hospital gala. Ramses texts me to get together the same night, but I tell him I'm busy and we set a date for Friday instead.

Everything is going well with Sean, a soft-spoken widower with gray hair and horn-rimmed glasses, until we walk inside the Rainbow Room at Rockefeller Plaza and I see the banners strung everywhere:

Lenox Hill Children's Hospital

And underneath, in a tasteful but highly legible font:

Sponsored by Obelisk Investments

I look around wildly for Ramses. It doesn't take long to search a room for something that big—when I see he's not there, I let myself breathe again and recognize that he probably doesn't attend every event his company sponsors.

"Something wrong?" Sean says.

"Nope." I grab a glass of champagne and gulp it down. "Everything is perfect."

Sean leads me to his table right up at the front of the room. He introduces me to our seat-mates, then we all make chit-chat until the lights drop and the talking begins.

The first speaker is Tom Brewer. I've got a big position in his biotech company, but he doesn't say anything useful, just spouting all the same jargony shit you'd get from a press release.

I must have attended a hundred events like this by now. Maybe more. I think of the endless string of nights almost exactly like this—rolls on the table, tiny spheres of butter, ice water, red wine or white. Video screens above the stage, slide shows, awards, clapping, polite conversation turning into less-polite conversation as the drinks take hold.

How many people have I met that I'll never see again?

How many times have I spouted off my bullshit—fake names, fake careers, fake *how did you two meet* stories...

Sean has asked me to pretend that I'm a hospital administrator from upstate. Usually, it's a bad idea to pretend to be in the same field as the people you're lying to, but I've dated enough doctors that I could probably remove an appendix.

The guy on my other side is a pharmaceutical rep, which is gold for getting info on drugs that haven't been released yet. I'll take my chance to grill him next time Sean visits the bathroom.

That shouldn't be long—he's downed three glasses of chardonnay and is signaling the server for a fourth.

"You look so pretty tonight," he says, resting his hand on my wrist. "Genevieve used to wear a dress that same color."

Genevieve was Sean's wife. She died scuba diving in the Maldives.

"You must have so many happy memories with her."

Sean's eyes go misty. "She was an angel on earth. We used to ski together in Aspen. She—"

I listen to Sean's flow of stories, nodding and smiling and commenting in all the right places. Escort work is 30% sex, 10% personal stylist, 20% keeping people company at events they don't want to attend, and the rest on-call therapist.

Sometime around the filet of sole, Sean clutches my hand and whispers wetly in my ear, "Sorry I'm rambling. I'm a little nervous. This is my first time since...since..."

Oh, fuck.

Widowers always cry the first time. Unless they hated their wife. Even then, sometimes they bawl.

"You're doing great." I squeeze Sean's shoulder. "I've got to run to the ladies' room."

I take a long time in the stall, just sitting there. Asking myself why every minute of this evening has felt so goddamn long. It's boring, sure, but these things are always boring.

There's nothing wrong with Sean, he's nice enough. Why does the thought of going home with him fill me with dread?

I've barely taken two steps out of the bathroom, hands still damp, when I run into a broad and extremely familiar back. Ramses turns, just as surprised to see me.

"Blake—what are you doing here?"

"Eavesdropping on Brewer," I quip, blurting out the first thing that pops into my head.

Ramses doesn't smile. He's scanning the room, looking to see who I'm really here with.

"So you actually did it," he growls.

"I told you I would."

Ramses expression is grim, his jaw set.

I put my hand on his arm.

"Ramses, I—"

Sean interrupts, approaching cautiously.

"Blake...you were taking so long...I was worried..."

"Sorry," I say. "I ran into a friend. Do you know—"

I turn to introduce them, but Ramses is already gone.

THE NEXT MORNING, I wake with a crushing hangover.

After Ramses stormed off, I returned to Sean's table and drank so much of the free shitty wine that we were both completely hammered by the time the tiramisu plates were cleared away.

Sean drunkenly confessed that he'd been lying to his daughters about having his wife's jewelry cleaned because he couldn't bear to give it to them yet. I told him about the time I accidentally took a bite of my boss's sandwich and then pinned it on the kid in the cubicle next to mine.

As I supported my stumbling and tearful date into a taxi, he admitted that he wasn't ready for any of this. I let him off the hook nice and easy, telling him to give me a call in a few more months.

I felt an intense sense of relief watching that taxi pull away from the curb.

Ramses' words have been ringing in my ears.

It's time to graduate...

He had his own selfish reasons for saying that. But that doesn't mean he's wrong.

Why have I kept doing this for so long? So I hit a hundred million faster?

That's not the real reason.

I like the hunt. I like tricking these men. And if I'm being honest with myself...these are the only relationships I know. The only person I spend time with who isn't a client or a call girl is Sadie.

The idea of cutting myself loose is terrifying.

I was in a dark place when I started this job. One bad day away from doing something irreversible. Magda opened a door into a different world—one where I had power, money, opportunities. But it came at a price.

They're not alone...but we still are.

Thoughts churning in my head, I tidy my apartment and water my plants. I bought a few last week, and I'm thinking of adding more even though I'm barely keeping these alive.

I open the windows so the sounds of street traffic and the scent of flowers can come inside. I moved to the Flower District on purpose because I thought fresh blooms on the table were the height of luxury—buying something to enjoy for a couple of days before it withers and dies.

I thought when I had money I'd buy flowers every single day. But it's been months since I bought a bouquet or even walked into one of the shops that line my street.

Maybe I should today.

That's what I'm thinking when I sit down at my kitchen table with my laptop and an avocado drenched in balsamic. I pull up my brokerage account and all my tabs, planning to check the status of the hundred different balls I'm juggling.

It takes about two seconds to see my account dropped by six million dollars.

What the fucking fuck?

I pull up my stocks, scanning the list, trying to figure out what just happened.

That doesn't take long either—Tom Brewer's biotech company just took a massive shit. The stock dropped twenty points in a single night.

My computer screen disappears behind a furious haze of red.

Ramses did this.

13

RAMSES

Blake comes storming into my office at 10:22, an hour after I expected her.

"What the *fuck,* Ramses!" is how she greets me.

She's wearing silk trousers, loafers, and a button-up shirt not quite tucked in. Her hair is in a messy bun and her cheeks are flaming red. The hectic, half-dressed look of her turns me on almost as much as the way she stomps into my office and slams the door.

"You slept in. Must have had quite the night."

"You jealous little bitch," she says, stalking right up to my desk and glowering down at me.

I stand up. Blake holds her ground, though she doesn't look quite so certain anymore. She grips the edge of the desk, watching as I close the space between us.

I wait until I'm right in front of her, looking down into her face.

"*Never* give away your position. Not even to me."

"Oh, go fuck yourself!" Blake shouts back. "This isn't a lesson!

You hit my stack because you're pissed that I picked up another client. Even though I told you from the beginning this is the deal!"

"You're damn right I did."

Her mouth goes slack with surprise that I'd actually admit it.

"And *that's* the lesson," I growl, backing her right up to the desk. "You're playing with people who can crush you like an insect. I could wipe your whole stack in a week if you really make me angry."

Her chin trembles with rage.

"You're threatening me?"

"I'm making you a new offer. I'll help you hit your number— I'll even teach you how to do it faster. But I want all of you to myself. No other clients."

Her face goes dark and she turns away from me, staring out the bank of windows. I've got all the blinds open, the view on display. I wanted her to see it the moment she walked in.

She wraps her arms around herself, shoulders stiff, staring downward.

I wait, saying nothing. Counting her breaths.

At last, she says, "I'll get rid of Sean, but I'm keeping Lukas."

I love a good counteroffer.

"Fine. But you're coming to the Hamptons with me."

Blake looks like she'd like to scream into a pillow—and not in the sexy way.

"*Fine,*" she mutters.

"Poor Sean," I let my grin slip through. "After everything he's been through..."

"Do you know him?" Blake forgets to be angry when she's curious.

"I know everybody."

"I'm starting to think that's true."

She's melting like frost in the sun, already returning from the window, leaning against my desk, peeking up at me from under her bangs.

I brush my fingers against hers.

"You know some people think he murdered his wife."

"No they don't!"

"They will if I keep spreading that rumor around."

Blake laughs that delicious, wicked laugh of hers, linking her fingers with mine.

"You better be serious about these lessons...I want my six million back."

"You'll make a fuck of a lot more than that if you listen to me."

THE REST OF THE WEEK, I'm on fire. When I'm not with Blake, I'm slaying everything I touch, riding a bull market to one of the most profitable weeks of my life. It's almost enough to make me think all those superstitious fuckers were right—Blake is lucky.

I don't actually believe in luck.

What I believe in is momentum—wins create more wins. And I've never felt more like a champion.

All day long I look forward to the moment when the elevator doors open into my apartment and I call out for my little Minx. She comes running to me, face glowing, and I scoop her up in my arms and cradle her against my chest, carrying her into the living room.

I haven't gotten tired of our game—quite the opposite. Each time we play, it feels more real and more right.

I'm obsessed with the way she lies across my lap, letting me touch her any way I want. Touch has always been my strongest sense—I don't feel like I've really seen something until I've put my hands on it.

My Minx gives me full access—hours of stroking, touching,

teasing, exploring...I make her come a thousand different ways, sometimes soft like a sigh, sometimes building like music, sometimes exploding under rapid fire fingers.

She's an instrument I'm learning to play. Soon I know her as well as the guitar in my bedroom—every curve, every sound she makes.

I'm even learning to read her face, though Blake is so good at pretending. When she comes over one Tuesday evening, I can tell she isn't feeling well. She's a shade or two paler than normal, her eyes slightly tired.

"What's wrong?"

"Nothing."

I was home before her, so she hasn't changed into her cat suit yet. We're sitting at the kitchen bar, sharing the charcuterie board laid out by my chef. Blake picks at the dates and candied almonds, not eating much. When she thinks I'm not looking, she presses her hand against her side.

"You're not feeling well."

"It's nothing," she says again. "Just...I'll probably be out of commission for three to five days, starting tomorrow."

"Oh," I laugh. "Sorry about that."

"Joys of being a woman."

I think for a moment, then I lift her off the stool, carrying her into my bedroom. I love carrying her, I can't explain it. I love how she snuggles in every single time.

I set her down on the rim of the bath and start running the water.

My bathroom is dark stone. The tub looks like a hollowed-out boulder.

I slide off Blake's shoes then start undressing her. She lets me do it, smiling silently. I haven't grabbed her collar, but we're slipping into the scene anyway.

The tub fills quickly, steam rising off the surface. I lower her into the water. She lets out a low moan of pleasure and relief. Her skin is slippery and soft, her body buoyant in the water so full of tiny bubbles that it seems carbonated like soda pop.

She twists to let the faucet run down her spine, then turns to let it flow directly over her bare breasts. She lies back with her head resting on the edge of the tub.

Her bangs go springy with humidity, little curls appearing around her face. Her cheeks flush dusky pink.

I run my hands down her body beneath the water, rubbing out the tight muscles in her legs. Reaching underneath, I press my fingers on either side of her spine to release the tension in her lower back.

"Oh *Jesus*," she groans.

I soap a washcloth and wash her feet first, scrubbing gently on her soles, even between her toes. She smiles and bites her lip, trying not to giggle when it tickles. Her feet have high arches, long toes, the nails manicured the same rich, dark wine color of the suit she picked out for me.

I lift her leg out of the water, running the washcloth up the beautiful curve of her calf, over her knee, up her thigh. Her body is calligraphy, each line swooping into the next.

I set her heel on the rim of the tub and lift her other leg, opening her thighs, revealing the gorgeous cunt in between. Her little kitty is the prettiest pussy I've seen—dark on the outside, pink on the inner folds. Her clit is the size of the tip of my pinky and pokes up from under the hood. I tease my thumb across it, making it swell in the shimmering steam rising off the water.

She groans, eyes closed, head tilted back.

I massage her pussy with my hand, my fingers warm and wet from the water. Her wetness is slippery like oil. I rub it all around her lips and labia and in circles on her clit, stroking upward with my thumb, mimicking the motion when she grinds on me. She rocks her hips, eyelids fluttering.

Her legs are wide, knees hooked over the rim of the tub. I pull the faucet over so the water flows directly onto her spread pussy. She gasps and turns the heat down a degree or two. Then she leans back, letting the water pour down over her clit.

Without me asking, her eyes meet mine through the silvery steam. She holds my gaze while her face flushes with heat. She rocks her hips against the faucet flow, the rise and fall of her bare breasts speeding.

"Use the water," I say. "Nothing else."

She spreads her legs wider and lifts her hips so the water thunders down in just the right place. The dark tile is opaque with fog, the bathroom hotter than a jungle. I'm sweating through my shirt, so I pull it off and throw it aside, never taking my eyes off her for a second.

She's fucking the glossy stream of water, panting and rolling her hips against it, the water breaking and spraying off that beautiful erect clit.

I push one finger inside her.

That's all it takes—she starts to come, pressing down against my finger like she's riding on my cock. The faucet flows over her pussy like melting honey, running all the way down my arm.

She slows down, grinding her pussy against the flat of my palm, rubbing out the last bits of sensation. The tendons stand out in her neck and her nipples point at the ceiling.

When she's done, she sinks down all the way under the water and disappears.

She rises a moment later, her wet hair washed back off her face, baptized.

She smiles at me and slowly shakes her head.

I know exactly what she means.

I'm grinning back in just the same way.

We discovered something together. And it's fucking incredible.

Has anybody else played this game?

Not like us.

"Good kitty," I say.

Blake throws back her head and laughs.

I fucking love that laugh. I'll do anything to hear it. Jokes, impressions...I'll offend anybody, take the piss out of my own best friend just to see her smile.

I strip off my pants and jump in the tub with her, making water slosh all over the floor.

I don't care. Everything disappears when I'm here with her.

It's the only time the noise quiets. The only time my brain is clear.

Green eyes are all I see, staring into mine.

I kiss her, long and slow.

Her lips are warm and swollen from the water. Her hands are warm too. They press into the muscles of my back with surprising strength. Her legs go around my waist, and she positions her hips to let my stiff cock slide inside her.

I let out a sound as I slip into something hotter than the water, something that clamps around me and squeezes my cock all the way up, even around the head. I don't know why men ever talk shit on promiscuous women—they know how to ride. Her muscles inside are strong like a hand, warm and wet like a mouth. She milks me with her pussy, each stroke so intense that I struggle to control myself like I never have before.

The tub is huge, there's room for both of us without hitting the side walls. Each time I drive into her, water sloshes over the rim like a tiny tsunami.

A normal woman might say, *You're making a mess* or *You're going to flood the floor below us.* My little Minx doesn't say anything because she's deep in character.

She protects the fantasy for me. And for herself as well, I think.

We enjoy it the most when it feels real. When we're immersed, like in warm bathwater. You have to get all the way in to float.

I let go. I think of nothing but this creature in my arms.

I've never felt this kind of pleasure. It goes on and on, the best moment of sex, but it's all best moments. Each time we fuck is better than the last, and I think, *nothing can possibly top this*, but somehow the next one does.

What's the end of it?

I don't know. I don't want an end.

I don't want this to end.

I explode inside her.

My orgasm triggers hers. She loves when I come inside her; it makes her feral for hours after.

I watch her come, and she looks back into my eyes, our faces inches apart. I drive into her, slow and deep, making waves of the water.

DEEP.

DEEP.

DEEP.

Each thrust is the tide of her orgasm, relentless as the ocean. Give it enough time and it will wash everything away.

She can't hold my gaze—her eyes roll back and she makes a long, helpless sound, nails dragging down my back. All day long I'm hard at the office, just from the feel of my shirt sliding over those scratches.

When she comes, the most incredible scent rises from her skin. It's everything I love about rain and about her. I breathe it in and I'm awake.

I thought I was done—not even close. I blow it all in flashes of light and image, like that's how universes are made.

She holds me tight, touching me all the way down.

I whisper, "I worship you," in her ear.

The Egyptians of old worshipped cats—and I'm the mother-fucking Pharoah.

She's my Bastet, goddess of protection, pleasure, and bringer of good health.

I've never felt better, skin glowing, chest out like a champion.

Those other men thought she was lucky?

I know the truth.

Blake is powerful.

WE SPEND the rest of the night looking over my watchlist together. I'm doing something I've never done before in my life: opening my books and sharing everything.

Blake has a tiny stack, so it doesn't matter; she can't affect the market. But she's connected to people who could. I'm trusting her with my next six months of moves.

She knows what a big fucking deal this is, and she keeps her hand on my thigh the whole time. Stroking. Squeezing. Sometimes letting her fingers brush over my cock when she's asking a question and she wants me in a generous mood.

I tell her, "The stock market is the most toxic relationship you've ever had. It is emotional, based off fear, happiness...something as simple as the United States doing well in the Olympics can put everyone in a good mood and stocks get a boost for the next two weeks. Individual stocks will do well based on company performance, but by the time the earnings report comes out, the damage is done and there's no money to be made. You need to identify emotional patterns and predict how other investors will respond. That's what momentum trading *is*—it's emotional trading. And it's done on a day-to-day basis using the most current information."

Most of that she already knows, but she nods and pays attention anyway. 'Cause she knows I'm walking her down a pathway strewn with gold.

"Hedge fund managers aren't day traders, and they're not long-term value investors. They're swing-trading, which is in the middle. It's saying I think this company will shit the bed on their earnings in two weeks, so I'm going to buy their competitor's stock today and short *their* stock. And when the earnings report comes out, I should make money on both. I think this construction company is going to get this government contract, so I'm going to buy it today and sell it in three months when they get the contract. Big money means big moves. But it also means I'm changing the very thing I'm studying—I can't do anything without people noticing. I'm a market-maker. And soon, you will be, too."

She looks into my face, hers as vulnerable as I've ever seen it.

"You really think so?"

"Of course I do. Don't you?"

She grins and punches me playfully on the shoulder. "Yeah. But I'm an arrogant asshole."

I laugh but shake my head. "No you're not."

She looks steadily into my eyes. "How do you know?"

"'Cause it takes one to know one. And *I* actually *am* an arrogant asshole."

That makes her laugh, rich and low.

I'm an addict, I have to have it. More, more, more, more, more.

Quietly, Blake says, "That means a lot to me. Especially coming from you. Everyone thought I was stupid. Worse than stupid."

I go still because this is the first time Blake has voluntarily brought up something from her past.

She says, "I didn't talk until I was five. They thought I was retarded. I know you're not supposed to say that word now, but that's what they called me for years. Even when they realized I could do algebra better than their eighth grader, they called me *the retard that only knows numbers.*"

I know she's talking about her foster family. I can't breathe, can't speak, but fuck do I want to.

"Honestly," she says, looking blankly at the coffee table, not in my face anymore, "They were right. That's what I'm good at. The other things are fake. I'm not good in social situations. I never feel comfortable. It's all an act, one that I practice and work at. And I still fuck up."

I take a chance and stroke my hand gently down her back.

"Everybody's acting in social situations."

She lifts her chin to look at me. "How do you know? Just because *you* are? That doesn't mean anything—you're strange, too."

"I like to think of myself as exceptional."

"Of course you do," she snorts. "That just proves my point— how many other people do you know who would say that about themselves?"

I grin. "Not the same ones *I'd* call exceptional."

She can't help laughing. Neither of us can—anything seems funny through the right lens. And that's what Blake is—she's a mood that changes how I feel about everything else.

I put my arm around her and pull her close.

"I'm sorry anyone said that to you. You're brilliant. I've never met a mind like yours."

I take her chin, tilt it up, and make her look in my eyes while I say it:

"I admire you."

It's one hundred percent true—I admire the things about her

that I can't do. And I admire the things about her that I *can* do but she does better, or equally as good.

I don't say those words easily.

Blake knows it.

Her eyes go shiny and her body is still.

"Thank you," she says. Then she kisses me deep.

14

BLAKE

The two hours I spend on Ramses' couch looking through his books are a literal dream come true. The reality is even better than I imagined, which is rare. I reach deep with my fantasies.

Ramses goes deeper. He teaches me how his mind works, how he makes decisions. His stories are lessons with just enough hints for me to find the message myself.

He was right—he knows things I don't know, and I would have paid a steep price for what he freely offers.

In return, I tell him everything I've learned about the companies we both follow. The thrill I get when he writes some of it down, and even changes a few of his plays, is like nothing I've known.

No, scratch that. The best moment of the whole night is when Ramses looks in my eyes and tells me he admires me.

Fucking hell. If he ever wanted to make me come, that's the way to do it. To hear those words from a man like him—I want to rub my pussy just thinking about it.

It's all a dream until I stand up from the couch and it turns into a nightmare. While we were talking, I was bleeding on his cushions. The patch I left looks like a murder scene.

"I'm so fucking embarrassed."

My hands are over my mouth. I must be as red as that blood.

Am I fourteen? I haven't made a mistake like that in ages. The bath must have brought it on early...

If Ramses looks disgusted, I'll die.

He barely glances at the blood before scooping me up, saying, "Back in the bath."

I squirm against him, saying, "Let me clean it! Fuck, I'm sorry, you're getting it on your arms..."

He holds me tight, forcing me to still. Forehead close to mine, he says, "I don't care. Look at me. Do I look worried? It'll come out. Or it won't. I don't even like that couch that much; you did me a favor."

How does he make me laugh when I'm feeling so low?

Just a moment ago I was drenched in embarrassment.

His arms fill me with his deep, steady calm. His voice vibrates from his chest into mine. "You think blood turns me off? Think again. I like anything that comes out of you."

He's carrying me into his bedroom, but instead of the bath, he throws me down on the bed.

"The sheets—"

He puts his hand over my mouth. "The only thing I want to hear out of you is if this feels good."

He slides a finger inside me. "Does that hurt? Are you sore?"

I'm tender but in a way that only amplifies the sensation. His finger is gentle and his tongue laps against my clit.

"How about this? Does this feel good?"

"More than good," I gasp.

"Let me know if anything hurts or you want me to slow down."

I lie back and let him lick me gently while his warm hand lies across my belly like a heating pad. It feels so soothing, I could cry, if I was *ever* going to let myself cry in front of Ramses again.

Maybe a little moisture leaks out the corners of my eyes, but that just happens when you lie down sometimes. It doesn't mean anything.

I think of how Ramses looked at me while he taught me on the couch. I think how his eyes crinkled up when I gave the right answer or said something clever.

I admire you...

I start to come, soft and slow.

Ramses doesn't stop; he fucks me carefully with his fingers until his hand is drenched in red.

I close my eyes and all I see is red. All I feel is pleasure.

"You *are* an animal," I say when I can speak again.

Ramses only grins.

We're all animals. We like to think because we have thumbs and can talk, we're above them, but we're not. We have impulses and desires. And unlike animals, we can pretend to control them. Sometimes.

But those impulses are POWERFUL. When we repress them, that's when we have the least control. Because they will break free.

Ramses fucks me like an animal on that bed, and I don't think once about the sheets or my goddamn cramps.

I'm lost in the pleasure and the frenzy.

WHEN WE'RE DONE, me lying on the great slabs of his chest and Ramses gently stroking my hair, he says, with a strange hesitancy in his voice, "Would you come with me to this thing I've got to do?"

"Sure. What is it?"

"I built a high school to replace the one I went to. It's a good school, great teachers, but everything they've got is shit. I'm speaking to a pretty big crowd, and I thought it might be nice to have you in the front row."

I sit up on my elbow, checking his face. "You're not nervous, are you?"

I can't imagine Ramses nervous.

"Not really," he laughs. "But it'll be a fuck of a lot more fun if you're there."

I frown at him. "Are you secretly a good dude? Building hospitals, schools..."

"Oh, don't worry," he grins. "I'm gonna make 'em name it after me."

I laugh, snuggling back against his chest. "Thank god. If nothing's in it for you, I get nervous."

"*Ramses Howell High*," Ramses says like he can already see it written in stone.

"That's hot."

He wraps his arms around me, keeping me close. "I want to show those kids that's where I came from. It's where I learned what I could be. Where I started hustling with Briggs, where I started to have self-esteem that I could be successful."

I'm warm all the way through, Ramses' passion radiating into me.

"You think there's someone there who could be like you?"

"Probably not." He laughs because he really is that arrogant. "But I want them to be better. I want them pointed up instead of down. I want to show them it can be done."

I kiss him, and kissing turns to sex.

Afterward, I'm back in his arms, a starry sky outside the windows, a cocoon of warmth all around. Ramses' hand cradles my lower stomach, banishing the cramps.

I fall asleep with him wrapped around me, and I stay there all night long.

THE NEXT TIME I visit Tabitha, she takes one look at me and knows exactly what's happening.

"You fucking idiot."

Tabitha looks awful. She's hunched over, velvet dressing gown clutched around her with one claw-like hand.

I can see myself in the mirror behind her. I'm blooming. Everything about me looks rich and alive—hair, skin, eyes—and that's how Tabitha is catching me. That's how she knows I'm falling again.

Because falling feels like living. It feels like eating and drinking and breathing and running and flying. Why did I starve myself so long?

"He's not like Desmond," I say.

Tabitha stares at me with irises as cloudy and faded as an old marble. "They are *all* like Desmond."

Anger rises in my throat. "Men or Johns?"

"What's the difference." It's not a question. "They take what they want or they buy it. We're lucky when they bother to buy it."

I stand up from her musty old chair, seriously annoyed.

"When did you get so hateful?"

I already know the answer. She became hateful when she became old and alone.

That's why I don't storm out of her apartment.

I stay and I make lunch for her with the groceries I brought. We eat together and play cribbage. I shuffle and deal when it's her turn—her hands have gotten worse.

Even if her word isn't gospel to me anymore, even if she's no longer my teacher, she's still my friend.

And I love her. I realize that as I see her at her oldest, sickest, weakest, grumpiest. I still feel that warmth when I look at her.

I put my hand over her wrinkled old claw. Her skin is soft and thin, blue veins bulging.

"Hey," I say. "I love you."

"Oh my god." Tabitha shakes her head. "What is he doing to you?"

15

BLAKE

I dress with particular care for Ramses' big speech.

I know this matters to him. I want him to see that it matters to me, too.

He's grinning when he picks me up wearing his brand-new burgundy suit.

"You got it!" I cry, running my hands over the material.

"Came just in time."

Ramses looks nothing less than spectacular in that rich, deep wine, just like I knew he would. Blue is his color, the one he picks most, but this red makes him look like an emperor.

I'm wearing a deep, dark teal that coordinates beautifully. It makes me feel like there's a cosmic connection between us tonight even though I laugh at that kind of thinking.

"Thanks for coming with me," he says, slinging his arm behind my shoulders. I don't think I could ever go back to bucket seats after this. I snuggle against him, slipping out of my stilettos so I can put my feet up on the bench.

Ramses was underselling when he said he'd be speaking to quite a large crowd. The light-strung lawn is packed with everybody who wants to look good supporting inner-city schools, from the police commissioner to the mayor.

The grand stone visage of the new high school rises behind with Ramses' name in letters ten feet high. He glances up at it once, hands in his pockets, smiling.

The moment he steps onto the lawn, he's flocked with journalists, glitterati, and finance types all vying for his attention. He keeps me tight against his side, arm around my waist. He doesn't care who sees us together—in fact, he's going out of his way to introduce me to everyone he knows.

He's grinning, his hair combed more neatly than usual, his face freshly shaved. He smells so goddamn good I'm getting high from proximity after an hour on his arm.

Briggs hurries up, his body stuffed into an expensive but ill-fitting suit. Briggs is built like a bulldog, a shorter but even broader version of Ramses. I'm pretty sure they lift together.

Briggs is handsome when he's not talking—the moment he opens his mouth, the most godawful New Yorker accent comes out. He's got high cheekbones, a broad face, narrow eyes and a slight snub nose. His lips are full. His skin is smooth and golden.

"I love watching all these rich bitches get their heels stuck in the lawn." He spots me and grins. "Except you, of course, Blake."

"Which part am I excepted from?" I laugh. "'Cause I'm definitely getting stuck in the lawn."

"Yeah, but I won't take pleasure from it," Briggs solemnly promises. "Have you picked me out a babe for the Hamptons?"

"Yup."

Magda was perfectly willing when I asked her, and I'd love her help wrangling Briggs if we're going to be spending an entire weekend in close proximity.

"Does she have..." Briggs makes a cupping motion under his chest, the universal sign for huge tits.

"The best you've ever seen."

"Yesss," he hisses.

His phone buzzes in his pocket.

"Fuck! This is—"

"I know." Ramses nods. "Get back quick, they're about to start."

Briggs hustles off, already answering the call.

As soon as he leaves, a cultured feminine voice calls out, "Ramses!"

Ramses' body goes rigid, his face stiffening like wood.

An elegant blonde approaches accompanied by a hatchet-faced man who looks oddly familiar. I get a rush of embarrassment and a ghost of pleasure when I realize he's the one who caught us fucking in the elevator.

The blonde lays her hand on Ramses' arm—the one I'm not holding.

"I'm so proud of you, son."

Cameras are flashing. Ramses looks furious, the hatchet-faced man barely less so. Only the woman is smiling—the one who apparently gave birth to my date.

"And who is this?" she says, turning that tight smile onto me.

"Blake Abbott," Ramses says, lips so stiff he can barely speak. He wraps his arm around me and pulls me closer. "My girlfriend."

That's the only moment when his voice has any warmth, when he says those two words: *My girlfriend.* My heart is beating so hard.

"Oh really?" His mother makes an expression I know all too well as she looks me up and down. "How long has this been going on?"

Whether she knows I'm an escort or not, I'm never popular with mothers. I think it's the tits, but it could also be my personality. We just don't click.

Ramses ignores her question. Through his teeth, he says, "I didn't invite you."

"Don't be silly!" She gives the fakest laugh I've ever heard. "Of course I'm going to support my son's philanthropic efforts. I'll be sitting right in the front row."

"With him?" Ramses spits, staring down her date. "Go fuck yourself."

He turns on his heel and stalks away from her, my hand clamped tightly in his.

"That was your mom?" I say, though I'm pretty sure we established that.

"Yeah," Ramses grunts.

"Why is she here?"

"For attention, of course." Then, slowing down a little, he admits, "And probably to try to make up with me."

I don't know if I should ask the next question, but I have to.

"What did she do?"

Ramses is so angry he's shaking. I've never seen him like this. I pull him away from the crowd, behind a screen of cream-colored florals.

"Hey." I put my hands on his shoulders and look into his eyes. "Are you okay?"

"Yeah," he says. And then, shaking his head, "No, actually."

I put my arms around his waist and hug him, cheek against his chest. His heart hammers against my ear. After a moment, he puts his arms around me, too, and slowly strokes my back. His heartbeat steadies, bit by bit, until it's back to a reasonable tempo.

"She left us," Ramses says. "She left my father for a better man. And that's what kills me—he is a better man. My father was a failure."

His voice is thick. His hands clutch me close.

"He put a gun in his mouth on her wedding day. She knew,

and she walked down the aisle with a smile on her face. Fuck her forever for that."

Each word is a stone in my stomach. When Ramses is finished, his shoulders slump like he passed some of that weight from himself to me. I hold him tightly, glad that he told me.

"I'm so sorry."

It's what Ramses said to me when I told him one of my most painful memories. And even though he wasn't responsible for that pain, his apology made me feel better. Because it's the only one I'll ever get.

Ramses sighs, his face pressed against my hair. "Thank you. Thank you for being here."

We stand there holding each other for as long as it takes for us both to feel better. Then I pull back just a little to ask, "Who's the grim reaper she's with?"

"Halston Reeves," Ramses says. "He runs Oakmont."

"*Ohhh*," I say with the particular pleasure of finally matching name to face. "*That* motherfucker."

"Literally," Ramses says.

That makes us laugh in the most immature way.

"Come on," I say. "You don't want to miss your own speech."

"They can't really start without me."

That's true, though the organizer looks extremely harried when she spots us at last. "Ramses, there you are! I was starting to get nervous."

"Don't worry," he says. "I'm only half-drunk."

The poor woman can't decide whether to laugh or cry.

"Only kidding," he says gently.

Ramses climbs the stage. I take my seat on the lawn chair three down from his mother. She beams up at him, all her teeth and diamonds on display. Her husband glowers.

Briggs drops in next to me, panting slightly, tucking his phone back in his pocket. He catches sight of Ramses' mother and mutters, "*What the fuck?*".

The crowd is full of the rich and successful, but I also see the faces of students—kids who have obviously dressed in their best, though they don't have tuxes and gowns or even button-up shirts. Still, they've combed their hair, tied their sneakers, and put on whatever cheap and lovely jewelry they have. They're watching Ramses, every one.

Ramses crosses the stage, huge and powerful.

As he reaches the podium, his mother calls out, "So proud of you, Ramses!"

Her voice is high and clear in the expectant silence. Everyone turns to look.

Ramses' face flushes. His shoulders go rigid and his notes crumple in his fist.

Everyone's waiting.

Still, he doesn't speak.

His mother fans herself with her program. Ramses stands behind the podium, trying to ignore her, but the motion draws his eyes again and again.

I could kill this bitch.

Instead, I do what I do best—I steal Ramses' attention.

I uncross my legs slowly and deliberately, showing him that this dress leaves no room for underwear. It's just a one-second flash, but he sees and bites his lip.

Now there's a different kind of color in his face. Did I just make Ramses blush?

His grin breaks through. He takes a deep breath, tucking his notes away in his breast pocket.

Looking at the students, he says, "Ramses Howell High...I've been looking forward to this day for a long time. But if there's one thing I've learned in business, it's to not be afraid to admit when you've made a mistake."

The crowd shifts uneasily. This is not the opener they expected.

The kids are perking up—he's caught their interest. They lean forward eagerly.

"When I first had the idea to give back to the school that made me, I couldn't help but put my name on it. I'm proud to be a Titan. I grew up where you live. I thought if I put my name up on that wall, it would inspire you."

As one, the crowd turns to look at the grand stone visage, at the seriph-carved letters, ten feet tall.

Ramses calls them back with his deep, rich voice:

"You don't need to see my name on a school to achieve something great. You already have everything you need."

There's a shift in the air, warmth as the students lean closer.

Ramses runs his hands through his hair, ruffling it.

"I grew up on these streets. I lived on Wyckoff Avenue. My best friend Briggs lived two blocks down on Cypress. He's still my best friend and colleague."

Briggs shifts in his seat, smiling sheepishly with his lips turned down.

"My favorite teacher is *still* teaching here," Ramses says. "He's the one who taught me about investments. Mr. Petersen, put up your hand."

An extremely elderly and kind-faced man in a green cardigan sweater puts up his hand. The students whoop and cheer—he's clearly popular.

Ramses looks at each of the kids in turn.

"You are smart. You have passion. When you go out into the world, you'll find there's a lot of phonies out there. But when you find something real and authentic, and you love it..." He pauses and looks right in my eyes then back to the kids. "Don't let anyone take it from you. Not even me.

"You're Brooklyn Titans. Titans are brave. Titans are powerful. Titans change the world.

"Now that I see my name up there in concrete, someone needs to take that down. Fortunately, I know the guy who paid for it, and he's happy to do it."

The kids laugh, and most of the adults, too, though some still look concerned.

"We're going to get my name off the school because it's not my school. It's yours. And Mr. Petersen, you're going to start an investment club. At the end of each year, there's going to be a competition, and I'm going to come judge it. The winning team will all receive a full ride to their school of choice. If you want to name something after me, call it Ramses' Investment Club. But don't let ANYONE touch the Brooklyn Titans."

The students roar, the crowd, too.

Ramses shouts, "And when you make it all the way to the top, don't forget to send the elevator back down!"

Now the cheers are howls. I'm looking up at Ramses, chest on fire. And he's looking right back down at me, giving me a wink. Because whatever they call the club, he's making it for me.

16

RAMSES

The rest of the summer speeds by in a beautiful blur. When I'm at work, I'm soaring, and when I'm with Blake, we're lost in our own private world.

She comes over two or three times a week to play Minx, and I steal hours with her whenever I can, meeting her for lunch between meetings or even breakfast on a Saturday before I head to the office.

I take her on other dates, too—box seats at the Yankees, dancing at The Bowery Electric, and out for dinner at April's new place when it opens. April brings us so many small plates to sample that there isn't an inch of spare space left on the table. Blake and I eat until we're begging for mercy, and even then, April still brings us three different desserts.

Blake has slept over at my house twice more since the night she fell asleep in my arms. I don't push her to stay, but I count it a victory every time I wake with her still curled up next to me.

She never said anything about me calling her my girlfriend. I didn't plan to say it—but it sure sounded right coming out of my mouth.

I want this to be real.

I knew it the moment I stood on that stage, my mind a raging blank while my mother smirked at me from her seat. I don't get thrown off my game very often, but I was a fucking mess that night.

Blake knew exactly what to do.

Picture the audience naked? No, picture the hottest girl you've ever seen flashing her pussy at you—that's how you get your mind right.

She wiped every furious thought from my brain so all I saw was her naughty face smiling up at me. Reminding me that I'm the best 'cause I have the best sitting right there in the front row.

I knew exactly what to do after that.

Titan High is back up on the school's façade, and Mr. Petersen is already fielding applications for the investment club he's starting in September. The thought that one of those kids could be the next Ramses or Blake, the next brilliant brain who just needs one hard push to escape the gravity of poverty and launch into space...that perpetual possibility, fresh and alive, is making me so much happier than my own name in cold, dead stone.

The final Friday in August finds me waiting outside Blake's building, the top rolled down on the Lincoln to soak in the bronze-colored sun.

My phone buzzes.

> I'm running a few minutes late—you want to come up?

I'm out on the sidewalk before I've finished reading. I've been itching to see inside Blake's apartment.

I hold the front door for a woman lugging groceries and tail her up the stairs. Blake looks startled when she answers my knock.

"How'd you know which door was mine?"

"I've known for ages."

"And you never surprised me? How restrained of you."

I grin. "It took everything I had—I wanted you to invite me up."

"Well..." Blake smiles. "What do you think?"

I look around at the wide-open space. Blake has a classic loft, two stories high, the walls gray cinder block but the floors warm wood. The space is spartan—not a single appliance out on the countertops, nothing on the coffee table. The wall next to the windows is a riot of plants—ferns, fronds, potted trees, and long, trailing vines.

"You like those?" Blake says as I walk closer to her floor-to-ceiling jungle. "I've been adding to my collection. Haven't figured out how to keep the alocasia alive yet, but the philodendrons are pretty unkillable."

"Makes the air smell fresh—I should do that at my place." I'm glancing around at floor level. "I kind of thought you'd have a cat."

"I've been thinking of getting one."

"You should. It's life changing."

Blake laughs, exposing that long brown throat and all her lovely teeth. She's wearing an adorable outfit of eyelet lace, a blouse that ties in the front and a skirt of the same material. Her tan has deepened all summer long, making her eyes look green as spring grass. Her dimple has been showing since the moment I walked in the door.

Her apartment smells exactly like her, which means I want to live inside it forever.

Opposite the wall of plants is a wall of books, likewise running two stories high, with iron rolling ladders on both sides. The shelves are stuffed with biographies, fiction, ancient leather-bounds, even some old textbooks.

"Have you read all these?"

"Most of them," Blake says. "It's the only way I can get to sleep at night. But then I read until three in the morning."

"I have trouble sleeping, too." The words are out before I realize that hasn't been as true lately. Especially the nights Blake stays over—when she sleeps in my arms, my dreams are too dark and sensual to depart.

I run my fingers down the motley mix of spines, trying to find the books we've read in common.

"Did you like this one?" I pull out Dale Carnegie's *How to Win Friends and Influence People*.

Blake's copy is battered and yellowed, a price written in pencil on the interior flap. Most of her books look like they were owned by someone else first.

"Loved it," she says. "Isn't it funny how a book written a hundred years ago is truer today than it was then?"

"People don't change that much."

"Not in the things that are true about all of us." She smiles. " Like how much we love to talk about ourselves."

"Not you," I contradict. "But everything I've learned about you was worth the wait."

She has no photographs on display, no mementos. The most personal thing in the space besides her books is the art on the walls—dozens of prints hung gallery style in great splashes of color. Some I vaguely recognize from the one-and-only art appreciation class I took in high school.

I point at lush redhead in a green velvet dressing gown. "Who's that?"

"*Bocca Baciata*—the mouth that has been kissed."

Sure enough, the girl's painted lips are redder than her hair and slightly swollen.

"So...was she?"

"Probably," Blake laughs. "The model was Dante Rossetti's mistress."

I struggle to recall a lecture twenty years past. "Weren't most of the models sex workers?"

Blake shrugs. "The line between work and sex work has always been blurry for women."

She gazes up at the painting, unperturbed, while weight settles on my chest. My tongue wets my lips.

"When was the first time you crossed that line?"

Blake turns, her inky hair swirling and settling around her bare arms.

"Depends how you count it."

"How do *you* count it?"

Her eyes hold mine, clear and unblinking. "I was thirteen."

My stomach does a slow and queasy roll. Whatever I was expecting her to say...it wasn't that.

Not for one second did I feel guilty for paying Blake for sex—not until this moment.

"Don't." Blake says, that line of fury appearing between her eyebrows.

"Don't what?"

"Don't look at me like that."

"Like what?"

"Like I'm a victim."

"I'm not." I wipe my hand down my face. "It's just—thirteen? Jesus, Blake."

"I'm twenty-seven now. That was more than half my life ago. What we're doing here," she gestures between us, "has nothing to do with that."

I know Blake is an adult and I know she doesn't want my pity, but I can't shake the image of a much younger version of her nervously biting her lip while some fucked-up version of me pulls a hundred-dollar bill out of his wallet...

"This is exactly why I don't talk about it," Blake says, arms crossed over her chest. "I don't need a white knight. And I sure as fuck don't need you feeling guilty."

"I know." I try to remove whatever look on my face is giving me away. "It just makes me want to fucking murder someone, that's all."

"Perfect," Blake snorts. "'Cause we'll be seeing Desmond in a couple of hours."

I make a face. "I forgot that."

"And it's all your fault." Blake links her arm serenely through mine. "So you're the one who has to talk to him."

She stoops for her weekend bag. I snatch it first.

"I can carry it!"

"Not as easily as I can." I sling the bag over my shoulder and pull her close with my free arm.

It's not until we're down at the car that I realize that Blake was already packed and dressed. She wasn't running late at all. Which means she invited me up...simply because she wanted to.

She says, "What are you smiling about?"

"I was thinking how next time I come over, you should cook for me."

Blake shakes her head. "I only cook for myself."

"But that's the whole point." I sling my arm behind her as I pull away from the curb. "That's why you go to all that trouble—so you can share the meal afterward. And get praised for your mad skills."

I learned in our very first encounter how much Blake loves compliments.

But her expression is puzzled, even a little disturbed.

"What's wrong?"

She lets out her breath. "Sometimes I forget how weird I am. I've never cooked for anybody—not once. When you say that's the whole point—maybe it is for everybody else. There's all these common, everyday things with family and friends and human connection...I missed it. I never learned. And sometimes I think I never will."

"You can change anything you want to change."

"Can you?" It's a genuine question—Blake looks at me, face naked. "They did this experiment on kittens once—sewed their eyelids shut for the first six weeks of their lives."

"What the fuck?"

"I know. Point is, when they opened their eyes six weeks later, they couldn't see. They were blind forever. Because the part of their brain that withered and died in the dark couldn't ever recover."

I put my hand around the nape of her neck and draw her close so I can kiss her sun-warmed lips.

"You're not a blind kitten. Your eyes have never been wider. I'm watching you experience the world in a new way, and I *know* you are because the same thing is happening to me. I had my eyelids sewn shut, too. But we're not broken beyond repair. We can still change—we're doing it together. Look at where you are, Blake."

I gesture all around us at the towering buildings, the ancient sugar maples, the bustling sidewalk cafes, all the sights and scents and sounds of Manhattan, alive and vibrant from the open convertible.

"Look how far you've come. You're here where everyone wants to be, on top of the world. But this isn't your final form— ten years from now, we should both be better than we are today. And I'm more motivated when I'm with you than I've ever been before."

Blake looks at me, eyes wide and glinting, lips redder than the *Bocca Baciata.*

"You change how I feel," she whispers. "Things I thought were carved on my soul melt away and become something new when you look at me. When you touch me like that."

My hand rests heavy on the back of her neck, the tension beneath slowly releasing.

When she's fully relaxed, I finally ask, "What happened to your family?".

The answer wasn't in Briggs' file. All I know is what Blake already told me—she was in foster care. And eventually, for eighteen months, in Crossroads Juvenile Center.

Blake's voice drops, barely audible over the music on the radio and the wind flowing around us.

"I never really had one. My mom got pregnant at sixteen, same as *her* mom. My grandma was barely older than I am now," Blake gives a bitter laugh, "and even less interested in dealing with my mother's mistake than she was in dealing with her own."

Her face settles into that look of distant dullness that comes over her when I force her to dig through her memory banks.

"But of course, it's not that simple. If you knew where they came from, what they'd been through themselves...Coney Island was an upgrade. Everybody picks their escape. Grandma's was alcohol. My mom's was meth. Grandma's still alive. But my mom was looking for a rabbit hole so deep she'd never come back. And one day...she didn't."

Blake closes her eyes.

"She'd already stopped coming to see me a long time before that. In a way, it was better. The hours I wasted on porches waiting for her..."

The thickness in my throat makes it hard to speak. "I wish I could go back in time and take care of you."

Blake shakes her head, rejecting the idea.

"It made me who I am, and I mean that in the most literal way. I used to live in a different world than this one. When it all got ripped away..." her hands make motions in the air around her face, snatching, tearing, "When I was alone here in the real world, that's what forced me to change. The lessons were brutal, but that's how I learned."

Her back stiffens under my hand, the iron of those lessons threaded through every fiber.

"Everyone picks their escape," Blake repeats. "Mine used to be money. Now...it's Minx."

She says it almost like it's a surprise. Like she hadn't fully realized until this moment how much the idol in her mind had been supplanted by something that lives and breathes and grows and changes every time we visit it. I don't get tired of Minx because Minx is *us* experimenting together. It's whatever we want it to be, whatever we need it to be.

I place my hand over hers. "I feel the same."

We were both chasing the same target—the number in our minds that means we made it.

I hit mine and immediately started looking for another. Why? Because I didn't actually feel like I made it.

I felt...exactly the same.

Nothing changed until I met Blake.

Now *everything* is changing. And for once in my life, I don't have a plan. All I can do is hold on tight to whatever this is and pray I don't fuck up.

We're driving out of the city, down the beckoning finger of Long Island, an island that isn't an island at all anymore. Anything can change.

Quietly, Blake says, "She put me in foster care when I was four. For a long time, that's what fucked me up the worst. Most kids in care were taken. They'll tell you about the day the authorities showed up and abducted them from their school, their empty apartment, their screaming parents...My mom dropped me off."

Blake's situation was far worse than mine, but one thing we both experienced was the day our mothers left.

I say, "You don't ever forget the shape of someone's back when they walk away from you."

Blake nods, lips pale and pressed. "She was the only person I felt any connection to. The only person I could communicate with. We had these little signs for food or a drink or my favorite blanket. Everybody else, I couldn't even understand what they said. She'd get down low, hold my face, talk slow..."

I wonder if Blake has a picture of herself at that age. The image of her tiny and vulnerable is torturous, the words in the air like the chirping of birds.

"I went everywhere with her. I'd wait in rooms and closets while she was doing whatever next door. We slept together in the same bed. It was like I was a part of her and she just...cut me loose. She was the lizard and I was a piece of its tail left behind."

I think of Blake surrounded by babbling strangers, unable to ask what had happened to her mom or if she'd ever come back.

They wouldn't know how to take care of her. They wouldn't know what she liked.

You have to pay attention to understand Blake. I like to tease her, pressure her, push her limits, but I'm not blundering around like a fucking rhinoceros. I'm testing those limits carefully, watching her expression, her body language, her breathing. Sometimes I know what she's feeling before she does.

But I fuck up, too, because I'm still learning.

I don't want to spook her when she's sharing so much. So I keep my mouth shut and deal with my emotions by imagining I could have found her, whisked her away, taken care of her. Where was I, what was I doing then?

I was living just a couple of neighborhoods away in an apartment in Bushwick, and I was twelve years old.

Jesus. My mom left that same year...

Blake whispers, "I missed her so much it was like a sickness. I wouldn't eat, they had to put a tube in my arm. Then, later...I hated her. I was so fucking angry. And sometimes I still feel that way. But other times I think...maybe the day she dropped me off was the one day she wasn't selfish. The day she did something hard for me because she hoped it would be better."

There's a long pause before Blake adds, "It wasn't."

I rest my hand on her hair and pull her close so I can kiss her on the temple.

Trees stream by the open car. The traffic is blessedly clear because we left early in the day when most people are still at work.

Even fuckers rich enough to have a house in the Hamptons still get dragged into the office on a Friday, from their own compulsions if not from a boss. That used to be me—I would have gone today, but the pull to see Blake was stronger.

And that's why I'm driving through air warm as honey, Blake's bronze body curled up next to me on the seat, her mesmerizing voice telling me what I've wanted to know for so long. I'm here to hear it because I let go of the idol and grabbed for something real.

"Tell me everything," I say, my arm wrapped around her shoulders.

Blake leans her head against my chest.

"I bounced around a couple of places. The second couple I stayed with, I actually liked. The wife was an estate planner and the husband worked in finance. They were home all day long, so I was never alone, but they were quiet, just tapping away on their computers, whatever room they were in. The fridge was full, the pantry was stuffed, they let me take whatever I wanted. The whole house was a library, books in every room, sometimes even stacked on the floor. She'd let me take them down and flip through them, any book I wanted. I wasn't talking yet, but that's when words on a page first started to make sense. When she read to me."

"What did she read?"

Blake laughs. "Jurassic Park. I was obsessed with dinosaurs, and when I saw the cover, I brought it right over. She read the whole thing over a couple of weeks, probably without knowing if I understood a word."

Blake clings to me, remembering this woman who showed kindness in a time when she was still floating, lost in the disconnect, when all her world was confusion and abandonment.

"And the husband..." she smiles, remembering. "What *he* was doing made sense to me way before that. He put this little chair in his office, a tiny rocking chair. I'd sit behind him and watch the numbers on his screen."

Her happiness is painful because I know it didn't last.

"Why didn't you stay there?"

She huddles against me, her sandals slipped off and abandoned on the floorboard so she can tuck her bare feet beneath her.

"They had a daughter together who died a few months after she was born. I used to go into her nursery and look at her pictures all over the walls. Ingrid, the wife, would come in and tell me what a good baby Nora was, how she smelled like heaven and how early she laughed..."

Blake sighs, her head heavy on my chest.

"I think I was supposed to fill that hole. But the fighting got worse. At first, they'd do it at night after I was in bed. Soon it was all the time. The husband thought I didn't understand. He'd say, *She's not Nora, she's never going to be Nora*...which was true. In all the ways he meant it."

I stroke Blake's hair, glad she's lying against me so she can't see my face.

"When they split, Ingrid might have wanted to keep me, I

don't know—the foster system won't leave kids with single adults. The next place was a lot worse. And the one after that, the one where I stayed...that was worst of all."

I'm stroking her hair, soothing her. Soothing myself. Because the feelings inside me are ugly in the extreme. I want to hear more, but for once I'm not going to ask. I'm not going to dig in her most painful place. Those bones can stay buried forever, as far as I'm concerned.

It's Blake who goes on, who *wants* to go on now that we've started. She clings to me like I can protect her from everything that happened before—or at least protect her from the memories.

"I hated the Claydermans. They were the worst kind of foster parents, the ones who treat it like a job and take as many kids as they can get. Their house was constant noise—the parents yelling, kids fighting, dogs barking, TV blaring. Everything was monitored, locks on the fridge, endless charts of chores. Some of the other kids were fucked up worse than I was, especially the teenage boys. It was terrifying, like living with stray dogs and half of them have rabies."

I really don't know if I can handle this. I clutch the wheel to keep my hand from shaking.

"But it was Davis, the father...he's the one who really figured out how to get to me."

Blake stares at the road, eyes flat and unmoving.

"Before, he treated me like the rest of the kids—as a resource. Free babysitting, yard work, cleaning up after them, the pets, the other kids...But then, puberty hit." Blake gives a laugh that isn't a laugh at all. "And I got hot."

For once, I see her strange and powerful beauty for what it really was to a girl in her situation—the worst kind of curse. A lure to the dark desires of every cock that crossed her path.

"At first, it was helping me—Davis gave me my own room. I

thought he was protecting me from the others. Until I realized what he actually wanted."

I take short, shallow breaths, awash in all the queasy feelings from before times a thousand. I don't want to be anything like this degenerate piece of shit.

"I might have told him to fuck off—I hated that place anyway. But Sadie—" Blake makes a stifled sound and stops talking.

"There was another girl," she says at last. And then, very softly, "My sister. Not by blood. But we decided...that we were."

My chest burns. I kiss Blake on the crown of her head.

"If I told anybody what Davis was doing, we'd be split apart and sent off to new places and I'd never see Sadie again. She was little—little like I was when I came. My mom was already gone; Sadie was all I had. And I was all *she* had. So I made a choice."

Blake lifts her head and looks at me, finally answering my question in full.

"When I was thirteen, I started giving him a blowjob a week. That was the deal we made. He didn't push for more, and I didn't tell anyone. And that went on for three years."

"That's not—" I have to stop and try again. "That's not a choice. You were a kid."

Blake shrugs. "Less of a kid than most."

I can't stop myself now that we're both at the bottom of the well.

"What happened?"

Her lip curls, showing a flash of teeth. "He didn't keep his side of the deal."

"He tried to take more?"

"And I gave it to him—six times with a kitchen knife."

I let out the breath I was holding, suffused in red hot pleasure. "Good girl."

"The judge disagreed. He sent me to Crossroads."

"I know," I admit. "It was in Briggs' file. But that was it, that's all I know that you didn't tell me."

Blake shrugs. "You didn't know me then. And I didn't know you."

"But you do now." My fingers stroke her bare shoulder.

Her dimple peeks into view. "I'm starting to."

I smile the kind of smile that used to come once or twice a month but now seems permanently painted on my face. "And do you like what you see?"

Softly, Blake says, "*Like* doesn't quite cover it."

All of a sudden, we're in our own tiny bubble of air. Blake looks in my eyes and I look in hers, and we say nothing at all because we've gotten so good at talking without words.

I kiss her. The kiss goes on so long that the car swerves.

"You better get autopilot if you're gonna act like that," Blake teases when I've narrowly avoided killing us both.

"But then we'd lose the bench seat."

"Changed my mind." She snuggles against me. "That's worth dying for."

As we pass through Westbury, I feel peaceful enough to ask, "What happened to Davis? Is he dead?"

"No," Blake says, sounding slightly miffed.

"Did you ever tell anyone what he did?"

She shakes her head. "Even Sadie doesn't know. I never told anyone until you."

I don't know how that could make me feel so good under the circumstances.

It must be this: Blake's trust is worth more to me than anything I own.

I let myself slip into a Batman-style fantasy of driving to Davis Clayderman's house in the middle of the night to exorcise some emotion.

"Do you ever worry he might do it again?"

Blake snorts. "Not where I stabbed him."

I laugh at the satisfied look on her face, and she laughs at me laughing because the asshole portion of our Venn diagram overlaps beautifully.

17

RAMSES

"Your turn," Blake says.

"What do you want to know?"

"Tell me...." She peeks up from under her bangs. "Tell me something you've never told anyone before."

I search for the right memory to offer in return for hers.

"I'll tell you something kind of embarrassing."

"Perfect." She grins.

"As I mentioned...it was my dad who picked my name."

Blake nods, settling back against the seat, gazing up at my face.

"My parents were kids when they met. They worked at the same waffle house, my mom as a waitress, my dad in the dish pit. My dad was a dreamer—he had all this ambition, all these ideas. My mom got pregnant accidentally and young—not as young as yours but young enough that she'll still tell you how I ruined her body forever. They got married and moved in together. And that's when she started to realize dreams ain't worth shit when you've got bills to pay and a baby on your hip."

Blake smiles sadly, her hand on my thigh.

I tell her, "My dad's name was Chris and he hated it."

A laugh bursts out of Blake. She tries to smother it until she sees I made her laugh on purpose.

"So he named me Ramses and filled my head with dreams of the empire we'd build together."

Blake perks up, dropping her hand. "Was he Egyptian?"

"If you mean did we have relatives that once lived in Egypt, then yes. But neither one of us has ever seen a pyramid."

She's lost in giggles. "You call yourself the Pharaoh and you've never once flown your little jet over there?"

"I've been busy. And I'll have you know, my jet is anything but little."

I can't stop making her laugh, I'll do anything to hear it. And if I never get to the end of this story, who gives a fuck—all I want is this woman next to me, chortling at my expense.

"*Anyway,*" I say, pretending to be annoyed. "The trouble was... my dad isn't as smart as me. I figured it out when I was about eight years old. His schemes, his hustles, came to nothing because that's all they were—big dreams with shit plans to back them up."

"You still talk about him in the present tense," Blake says.

I stop to replay my own sentences.

"You're right."

"I do too, sometimes. Even though my mom's been gone so long."

Neither of us is laughing anymore.

Blake is a lens, magnifying whatever I'm doing with her. Making it the most close, the most intense it's ever felt—even when we're lost in fantasy.

Now she's pointed that spotlight somewhere I never look. And I can't ignore what I see.

"I didn't respect him. Sometimes I fucking hated him—especially after mom left. He'd lecture me, I should do this, I oughta do that...Once I started making money, I told him right to his face I didn't want to be anything like him."

I remember how he stopped talking. How his face slowly sagged, his shoulders, too. Like I'd taken all his bones away.

"I wish I never said that. What was the point? He already lost her. He was already spiraling."

I'm speaking my thoughts out loud, hearing them as they leave my lips.

Regret is a river that flows deep and dark and forever.

The things you can't take back...

The things you can't change...

My father killed himself later that year.

I feel Blake's hand, cool and soft against my cheek. She turns my head and makes me look at her.

"I'm sorry," she says. "I'm sorry she left and I'm sorry he's gone."

Sympathy is different when it comes from her—from her, it feels like understanding.

Blake wraps her arms around my waist and hugs me hard, her head against my chest.

I'm not trying to feel better. I'm not trying to be comforted. But the longer she hugs me, the more her warmth spreads through my body.

"Thank you," I say, one hand on the wheel, the other cradling her head.

We pass an amusement park, the distant loops of roller coasters silhouetted against the sky.

Blake sits up, her dimple flickering into view. "So, who *did* you want to be like? What was your bright, shiny star?"

She's asking 'cause she knows I had one.

Blake had one, too: the number in her mind and what it meant: a castle, a kitchen, a library...Those were the dreams she used to escape her reality. The goals that motivated her to work and work and work to dig her way out of the shit.

"That's what I was trying to tell you about. The day I saw the life I wanted..."

Blake settles against me, smiling.

♪♪ *Whole Lotta Money — BIA*

"So in high school, Briggs and I started buying cars at auction and flipping them. We got this '67 Spyder, fucking gorgeous. I would have killed to keep it for myself, but I was a broke-ass bitch then; it took my whole stack just to buy it, and we spent the summer fixing it up. In September, I sold it to a trader."

I can picture him perfectly, slipping behind the wheel of my car—bespoke suit jacket tossed carelessly in the backseat, tanned in April from wherever he'd been traveling, watch the same price as a Harvard education glinting on his wrist. He paid cash for the car, but it was his confidence I envied—the way he haggled me down, then threw in an extra grand 'for the air freshener,' to show me it was all a game to him, one he was winning effortlessly.

"Why is that embarrassing?" Blake says.

"'Cause looking back on it, he was nobody—probably just a floor trader like Jonesy or Pennywise. But he took my car, and when he drove away...it looked like he had everything I wanted."

"That's not so bad," Blake says. "I kind of thought you got into finance to show up Halston Reeves."

I shake my head. "When I picked my future career, it was really just 'cause I envied some random guy."

Blake grins. "I like that better."

Her hand creeps across my lap, easily finding my cock inside my slacks. Her sharp nails trace its shape, rubbing against the ridge where head meets shaft.

My cock swells until it's extremely uncomfortable inside my

pants. Relentlessly, she traces every inch—back and forth, down the shaft, up the head—until I'm throbbing like a drum.

Blake unbuttons my pants. The zipper breaks like a dam, my cock leaping free, hot in the cool air. Blake takes the head in her mouth, smothering me in velvet lips. Instantly, everything feels twice as good—the sun on my skin, the breeze in my hair, the wheel under my palm. Everything is pleasure when my cock floats on the flat of her tongue.

She unclicks her seatbelt so she can kneel on the seat, head bobbing in my lap, ass up toward the side window. I rest my hand on the small of her back in the patch of sun-warmed skin between her blouse and the waistband of her skirt.

I'm driving in the far left lane, fast enough that most people don't notice what's happening one car over. Traffic is sparse, the other drivers are cocooned in their own little world.

But Blake's ass against the side window is hard to ignore. We pass a twenty-something guy in a Civic who glances over then freezes like he saw a deer. Only this is a motherfucking unicorn.

I let my hand slide down so Blake's ass fills my palm, pressing the gas so the car surges ahead.

We fly down the road, Blake's mouth drenching my cock. The wind strokes like fingers through my hair and across my skin. Pleasure creates more pleasure, that's what I'm learning.

The guy in the Civic can't help himself. He's accelerated to match my pace, keeping his car right next to mine so his eyes can roam Blake's body while she gives me the kind of blowjob a man could only dream of receiving once in his life. This might be the closest this kid will ever get.

I let him watch for a good minute and a half before zooming ahead, grinning to myself.

The car roars down the highway, Blake attacking my cock. She sucks like a demon, stroking with her hand. It's a battle between my attention on the road and the climax she's determined to force out of me. She's not even buckled; I could crash and kill us both.

It's the risk that makes me harder than iron, her mouth pushing me closer to the edge. I'm riding the line, eyes fixed on the asphalt while my hips thrust into that warmth and wetness, my free hand clamped behind her head.

She sucks harder, faster, her hand pumping in time with her mouth. But it's the noises that get me, when she starts making eager little panting sounds, hungry—no—*ravenous*...

The first spurt hits her tongue. She grips the base of my cock and grunts with pleasure, sucking hard on the head. I explode into her mouth, both hands grabbing for the wheel.

The world becomes a streak of light and color as we blast down the road, time warping with each stroke of Blake's lips. The wheel seems to shake under my hands, or maybe I'm shaking—all I know is the pure and perfect pleasure of bursting all over her tongue.

Blake sits up, grinning, wiping her mouth on the back of her hand. "You didn't kill us."

"I still might, so buckle up."

Everything feels loose and wobbly, especially the wheel under my hand.

Blake's face glows with satisfaction. "I don't know if I've ever felt you that hard."

"Well..." I can't hide my grin.

I tell her what happened, all the same feelings surging over me again—the exhibitionism of taking my cock out in an open-top convertible, the pleasure of the wind and her warm mouth, the thrill when the other car pulled level with ours and I watched that kid's eyes pop out of his head.

Blake sits on her knees on the seat, the wind making a tornado out of her hair. The brightest bits of green in her eyes glint like glass.

"He was watching? How long?"

"As long as I let him."

She presses both hands against her cheeks, embarrassed but more aroused. "What did you do?"

"I gave him a look like that," I raise an eyebrow and give a little jerk of my chin, "to be like, *Yeah, it's exactly as good as you think it is.*"

Blake roars with laughter, delighted by this mini narrative that occurred right behind her back. Or behind her ass, I suppose.

"Fuck, that turns me on."

Her cheeks are pink, her shoulders too. Her body looks so goddamn good in that tied-up top. When she moves it looks like dancing, even when she just lifts a hand.

She touches the St. Christopher's medallion dangling from the mirror.

"Was that your dad's?"

"Yeah. He gave it to me when I was a kid. After my mom left, I took it off and threw it in a drawer. Then, when he—I found it when I cleaned out his house. And hung it on that mirror." The medallion glints like a winking eye. "Even though it kinda makes me feel like shit every time I look at it."

"That's probably why you hung it there."

I look at Blake, startled.

She says, as if it's obvious, "You're kind of a masochist. The hours you work, the way you train that body...I've seen those boxes of chicken and rice stacked up in the fridge."

"That's discipline, not masochism."

"Okay," Blake shrugs. "But I know what punishing yourself looks like."

"I prefer punishing *you*." My hand snakes out to grab the base of her neck.

"Do you?" Blake gives me her wickedest smile. "Because I think you like rewarding me even more..."

She leans back against the seat, parting her knees. The lacy skirt barely covers the tops of her long, brown thighs. A delta of smooth cotton peeks out between.

♪♪ *Go To Town — Dojo Cat*

"Unbutton your top," I growl.

Blake's fingers tease open her buttons one at a time, revealing another inch of skin. She unties the front of the blouse and lets it fall open, baring her breasts. Her nipples tighten under my stare.

"Good girl. Now slip your off your underwear and put your heels up on the dash."

Obediently, Blake hooks her thumbs in the waistband of her thong and pulls it down her thighs. She tosses her underwear on the floor of the car, then sets her bare feet up on the dash, toes against the windshield.

I touch her pussy, sinking two fingers deep into her pillowy warmth.

"You dirty little slut—did you get that wet sucking my cock?"

Blake lifts her hips, squeezing around my fingers. She closes her eyes and groans softly. I press inside her, sliding my fingers slowly in and out, feeling how warm she is, her interior walls throbbing...

I inhale her scent off my hand, the bouquet of her arousal complex like wine. I taste her slippery wetness, letting it dissolve on my tongue.

We're driving through farmland with roadside produce stands and tiny truck stop cafes. Blake reclines, her bared body mimicking the rolling shape of the hills. Her painted toes glint jewel-like in the sunshine dazzling off the glass.

"Spread your legs," I order.

She butterflies her knees so I have open access to her wet little cunt. I part her lips with my fingers, exposing the delicate pink interior to the sun and the air. Blake gasps, her pussy pulsing helplessly. Her knees draw together. I push them apart, barking, "Keep them spread."

Blake casts darting glances at the other cars, her arousal battling with her embarrassment, cheeks flaming and pussy gleaming.

Most of the vehicles are too low to see what we're doing, but anybody in a semi-truck has an elevated view. As we gain on a 16-wheeler, the driver watches in his rear-view mirror.

"Spread that pussy and fuck my fingers."

Blake lifts her hips off the seat, her feet up the dash like she's got her heels in stirrups. She rides my fingers, back arched, bare tits pointed up at the sky.

I zoom past the semi-truck, the driver's mouth hanging open, his nose pressed against the side window.

Making men jealous is my new favorite kink.

Women could never understand the level of competition between men. Our world is comparison. Whether it's chicks, whips, kicks, or dicks, we want to know how we measure up.

I've made this drive many times in this car. This is the first time I've had someone with me.

That driver and I are living two completely separate lives, passing each other for a moment in time. I'm getting off in the Hamptons, he's probably taking the next exit to deliver avocados. He already knows which of us is winning. But today, it wasn't, *Oh look, that guy has a nice car*...now it's *That guy has everything*.

I'm not the first classic car he's driven past; he does it all day long. In fact, he probably sees someone getting road-head once a week. But he's never seen anything quite like that.

Comparison is the checkpoint to measure your own success. Look who I am, look who I've become, I used to drive this car on this road...but now I have this fucking phenomenal woman with me, and life couldn't be better.

Blake feels like a trophy, but she isn't. I've stayed at the bougie resorts, eaten at the best restaurants, spent time with impressive people. It doesn't feel like this.

Blake understands things about me that no one else does.

Something in us is wired the same, and it flows between us like a current.

Sex has gone so far beyond sex. It's bonding, it's relaxation, it's play, it's deep and dark catharsis.

My fingers make wet, sloppy sounds as I pump in and out of Blake's cunt. My cock spills out of my half-zipped pants.

We fly faster and faster down the road, the engine a low growl, the rush of wind fighting the heat of the sun. Blake's bare skin blazes like metal, sweat on her breasts. Her cheeks are crimson, her pussy clamps like a vise on my hand.

My arm is steel, bicep burning. I wouldn't stop even if I were about to lose a hand.

Blake rides the edge, jaw clenched and teeth bared like she's biting a wire.

"Come for me," I say, and I watch her explode.

18

BLAKE

Ramses and I stop for lobster rolls in East Hampton, then we make the short drive to a blue-shuttered house set back from the road in a grove of magnolias. The mailbox says *Sundune*.

"Is this yours?"

Ramses nods. "It's a bit beat up, but I like being on the edge of everything."

Sundune is nowhere near as grand as Desmond's estate, but it's much more private, set on a blustery spit of land at the very tip of the peninsula. The tangled garden gives way to bone-white dunes and rushing surf.

Briggs pops out the front door as soon as we pull up, grabbing our bags out of the trunk and helping Ramses carry them inside.

"Where's my date?" he demands.

I say, "She's coming on the train."

"She'll be here before dinner?"

"Yeah, in an hour or two."

"Good." Briggs nods. "Did you tell her to dress slutty? I'm gonna peacock all over this party."

"Yep," I say, keeping my face carefully smooth.

Ramses gives me a sharp look.

When Briggs is out of earshot, he says, "You invited Magda?"

"Yeah, but she cancelled this morning," I admit. "I had to find a last-minute replacement."

Magda's mom got a respiratory infection. I wasn't annoyed, but I did have to scramble to find somebody who was free the entire weekend.

"Briggs won't notice," Ramses says.

I grimace. "He might."

I head into the bedroom to hang up my clothes. I brought way too many outfits 'cause I'm nervous. Putting Ramses and Desmond in a room together is a supremely bad idea, especially when I know Ramses only brought me here to piss Desmond off.

Ramses already hung up his shirts and trousers, crisp on their hangers. Now he's stowing our suitcases neatly in the hall closet. His toiletries line up like soldiers beneath the bathroom mirror.

Everything he does is intentional. That's what makes him powerful—he's in control of his world.

I hang my dresses next to his shirts, amused that his shirts are longer. He's so big he makes everyone else look small.

I like how our clothes look in the closet together, like our shadows are hung up next to each other. I like sharing a double sink, Ramses on the left, me on the right.

Most of all, I love knowing I'm going to fall asleep in his arms tonight. I've only let myself sleep over at his house three times. It was the best rest of my life, warm as toast and safe as a gold brick in Fort Knox.

It scares me how much I'm enjoying my time with Ramses. Happiness scares me. I'm not used to it. And I'm terrified how painful it will feel when it's ripped away.

I don't know when it will happen or how it will all blow up in my face, but this I know for certain: nothing lasts. People change, they age, they die, they decide they don't want you anymore. We come into this world naked and alone, and that's how we leave it.

Still, this morning, I cut the last cord tethering me to sanity—I called Lukas Larsen and ended our arrangement.

I haven't told Ramses yet.

Half of me can't wait to do it, but the other half is hiding, afraid that even Ramses doesn't realize how much he's driven by the chase. He thinks he wants me now, but once he has me, am I just a checked box?

That's the gremlin in my mind.

But nothing ever felt so right as the drive down that highway. I opened myself up to Ramses—in every sense of the word. There's a bright and reckless freedom in risking that kind of harm.

He pokes his head into the closet.

"What's taking so long?"

"I was trying to decide what to wear tonight."

"I like what you have on."

"I don't think it's fancy enough. Plus, I got sweaty on the way up."

Ramses grabs hold of me, nuzzling his face against the side of my neck. He licks right below my ear, tasting the salt on my skin.

"I like you sweaty."

Heat spreads everywhere he touches. I put my arms around his neck and kiss him deep, tasting my own salt on his tongue.

When we break apart, Ramses says, "Briggs is picking up his date. Wanna tag along?"

"We'd better."

I follow Ramses back downstairs, over creaky floorboards swollen with salty sea air, sand in the crevices.

Briggs waits for us in the kitchen, pouring drinks.

"What's this shit?" Ramses examines the bottle with displeasure.

"Liquor stores are empty," Briggs says. "The Hamptons are

flooded now that everything's open again. They're saying it's gonna be the biggest party season since Gatsby—there's a state-wide shortage of rosé and chlorine."

Ramses takes a sip of his drink, makes a face, and pours the rest down the drain.

I gulp Briggs' terrible Scotch, hoping it will take the edge off my nerves.

Briggs downs his double even quicker, though he doesn't look nervous in the slightest.

"God, that's swill," he says, chucking the rest of the bottle in the trash. "Let's steal something better from Desmond."

"We'll take my car." Ramses grabs the keys.

It amuses me that he won't even let Briggs drive him.

Briggs rests his hand on the frame and leaps into the backseat of the convertible like he's never heard of Scotch. He's annoyingly athletic and I've never seen him look awkward.

Ramses drives us to the Montauk train station, which looks like a big white farmhouse. The double-decker train pulls up, and a shocking number of people spill out.

"See?" Briggs says.

The weekenders hustle off the platform with bags slung over their shoulders, coolers and beach towels tucked under their arms. I scan the crowd for a familiar blonde head.

Sadie comes skipping down the steps in a purple top, bright yellow shorts, and heart-shaped sunglasses, her hair in stubby pigtails. Briggs stares at the mosquito bites on her chest with an expression of horror.

"*What the fuck, Blake?*"

"Briggs, this is Sadie. Sadie, this is Ramses."

"Hi!" Sadie chirps. Her nose is sunburned and peeling.

Briggs pouts while Ramses seizes Sadie's hand and shakes it. "I'm so glad you could come!"

Sadie gazes up at Ramses, wide-eyed, then turns and mouths *Goddamn!* at me.

"*Blake!*" Briggs hisses in my ear. "*I specifically asked for blonde, tall, huge tits, super filthy, and Catholic! You only got one out of five.*"

"Actually, I got two out of five."

Briggs pauses. "Which two? *Wait, which two, Blake?*"

I sidle closer to Sadie so I can cut her off before she lets anything slip.

She's talking to Ramses at warp speed but only about cronuts, so we're safe for now.

"Donuts are my literal favorite thing, and croissants are definitely in my top six, but somehow, when you put them together—"

Briggs squints at Sadie. "You look familiar."

Sadie, who is a terrible liar, makes a face like she swallowed a frog. "Maybe we've been at some of the same parties. Stockbroker parties. On Wall Street."

I step on her foot to tell her to shut the fuck up.

"Ow!" Sadie says. "Why are you stepping on me?"

"Should we get going?" Ramses grins. "Briggs, be a gentleman, help her with her stuff."

Briggs looks like he'd rather lie down on the train tracks than touch Sadie's rickety rolling suitcase and the pile of beach gear stuffed in two CTown shopping bags.

"Better let me." Sadie cheerfully hoists her suitcase. "The handle comes off."

"I think you can afford a new one," I tease her, taking her shopping bags. "You made bank this year."

"Yeah," Sadie murmurs so the men won't hear. "But I kinda spent it all…"

"*What?*" I whisper-shout. "What did you buy?"

"Flightline," Sadie says with guilty glee.

"Sadie…"

"I know, I know! But he's incredible, Blake, I'm telling you, we're just getting started—"

Racehorses are the biggest gamble in existence. It's roulette with sweat and saddles. And my sister is telling me she just spent her life's earnings on a colt who's barely won a handful of races.

I'd like to rip her a new one, but it's only a few steps to the car, which is probably why she chose this moment to tell me. I chuck her bags in the trunk, scowling.

"Nice ride!" Sadie perches on the backrest of the convertible with her feet on the seat. "I can work on my tan."

Sadie's "tan" is a pink flush mixed with a whole lot of freckles.

Briggs is livid.

"Why does she look like the roommate who never leaves the house of the girl you were supposed to bring?"

"You should be so lucky to be on a date with Sadie," I hiss. "She's the best goddamn person you'll ever meet."

Ramses is in heaven. Nothing amuses him more than sticking it to Briggs.

"I love your sunglasses," he says to Sadie. "Where'd you get them?"

"I found them on the subway. Can you believe somebody left these behind?"

"They must have been devastated."

I can't tell if Briggs is more disgusted by the orphaned sunglasses or by the fact that Sadie takes the subway. He's sitting as far away from her as possible while she balances on the backrest with the wind blowing her pigtails in a handlebar shape like Pippi Longstocking.

As soon as we reach Sundune, he bolts from the car.

Sadie leans over the seat to whisper in my ear, "He's still gonna fuck me, right?"

19

BLAKE

The private road to Desmond's house is like driving three years into the past. The manicured lawns and weeping willows are just like I remember, and the white stone facade hasn't changed in a century.

Even Briggs is awed.

"Oh, shit...so the Lowes are *rich* rich."

"Yeah," I say. "I think his great-grandfather invented imperialism."

Ramses snorts. He doesn't look impressed.

"Come on," Briggs says. "He's got the nicest place in the whole damn Hamptons. You'd buy it."

"Yeah, I'd *buy* it," Ramses says. "Desmond didn't."

"He's got stables..." Sadie sighs.

"And his own driving range," Briggs points out. "With caddies."

Ramses is unperturbed. "Briggs, remember how hard we worked that one summer because we were obsessed with buying matching Rolexes? And you were like, why don't we just get some fake ones on the street? But we didn't. We busted our asses all summer long, and in the fall, we wore those Rolexes like goddamn Olympic medals because we *earned* it. Yeah this place is gorgeous, yeah it's grandiose, but I'd rather wear a watch I earned than act like this is mine."

Briggs laughs. "Are you calling a seventy million manor a fake Rolex?"

"Yeah, I am," Ramses says. "Because generational wealth isn't authentic. Desmond is a money manager, and he's damn good at his job. But he never had to hustle. He's walking around acting like he built this—he wasn't even alive when they bought it."

I look at Ramses. His expression is calm and unconcerned. He's not just talking shit to make himself feel better—I honestly think if someone handed him the key to the front door, he wouldn't take it.

It's a far cry from how I felt when I first drove up to this house. I was intimidated. Ramses knows his worth.

He parks in the mass of gleaming cars surrounding a ten-foot fountain. The party's already in full swing, guests carpeting the back lawn. I wave to someone I know, a fellow working girl. Briggs mutters, "Why couldn't you have brought *her?*"

He's being damn ungrateful 'cause Sadie actually looks pretty hot. I lent her one of my dresses and styled her hair in cute beachy waves.

Briggs looks good, too—he's wearing a button-up and shorts that show the softball-sized bulges of his biceps and calves. His skin is smooth and golden, his face freshly shaven.

But it's Ramses who keeps yanking my eyes back again. He's got on a loose white linen shirt unbuttoned just far enough to show the swell of muscle below his collarbone. I finally understand why men are so obsessed with cleavage—every time Ramses moves or bends, I catch a little more of his warm flesh and my mouth waters...

As we make the rounds, I'm surprised by how many people I

recognize. There's everyone I knew before, plus dozens more I've met through Ramses. A new friend from the investor's club calls me over with a mojito in each hand. "Blake! Come here! There's someone I want you to meet."

Angelique introduces me to the Fed chair, whom I've seen at parties but never spoken to before.

Ramses circulates in close proximity, chatting with everyone he knows. When our eyes meet, he smiles and gives me a little nod that feels like a fist bump. He thinks I'm doing well, and that makes me grin and stand up a little straighter and think of funny things to say to Angelique.

There's no drug like the high of impressing him.

Tonight is the night to put on a show. This party's a who's who of movers and shakers. The snatches of conversation I overhear are rich with tantalizing hints of information. But I'm not just overhearing—I'm talking to the big dogs, getting direct interaction in a way I never did before when I was just a date on someone's arm.

It's pretty obvious how most of the guests secured their invitation—if they're not loaded, they're famous and gorgeous. The only person I'm surprised to see is Sinjin Rhodes. Desmond loathes him, going back to their boarding school days. I can't imagine Des would invite Sinjin, even to show off.

An hour later I get a hint—one of Desmond's traders mutters to his friend, "What's *he* doing here?"

The other trader glances at Sinjin and grins. "Des is fattening the pig before the slaughter."

"He's pulling the trigger?"

"Monday."

I snatch up that little tidbit and share it with Ramses the moment our paths cross again.

"What do you think he meant?"

I love watching Ramses' mind work. His eyes go still while a slow smile spreads over his face. "I'm not sure...but I have some ideas."

Party turns to bacchanalia. Desmond has pulled out all the stops—he's got taco trucks serving sliced Wagyu on hand-tossed corn tortillas. Down on the beach, a tiki bar pumps out pineapple margaritas garnished with edible flowers. A raised dance floor hovers above the sand, strung with lights, while some of the braver guests skid across the water on jet skis and hydrofoils.

I've managed to avoid the host—Desmond's busy, surrounded by sycophants and servants, keeping the party running and trying to woo the whales he invited here on purpose.

I catch up with Sadie by the sushi chef.

"Oh my god, Blake, he'll make anything you want! He's got bluefin tuna! I think that's endangered! I just cost Des like eight hundred and seventy dollars."

"He can afford it."

Briggs appears at my elbow, fidgety and annoyed. "Show me how to get into the palace—I want a real bathroom."

"They've got 'em over there." Sadie points to the facilities behind a screen of florals.

"I'm not using a porta-potty, no matter how pretty they make it," Briggs snarls.

"Relax," I say. "I'll show you."

Before I've taken two steps, Ramses slips an arm around my waist. "Where are you headed?"

He's been letting me network outside his shadow but watching all the time, right there if I needed him. He was probably listening to half my conversations and will have things to tell me when we're alone.

"I'm getting Briggs a flush toilet," I say. "We can go in over here."

Desmond is keeping the party outdoors to protect his marble.

I lead the others through the servants' entrance then down hallways I walked every weekend the summer Des and I dated.

Ramses sees how well I know my way. A certain mood comes over him. He looks the same, but I can feel it—lightning in the air.

"I can't believe this place..." Sadie whispers.

I shrug. "I remembered it a little bigger."

Ramses soft snort makes me glow.

I show Briggs to one of the innumerable guest bathrooms. Before his hand touches the knob, the housekeeper swoops in.

"Hello, sir, did you get turned around? I can take you to the—"

"Sorry, Hattie, I told him he could come in."

Hattie turns, surprised and pleased. "Blake! I didn't know you were coming. Are you staying for the weekend?"

"No—not here."

"Oh. I hoped—well, I'm glad to see you."

I hug her because I'm glad to see Hattie, too. We used to talk all the time while Des was working. Sometimes I'd help her tidy up, though she hated that—she'd only let me if Desmond was safely shut up in his office on a call.

"How are your boys?" I ask.

"Taller than me now. Taller than their teachers, even!"

Hattie only comes up to my chin, so her second boast is much more impressive.

"I want to see pictures. The party's spectacular; I can't believe you're still standing."

We both know who did the work to make it sing. Hattie looks exhausted. "He hasn't complained yet, so I must've done okay."

Hattie refers to Desmond as "Him" or "He" like it's perfectly obvious who we must all be talking about. And when it was just me and her and the other servants, that was true.

"Do your friends want to see the house?" She perks up. "I could give you a tour."

"Oh no, I don't—"

"I'd love a tour."

I turn around to stare at Ramses. He smiles at me while my brain yells DANGER! DANGER!

Sadie claps her hands. "I love tours!"

She's been staring everywhere like she's at Disneyland. Actually, Sadie's never been to Disneyland. Neither have I. She's looking how I imagine she would look, five-year-old Sadie alive and delighted in her face.

"I hate tours," Briggs groans, coming out of the bathroom. "Fucking kill me."

I elbow him in the ribs. "Not 'till you've seen Des' trophy room."

"Please be joking."

"Oh, I wish I was."

Desmond's mansion really is something else. It's like his ancestors were trying to recreate the sort of English palace someone like Mr. Darcy would have walked through—while they were living across the bay from Fitzgerald, creating his own brand of literary hero.

In truth, I prefer Ramses' beach house. That at least feels like it belongs with its old net hammock on the porch and sand slung across its floors. Hattie wouldn't allow a speck of sand—that's why the doors to the manor are kept closed. Des' windows look out onto a beach you can't hear or smell.

This house is a museum. Hattie shows us the music room and the solarium. Sadie only gives a shit about the memorabilia.

"Did you hear that, Blake? This is Shaq's shoe! I could canoe in it!"

I yawn. "Des is a whore for celebrities."

It's one of his strange weaknesses. He's fascinated by stars, especially the ones who embody that potent mix of personal charisma that seems to shoot them to icon status.

If I'm going to put on my Freud hat, it's probably because Des himself, for all his good looks, for all his wealth and intelligence, still lacks that spark, that thing that makes people turn and look when you walk into a room.

"What's this?" Ramses murmurs to me. "Prince's couch?"

He nudges his knee against the purple suede upholstery.

"Actually..." I say. "It is."

"Are you serious?"

When he sees that I am, Ramses laughs. His laugh comes from his chest. I feel it in my bones like a drum.

We're deep in the manor, in Desmond's private rooms where he keeps his treasures. I was one of those treasures, once. Or so I thought...until it was time to show me off.

Some darkness must have fallen over my face—Ramses zeroes in.

"What happened with you two?" he growls, close to my ear. "I know all the reasons Desmond's a shit, but you liked him once. How did he fuck it up? Tell me so I don't do the same."

I smile and shake my head. "You don't do anything like he does."

Ramses puts his hand on the small of my back and pulls me close. "Tell me anyway."

I glance at the others. Sadie is oohing over anything she's never seen before, which is everything in this goddamn place, the most attentive tour recipient Hattie has ever enjoyed. Briggs has become interested, despite himself, in Des' multi-million-dollar collection of baseball cards set in handsome rosewood cases on the far wall.

"It was here, actually. The day I realized how fucking stupid I'd been."

I remember that long, lovely summer. The one and only time I thought I was in love.

"Desmond wooed me like I'd never been wooed before: necklaces, earrings, purses, shopping sprees...he took me to Paris and told me he loved me over a candlelit dinner at the top of the Eiffel Tower."

Ramses' lip curls. I laugh.

"Yes, it's cliche, yes, you're much more creative. But to me, at the time...it felt like a fairytale."

I was twenty-four. I'd only been an escort for a year.

Desmond swooped in like a white knight, promising me everything I'd ever dreamed of.

"We came here every weekend. I loved being right on the water; I was learning to surf. Des worked a lot, but when we were together, he treated me like a princess."

I stop, thinking of those long summer days. I wasn't trading as much because I'd cut loose all my clients and stopped going to parties and events. I spent a lot of time in these pristine white rooms, reading. Alone.

Ramses' hand brings me back. He's touching my cheek, looking into my eyes. Connecting me to him.

He says, "You're not a princess."

I could be offended but I know it's true.

"Then what am I?"

I'm hoping he doesn't say, *a queen.*

Ramses slow grin makes the rest of the room disappear until all I see is him.

"You're a hunter. Like me. I saw it the moment you walked into the Belmont. I've been watching you do it here all night. It turns me on."

I feel a deep and visceral thrill when Ramses says we're alike.

For everything that divides us, at our core we're the same. We have the hunger. And the teeth and the cunning to feed it.

Ramses' face has never looked more attractive close to mine, the sea-deep blue of his eyes, the shape of his mouth in that lean, hard jaw. He is ferociously himself. Desmond's mansion is nothing compared to the fire in his chest.

"Though sometimes..." he murmurs, "it's hard to tell who's hunting who..."

When he kisses me, it's not hard to tell at all. I'm devoured.

He lets go, and the rest of the world falls slowly into place again.

"Now tell me what that idiot did to lose you."

I give in so easily. Because it feels so good.

"We were here. He asked me to move in with him. I hadn't answered yet when we heard Hattie at the door. Des wasn't expecting anyone. We walked out to see. This old lady strolled in, dripping diamonds and scarves. Immediately...he dropped my hand."

The look of swift satisfaction that crosses Ramses' face is smoothed to sympathy, but not before I catch him.

"His grandmother came to surprise him. Desmond introduced me as a friend. I said nothing in front of her. When she left, I took the train home and broke up with him. He said our relationship was real, but it wasn't. I was still his dirty secret."

Ramses doesn't attempt to hide his smugness. "I'd show you off to anyone."

"You already have. You flaunted me to your mom."

"I wasn't flaunting you. I was *proud* of you."

My whole body burns. I'm terrified of how good that makes me feel.

Ramses touches my cheek with his hand.

"For a man who runs a hedge fund, Desmond missed the opportunity of his life. And I can see it on his face every time he looks at you."

IT'S full dark when we head back out on the lawn, strings of golden lanterns revealing how drunk everyone has become. Apparently, that rosé shortage was due to Desmond—he's got fountains of it flowing everywhere I look.

"Do you want a drink?" Ramses asks.

"I'd love some water."

"I'll be right back."

I watch his broad back cut through the crowd, even the tipsiest guests making way.

"I'm hungry," Sadie says.

"Didn't you just eat eight pounds of tuna?" Briggs says.

"Gotta feed the beast." Sadie flexes her bicep. She's skinny as a whip, but her arm is roped with muscle.

Briggs raises an eyebrow, impressed. "Where'd that come from?"

"Duh, from riding," Sadie says then claps a hand over her mouth.

Briggs narrows his eyes. The pieces click together at lightning speed.

"You're that jockey!" he shouts. Then, whipping around to point at me, "That's how you knew about that horse!"

"*My* horse," Sadie proudly proclaims. "I bought him."

Briggs looks like he just solved the Kennedy assassination. "I knew I'd seen you before! Are you even a hooker?"

"Don't say that," Sadie snaps, which only confuses him.

"She's my sister, idiot."

Briggs frowns. "You don't have any sisters."

"The fuck I don't."

Sadie squirms. She hates anything that sounds like a fight. "I'm gonna get a taco."

"I'll come with you," Briggs says, surprising Sadie to a comical degree.

Behind his back, she turns and mouths, *Fuck yeah!,* at me.

"Now, tell me who you like for the Gold Cup..." Briggs says.

Sadie is pretending to hump him from behind for my amusement. Or maybe for herself, it's hard to tell.

"Who do I like for the what now?" she says, falling into step.

Ramses is still waiting in line for water. I can tell from the set of his shoulders he's annoyed about it. I smile because he waits anyway. For me.

"I'm surprised you're here," a voice says in my ear.

I know it's Desmond before I turn. Partly from how he touches my arm, which is very different from how Ramses does it, and partly because I knew he'd take his chance the moment he thought I was alone and unprotected.

His face is too close to mine. I've gotten used to looking up at Ramses even in my tallest heels. Des is pretty like a girl. His lips are red.

"Not by choice," I say.

Desmond laughs. "Please. We both know you do whatever you want."

His hand is still on my arm, his thumb sweeping back and forth like my skin is fabric and he's examining the quality.

"If that were true, I would've told dear old granny how much you like to eat ass."

Desmond wrinkles his nose. "Classy as ever."

"That's right. I haven't changed a bit, and neither have you. I saw Hattie's still driving that old Kia. Why don't you give her a raise, you fucking cheapskate?"

Desmond ignores that last part as he ignores anything he doesn't want to hear.

Low and urgent, he says, "How long are you going to keep

punishing me for one moment? I was surprised. If you would have given me time—"

"What?" I snap. "You could have worked your way up to not being embarrassed of me?"

His fingers dig in. "You want me to parade you around like *he* does?"

"No, Des. I don't want anything from you. Except for you to let go of my arm."

"*Right fucking now.*"

Ramses' growl makes Desmond drop his grip like my skin went red-hot.

He tries to hide how hard he jumped.

"Enjoying the party, Ramses? Can't really throw one like this in a *penthouse,* can you?"

Only Desmond could make a penthouse sound like a parking lot.

Ramses stands so close that his heat bakes my back, towering over me. Daring Desmond to so much as breathe on me again.

"You're right, this place is pretty spectacular. I wish my grandpa would have bought me one instead of being a plumber."

I laugh at the look on Des' face and the way the front of Ramses' thigh presses against the back of mine. I'm invincible when we link up.

"There's a lot of things you have that I'll never have." Ramses takes my hand. "But have you met my girlfriend?"

Desmond's eyes fix on our linked fingers.

"Sloppy seconds," he hisses. "From me and everyone else."

If I thought Ramses was angry before, that was nothing to the hardness that settles on him now. There's a look to a man who's been in not just one fight, but many. Ramses shifts his weight and the whole mood changes.

"Blake is the best," he says flatly. "And you know it, which is why you're over here trying to shoot your shot the second my

back is turned. I don't even blame you for that, though I'll damn
sure make you pay for it. But if you ever call her 'sloppy' again, I'll
fucking kill you."

"You'll *kill* me?" Desmond sputters. "For god's sake—"

"I don't know how you 'old money' people handle it, but the
way *I'll* handle it is I'll put you on your knees in front of all these
people you're trying to impress and make you apologize to her.
And *then* I'll fucking kill you."

Desmond looks like he just got slapped across the face with a
glove. He's white with anger, but he's smart enough not to say a
fucking word while Ramses is still loaded with charge.

Ramses sweeps me away with an arm around my waist. My
feet are touching the grass but in floating steps, all my weight on
the crook of his elbow. The night feels cooler, cleaner. The
lanterns are pretty again.

The moment we stop, I throw my arms around Ramses' neck
and kiss him.

"Thanks for standing up for me."

"I'm sorry I made you come in the first place. It was—"
Ramses catches himself, smiling slightly. "It's what I would have
wanted before."

"Not anymore?"

"No," he says simply. "Now it feels like a waste of time. When I
could be anywhere with you."

I know exactly what he means. I really didn't want to come; I
thought it would upset me to be back here again. Now it all feels
like a joke. Why did I ever care what Desmond's old grannie
thought of me? Or Desmond himself?

There's only one person I want to impress.

Ramses kisses me. His hands on my body tell everything
about what it means to be touched by *him*.

The lamps become fireflies. The surf becomes whispers. The
golden glow on his skin and in his eyes is a feeling that passes

into me when our lips meet—what it means to be alive and burning in the night.

This is real. This is worth risking everything I've earned or ever will.

"Let's get out of here," Ramses says.

I link my fingers through his, grinning.

"We will in a minute."

20

RAMSES

♩♪ *7 Rings — Ariana Grande*

Blake sneaks me back inside the house with a mad gleam in her eye. She shoves me down on the purple suede couch and starts ripping off my clothes.

I say, "Are we doing this in honor of Prince or to spite Desmond?"

She laughs. "Both."

She's pulling at my buttons, slipping her hands under my clothes, grinding against me as she straddles me on the cushions. She sucks on the side of my neck, her mouth fevered.

I'm in a strange state that's half arousal, half residual rage. I was two seconds away from knocking Desmond's head off his shoulders, and all that aggression is still swirling around inside me. Blake's wild mouth and the heat of her skin are whipping me into a frenzy before I've even calmed down.

I want to fuck her on this couch. I want to smash everything in this room. I want to fly her to Bali and have the vacation we should have had from the beginning. I want everything, everything, as long as it involves her.

The things I would do for this woman...

However dark I thought I was, I'm worse.

I grab her by the wrists.

"Tell me he's nothing compared to me. Tell me you've never felt like this."

"Never," Blake says, her eyes dark in the gloom. "It's not even close."

I release her wrists. She seizes my face instead, kissing me in the scent of leather and smoke.

I let my cock free, and she slides down on it like this is the way we fit together best. Like every part of me was shaped for her.

"I need you." I bite at her neck, thrusting up into her. "Give me everything."

"I'll give you what I never gave him."

Blake puts her arm around my neck and lifts herself so my cock slides almost all the way out. She grips the base and repositions the head against her ass instead.

I'm wet from inside her. Still, the pressure and friction almost tear off my skin. At least, that's how it feels as I inch inward a millimeter at a time. *This* is biting the wire. This is maximum voltage.

Blake is making sounds that might get me arrested, and not for trespassing. I grab a handful of her hair and silence her with my mouth.

I don't think I'm thrusting. I don't know if I'm moving at all. All I can feel is the most intense squeezing of my life, and I am not going to last long.

Her tongue tastes richer and filthier than it ever has. Her back is sweating. I'm experiencing a pleasure that must be illegal.

"Take it," she whispers in my ear. "You deserve it."

White-hot heat blasts through my brain—from the place

where her lips touch the rim of my ear, all the way down through my body and out through my cock.

I press upward into the deepest, deepest part of her, like I'm socked into her soul. Blake lets out a long, wrenching groan. She shudders in my arms.

I lay her down gently, careful not to make a mess as I pull out, but only out of respect for Hattie.

I hold Blake cocooned in the dark, cradled by the soft purple suede. Her breathing makes me calm, softer than rain, steadier than waves.

After a while, she asks, "Were you ever in love?"

"I thought I loved my high school girlfriend. Maybe I did, as much as you can at that age."

"What happened?"

It's so easy to tell her secrets in the dark. Things I've never told anyone...things I've never admitted to myself.

"She was always the type to flirt a little. I didn't mind at first, but once we got serious, it started to eat at me. She'd go 'study' with guys I knew, guys who were bigger than me, stronger than me, better looking than me..."

"Wait," Blake interrupts. "Who's bigger and stronger than you?"

I laugh softly.

"You've never seen a pic of me in high school, have you? I was tall but lanky as fuck. I was super self-conscious about it, actually. Briggs and I didn't bulk up 'till college."

"I can't imagine you scrawny."

"Believe it, baby! I wasn't the hottest guy in my school, not even close. Every girl I got, I had to work for it. Especially Ashley. It was the end of our senior year. We'd both been accepted to the same college. Right before the summer, she sat me down and said, starting in the fall, she wanted to see other people."

"What did you say?"

"I told her, no fucking way. If you want to be single, you can be single right now."

"You broke up?"

"Yeah. But once we were at college in the same dorm, she tried to rekindle. It was the first week, there were all these parties and events going on. She asked me to get together with her. I waited all day long, missed all the shit I could have been doing. Later I heard she'd been out with someone else."

Blake murmurs, "I hate wasted days."

"I was so fucking furious, I told her never to speak to me again. But a week later, she decided she'd made a huge mistake and came crawling back. She waited outside my dorm room for hours, crying in the hall. Not just one day. On and off for months."

"You wouldn't cave?"

"*No.* I had this fire in me because she'd fucked me over twice. But it was hard, the longer it went on. Her friends would tell me what a mess she was. She'd apologize and say all the things I'd always wanted her to say. She'd beg on her *knees.*"

I feel the slight shake of Blake's head. "You're stone cold."

"Not really. I just couldn't forgive her. Because she didn't pick me. And it fucking hurt."

Blake hugs me, pressing her cheek against my chest. "I'm the same way. When I'm done, I'm done."

I chuckle. "I saw that. Poor Desmond."

"He doesn't love me." She's quiet and certain. "He never did. And that day, I finally saw it."

"When you know what to look for, you can see anything." I think about how Ashley's head always turned when someone tall and good-looking walked into the room. "Can I tell you something, though?"

"Anything," Blake says, and I believe her.

"When Ashley was on her knees, pleading, making

promises...I used to have the most fucked-up fantasies of what I could get her to do."

Blake presses against me in in the dark, her mouth wet against my neck. "I'd do very bad things to get you back."

My heart thuds. "What kind of things?"

"I'll show you when we get home."

I love that she called it *home*.

"I've always had dark fantasies," Blake murmurs. "Even when I was a kid."

"Why do you think that is?"

"I don't know. Does anyone choose what turns them on?"

"Maybe not, but you can feed it."

"I like feeding *this*." Blake grabs the front of my shirt and kisses me hard.

I kiss her back until I'm not sure where she ends and I begin.

WHEN WE STUMBLE BACK out into the star-strewn night, the party has descended to Gatsby-level debauchery. Drunken stockbrokers race battery-powered porpoises through the surf while fire dancers wearing nothing but body paint light up the sand.

Blake grabs us each a slice of watermelon.

"For the road," she says, taking a huge bite of her wedge, juice running down her arm.

We're hunting through the crowd. Blake doesn't want to leave without checking in with her sister, and I've got instructions for Briggs. I expected to find him at the outdoor poker table or maybe over by the volleyball nets. All I see is a bunch of tipsy Brits and one extremely blitzed Pennywise.

"Ramses!" he shouts. "I bet Jonesy my watch that I could do a backflip."

"Yeah, how'd that go?"

"Not great," Jonesy says, holding up his wrist to show two Breitlings stacked on top of each other.

"Aw," I say. "Now you have a matching set."

"I'll win it back," Penn assures me.

"I also got his car," Jonesy says, jingling the keys.

Blake reappears with more watermelon but no Sadie.

"Where do you think she went?" she says with more curiosity than concern.

"Blake!" Penn calls. "Gimme some of that watermelon."

"I would..." Blake says, chomping down the last few bites. "But it's all gone."

Pennywise laughs uproariously. "Now I see why you and Ramses get along."

"'Cause we're both assholes?" Blake grins.

"I'd never call my boss that," Penn says. "Where he can hear."

"Come on." Blake links her arm through mine. "Let's check the beach."

We make a thorough pass of the dunes before leaving, but Briggs and Sadie are nowhere to be found.

THAT NIGHT I wake just once.

The doors to the deck are open, the gauzy curtains blowing in. The moon hangs suspended over its watery twin.

My heart is still beating from a tangled dream, fragments slipping away before I can make sense of them—my mother in her second dress, my father with grease on his hands, the door to our old apartment...my mother painted it blue, but the paint was cheap and in a year it was chipped and fading again...

You're not coming to my wedding?

Why won't you come?

He'll be fine, I need you there...

The old bitterness fills my mouth, and my mind starts to whirr, thinking of what I should have done, what I could have done, what I *will* do differently.

I want to grab my phone to check the time even though I know that shot of blue light will make it harder than ever to fall back asleep.

Blake feels me moving and rolls over onto my chest. Her face tucks up against my neck, her thigh slung over mine, her fingers twined in my hair.

I'm trapped on my back in a position that shouldn't be comfortable. But Blake's weight is calming, her heat necessary against the coolness of the sea. She smells of salt and watermelon and warm spiced tea.

I stroke my hand gently down her spine.

Instead of remembering the dream, I think of the look on Blake's face when I told her I was proud of her.

Soon I fall back asleep to the sound of the waves and her slow, steady breathing.

Bacon wakes me in the morning.

I slept so deeply, Blake snuck right out from under me.

I shuffle down the stairs, pulling my shirt down over my head but not bothering to try to tame my hair.

Blake has three skillets going on the stove top, frying bacon, scrambling eggs, and sautéing hash-browned potatoes. The scent makes me rabid and yanks Briggs and Sadie out of their beds, though they look like they've only been home a couple of hours.

Briggs' face is puffy with sleep, and he crashed with a Biore strip still stuck across his nose. Sadie's makeup from the night before is smeared down the left side of her face. The hair on that side has possibly been attacked by birds.

"Where'd you disappear to last night?" Blake demands. "And what happened to your knees?"

Sadie looks down at her skinned knees like she forgot she had knees at all.

"Football," she says.

"*Football?*" Blake has to save the bacon from burning, so she can't see the expression on Sadie's face.

Briggs is gazing carefully into his coffee mug.

"Where'd you go?" I say, mostly to watch him jump.

"Oh, uh, they had a poker game going down on the sand. Sadie's pretty good, actually."

"That's because she looks excited no matter what she has," Blake calls from the stove.

She brings over four plates, carrying them in that way that shows she's worked as a waitress at least once.

She sets mine down first, the bacon, eggs, and potatoes beautifully arranged with sprigs of rosemary for garnish. She's even mixed a pitcher of sangria.

"Not bad," Briggs says, spearing a bite of potato and chewing with relish.

"*Mmbbm brabrram mrabab,*" Sadie says, mouth stuffed.

Blake watches while I take a bite of the best goddamned scrambled eggs I've ever tasted, rich and buttery and melting.

"Jesus, you're never gonna stop rubbing it in my face, are you?" I say. "You make the best eggs."

Blake pours us all monstrous glasses of sangria. "To the best eggs!"

"To winning!" Sadie shouts.

"To quieter toasts," Briggs says, pressing his finger into his ear.

"To the best chef," I tip my glass at Blake.

"To cooking for someone else," Blake says, looking only at me.

We drink the sangria and eat all that delicious fatty food until we're no longer hungover and are well on our way back to drunk.

Blake lounges in her chair, smiling, her cheeks glowing pink.

BLAKE and I skip the rest of Desmond's wank-fest and spend the weekend doing whatever we want. This mostly involves fucking, sleeping, renting a schooner to sail to Shelter Island, and roasting clams on the beach.

I expect Briggs to join Penn and the others for at least the most tempting of Desmond's scheduled activities, but to my surprise, he never steps foot back on the silver-spoon estate. Saturday afternoon, he joins Blake, Sadie, and me on the schooner, and Sunday morning he volunteers to drive Sadie back to the city at a strangely early hour.

"Do you think there's something going on between those two?" Blake says as we're packing our bags.

"I'm not sure—they barely talked at breakfast."

"That's what made me suspicious," Blake says. "When does Sadie ever shut up?"

"She'd be a terrible spy."

"So would Briggs. Did you hear him complaining about the bacon? And the towels? And the dish soap?"

I laugh. "He was always like that—Briggs had to make money 'cause he's too picky to be poor."

"And Sadie will eat chips someone left on a train. So I guess I'm just imagining it."

"Probably," I say.

Though, earlier, when Briggs was changing shirts, I noticed his left side was striped with marks that looked suspiciously like a riding crop.

21

BLAKE

Late Sunday night, Ramses and I sail down a road black as a river in the moonlight. He's put the top up on the convertible, and I'm lying all the way across the bench seat with my head in his lap, the softness of his shirt against my cheek. I look up at his face. Every so often he glances from the road down to me, smiling slightly. His left hand rests on the wheel. His right roams over my body.

"You should stay over tonight," Ramses says.

The request pleases me. I expected him to drop me off, maybe a little glad to be alone after so many hours together. It would be natural, though I don't actually feel that way myself.

I want to go back to his apartment. I like it more than mine. Every part of it smells like Ramses and reminds me of him in mood and scale. Plus, we haven't played Minx in a while. I've been craving it.

Most of all, I love sleeping in his bed. It's bigger than a king, seemingly an acre across with heavy down comforters and cool, fresh sheets. When Ramses gets under the covers, he creates a kind of den with his mass. I curl up inside it, his arms around me, his thick chest against my back.

Usually, my dreams would make Salvador Dali freak the fuck out—stressful, twisted, disturbing. Some nights my brain is stuffed with so many nightmares that I wake hardly rested at all.

Not with Ramses. We sleep with his heavy paw cupped over my pussy, warm and comforting. He slips a finger inside me in the night and my dreams become sensual instead of horrifying. His scent fills my nose, his heat keeps me calm, and my wet dreams soak the sheets.

In the morning I wake with his head between my thighs, his tongue reminding me why it's good to be alive.

So he doesn't exactly have to twist my arm to get me to agree to sleep over.

"I'd love that."

"Good." He grins. "'Cause I need you at the office with me early."

"What for?"

"It's a surprise."

I make a face. "You've got a fifty percent hit ratio on surprises."

"That's some bullshit," Ramses growls, pinning me down with his hand. "When have I done anything you didn't like...eventually."

He lets his fingers dance up my ribs in a way that's *almost* torturous, then cups my breast in his hand, rough at first, then soft and caressing. He teases my nipple until I have to moan.

I wonder if Ramses has any smiles that aren't wicked.

WHEN HE SAID we had to be at the office early, I wasn't expecting five a.m. Ramses has to roll me out of bed and practically brush my teeth for me.

"This surprise sucks so far," I say when I've spat out the toothpaste.

"You'll change your mind when you see this..."

I hear the soft purr of the blinds. The panorama of glass reveals the dewy treetops of Central Park and the flat glitter of the bay. A streak of orange lightens the base of the deep blue sky. I join Ramses, watching the light spread.

His fingers link with mine.

Rafts of clouds illuminate, gold on the edges closest to the sun, still stormy underneath. The blue sky lightens and becomes transparent.

When Ramses turns, all the colors are caught in his eyes. I become very aware of how high up in the sky we are and how far I could fall.

"Okay," I say, kissing him softly on the mouth. "I'm having fun."

"Not as much as you will."

I've been to Ramses office once before to shout at him. Entering as co-conspirators is much more fun.

He's got a massive brick building in Hudson Yards, the top floor torn off and replaced with glass.

We're not even the first people here—the market doesn't open until 9:30 Eastern, but the traders are at their desks by 7:00 a.m.

Ramses runs his floor differently than Desmond—his office is much less opulent and his traders are hungrier. The noise and energy are immense.

Desmond has a private corner suite. Ramses' office is made of glass walls that can be frosted for privacy but look over his employees at all times.

His assistant brings in the mail with a strangely nervous look. Ramses takes it from her, plucking out a silver envelope. He glances at the postmark, and his face tightens. He pulls out the invitation, gazes at it stone-faced without seeming to read anything, then drops it in the trash.

"Do you ever get invited to parties you actually want to attend?" I tease him.

He blinks, and the anger breaks enough for him to say, "Maybe...when's your birthday?"

"Do you really not know?"

"Of course I know." He smiles. "You're a Gemini."

That makes me laugh. I didn't expect Ramses to be into star signs. "And what are you?"

"Sagittarius."

His pride makes me laugh even harder. "Is that a good one?"

"The best."

Now that he's in a mild mood again, I'm wondering if I have the guts to snatch that invitation out of the trash to see what pissed him off.

I lean against his desk, waiting for my chance to peek into the bin, where I catch the words, *10th Anniversary Celebration*, in ornate script. My stomach sinks.

Ramses pulls up his Bloomberg Terminal. He looks like a kid on Christmas morning. "Almost time!"

I don't bother to ask what we're doing. Ramses won't tell me, but he'll show me soon enough.

I can see he's pulling up the data for Gab, Sinjin Rhodes' company. He runs a social media platform everybody's saying is the next Twitter. But "everybody" says a lot of shit that never ends up happening.

"Watch," Ramses says.

As soon as trading opens, the price of Gab stock pops by two points.

Ramses smiles. "Desmond took the hook...now let's run the line."

His fingers flash across the keys.

I watch, numbers scrolling before my eyes.

Desmond's hedge fund just bought a two percent stake in Gab. Ten minutes later, he buys another fifty thousand shares.

That's when Ramses starts conducting his symphony.

I watch it unfold before me, an artist at the peak of his skill.

Ramses unleashes the traders first, with a bevy of small purchases that won't immediately be noticed. As the stock ticks up another two points, he starts making phone calls to everyone he knows.

Watching him work is fucking beautiful. He stands silhouetted before the bank of windows, sleeves rolled up, hands moving like a magician.

Ramses says, "Do you know what happened when Walt wanted to open a second Disneyland?"

I shake my head, smiling back at him.

"He opened a bunch of shell corporations and started buying up swampland in Florida. At first it was going great—he was getting acres for pennies on the dollar. But then a reporter noticed the purchases and spilled the story. The people who owned the last of the land raked Walt over the coals."

I laugh softly. "Never give away your position."

Ramses winks. "Not even to me."

By the time the market's been open an hour, Desmond's hostile takeover is in shambles. Ramses has pumped the stock up 30%.

Desperately, Desmond's hedge fund tries to buy the rest of the shares as fast as they can.

Ramses grins. "He's pot committed now."

Buy, buy, buy, buy, buy, Ramses hammers him again and again and again, each purchase driving up the price so the rest of the stock Desmond needs becomes increasingly expensive.

I can only imagine what this is costing Ramses in favors and cold, hard cash. He doesn't flinch as he hits his keys, each blow the cut of a knife for Ramses but a hatchet hack for Desmond.

"How long are you going to keep going?" I murmur.

Ramses looks at me, eyes dark and flat. "Until you tell me to stop."

I stare at the screen as Desmond's purchase balloons to more than double what he expected to pay. The last 10% of the shares he needs for a controlling interest cost him as much as the 90% that came before.

"Okay," I say at last.

Ramses hits him once more for 100,000 shares. "So he doesn't forget."

I shake my head, impressed and slightly sickened. "Remind me to stay on your good side."

Ramses has never looked more serious.

"That was a taste. Watch what happens if he touches you again."

22

RAMSES

The best week of my life is followed by two of the worst.

I'm flying high after my trip with Blake and the thrill of fucking up her ex together. She spends almost every night at my house, and I spend one at hers. We cook dinner together, then I lie with my head in Blake's lap while she reads aloud from *How To Win Friends And Influence People* so we can remember when we each read those pages thirteen miles apart in two of the shittiest neighborhoods of Brooklyn, dreaming of the day we'd carve our names next to the Carnegies of the world.

The next week, the market takes a giant shit. It's the worst three-day decline since 1987. That wouldn't be so bad, except that Halston Reeves takes the opportunity to gut two of the biggest investments I have going.

In a moment of unusual pettiness, I took my mother's invitation out of the trash, tore it up, and mailed it back to her. Apparently, Reeves didn't appreciate that form of RSVP because he started attacking my business with a ferocity that makes what I did to Desmond look like a pat on the back.

Reeves is a brawler. He's been in this business twice as long as

Desmond or I have, and he's fucking crafty. Now that he's declared war, I have to be on high alert everywhere, and I have to hit him back because an attack like that can't go unanswered.

When you become the guy people are afraid of, they don't deliberately take shots at you. You have less contenders coming after you because they know they'll be met with brutality.

Part of the reason my fund does so well is that when my rivals are deciding who they want to fuck over, they don't pick me.

If I don't hit Reeves back hard enough to send a message, the jackals will descend.

I could handle all that if I could keep my fucking focus, but my mother's anniversary is a rat gnawing at my brain. Each day it creeps closer, eating deeper into my psyche. Because it's also the ten-year anniversary of my father's suicide.

I tell myself that ten years is a long fucking time. I should be over it by now. In fact, I never should have let it affect me like it did.

But I start waking up in the night again. Staring at the ceiling, sickening silence blaring in my ears. Wishing I had asked Blake to come over instead of telling her I was too slammed with work.

I'm embarrassed for her to see me like this. I'm gripped by stomach cramps and a clammy sweatiness that makes me think I might have the flu, except it only seems to get worse.

By the time the weekend rolls around, I can't take it anymore; I have to see Blake even if I'm not at my best. I book us a dinner for Friday night, the night I'd be at that godawful party if I was *ever* going to cave to my mother's bullshit again.

All day long, I try not to think about the things I don't want to think about. I don't visit my father's grave. I've never been to see it —not since his funeral.

Reeves hasn't stopped his fuckery. Actually, he's ramped it up. He knows what day this is just like I do. My mother's tried to call me twice. Each chop Reeves takes at me is retaliation for her tears.

I want this to be a day like any other. I tell myself it is.

Through all the attacks, through the unusual infuriations I have to handle with my traders and Briggs and the SEC, I keep picturing Blake smiling at me across a candlelit table while the rest of the world melts away...

It's past seven before I can leave the office. I text Blake to meet me at my apartment so I can shower and change clothes.

As soon as the elevator doors open into my suite, I catch the scent of her perfume. My heart leaps. I drop all my shit on the floor and cross the room in three strides, scooping her up and breathing her in.

Her blue dress hugs her curves. Her hair is so shiny it looks lacquered, her bangs freshly trimmed, her nails filed to points, thin silver rings on her fingers. The feel of her in my arms instantly becomes the best part of my week.

"Are you starving? I'll hurry."

"No rush." She smiles. "I've got some emails to clear out."

Her laptop sits open on the coffee table, photos of the investment club pulled up on the screen. Blake confessed to me that she has a hard time recognizing faces. She practices matching pictures to names so she'll greet acquaintances correctly at parties. I've only seen her make a mistake once. She told me afterward it was because she'd been going off an old photograph.

The way she continually finds ways to back-door the obstacles of her existence impresses me. I know how hard it is for me to do what I do. Trying to do it at half my size, as a gorgeous girl with a bizarre brain, would be like trying to make it to the NBA one-handed.

I plug the sink in my bathroom and run the water so I can shave my face again. I want it perfectly smooth when I eat her pussy later. Fuck, I can't wait. I deserve it after the week I had.

I hurry into the closet to grab fresh clothes. While I'm in there, Briggs calls with more bad news. I retaliated against Reeves, and now he's fucking with my individual traders. Pennywise just took a massive hit. Jonesy is next, from the looks of it.

This is spiraling out of control. I need a way to punch Reeves back hard enough to hurt. No, to put him on his fucking ass...

My mind works frantically, my stomach cramping again. Unbidden, thoughts of my father flash through my head.

I failed at the only thing that matters to me...

I'm sorry, Ramses...

You were right to choose her...

The sound of water hitting the floor jolts me back. I rush into the bathroom. The sink has overflowed, flooding not only the countertop and floor but also the half-open drawers. My toiletries are soaked, the drawers so full that I'll have to bail them out with a bucket.

I stare at the mess, the sickening pressure of trying to fix this and everything else in my life finally crashing down.

Blake walks into the bathroom.

"Hey, I heard—"

She stops, staring at the disaster in front of her. When she sees my face, she shuts off the water and comes to wrap her arms around me. My heart is hammering so hard that she lifts her head from my chest.

"Baby, are you okay?"

I open my mouth to say yes. It's too heavy a lie. I shake my head instead.

"Come here..." Blake pulls me over to the bed.

I sink down on the edge. She puts her arms around me again, kissing me gently on the forehead. Her eyes search my face.

"What's wrong?"

There's pressure around my chest, iron bands strapped tight.

I keep seeing the water overflowing the drawers, flooding the floor, my razor blades and pomade and toothpaste all floating in the mess. I can't believe I did something that goddamn fucking idiotic. FUCK!

I put my hands over my face, blazing with shame.

"I don't want you to see me like this."

I expect Blake to draw back, to take her arm off my shoulders. I can feel her looking at me.

I must look like such a fucking fool. I'm sweating. My shoulders twitch. I know she felt that, too. Fuck, fuck, *fuck.*

It's getting harder to breathe. The bedroom presses tiny and close, then balloons out huge like I'm shrinking. My heart races, pounding in my ears.

The pressure is everywhere, tight on my chest, tight against my temples. The room goes dark. The bed drops like an elevator. My body jerks.

All that remains are Blake's arms wrapped around me. While everything else swells and shrinks, swoops and falls, she holds me tight, her breathing steady, her heart like a metronome.

"It's okay," she murmurs in my ear. "Everything's okay, I'm right here with you."

What's happening to me?

"You're okay. It's going to be fine."

I think I'm having a heart attack—

"Shh, it's okay, I've got you, I'm right here..."

Gradually, eventually, the pounding in my ears begins to slow. The waves of nausea grow further apart, and the room seems only dim instead of dark. I can see Blake's hand gripping my arm, and then I can feel it, too, along with her other hand stroking my back.

As soon as there's space to think, embarrassment is close at hand.

"Sorry," I mutter, trying to pull away.

"Ramses." Blake takes my face in her hands. "It's okay. I get panic attacks, too."

Do you ever hear something, automatically deny it, *really* hear it, think about it, get slapped with the truth, think about it more, change your whole idea of yourself, and then have no idea what to say?

I never thought I'd be a person who has panic attacks.

Then, all in a moment, I knew that was exactly what I'd had. Because Blake was there, and she saw, and she understood.

I'm afraid to look in her face. If I see disgust there, revulsion, even pity...it will destroy me. Because I can't bear to be weak in front of her.

But I have to risk it, or I can't look at her at all. I'll have to get up and walk out of the room. Because I can't hide anything in this moment. And I don't think she can, either.

I look into Blake's eyes—they're wide, clear, and searching. She cups my face in her hands, kisses me on the mouth, then presses her forehead lightly against mine.

"What is it?" she says between kisses, between touches. "What's got you so spun out? Is it work shit? Is it this stuff with your mom?"

If I felt hesitancy in her hands, if she pulled back at all, I'd notice. I'm hyper-sensitive, I'm watching. But her body presses against mine, her hands grip my arms, her mouth is as warm and eager as ever. More, as she feels me responding.

She's hungry for me still.

I sink against her, warmth flooding my chest. My arm slips around her waist; I rest my head on her shoulder and turn my face against her neck, inhaling.

Her scent brings me back over miles of ground.

"Today's the anniversary."

"Oh," Blake says.

That one little syllable contains all the weight in the world.

She hugs me with her arms wrapped as far around as she can reach.

I pull her onto my lap and kiss her, my hands thrust deep in her hair.

"My mother came to see me a few days before her wedding. You have to understand, before she left...my dad and I fucking adored her."

The images come, fast and painful. All of us dressed up in our best clothes to go to Blue Marble for sundaes. Tuesday night movies at matinee prices, sneaking in popcorn in our coat pockets. Dancing over the worn carpet in the living room, my mom adjusting my hand on her waist, *Be a gentleman, Ramses.* Me rolling my eyes, *What's a gentleman?* Her smiling up at me because I was already taller than her at twelve, *A gentleman is a patient wolf...*

I say, "An only child is an intimate participant in their parents' marriage. My dad worshipped my mom, and so did I. When she was upset—and she was often upset because my dad was unreliable, a liar, a schemer—I was roped into his grand schemes to win her forgiveness. I was trained to please her. I wanted to make her happy."

I think of her the day she left, still in the last flush of her thirties and achingly beautiful like a doll. Too fragile and flawless to ever look at home where we lived.

I think of the house I used to pass every day on the bus, the one that looked so fancy to me. I'd imagine how happy my mother would be if I could somehow buy it for her. How she'd never have to worry about a stove that smoked or creaky stairs or creepy old men who peed in the alleyway. She'd be proud to bring her friends over. Feverishly, I planned, even after she left, even when someone else bought the house, even when they tore out the rose bushes. I'd think if I could somehow get it, she might still come home...

My face twists.

"When she came to see me, that's what she said—*Don't you want me to be happy?* She cried and begged me to come to her wedding."

I think of her blue eyes looking up at me, wet with tears.

Blake says, "It wasn't wrong to go. Lots of people's parents get remarried. And yours had been divorced for years."

"I know. But I also knew my dad wasn't okay."

You were right to pick her...

Blake grips my hand. "That's not your fault."

I remember the water hitting the floor. I think of my own dumb shock.

Oops.

"I fucked up. I knew he'd be upset, but I didn't think..."

The bands around my chest haven't disappeared. In fact, they're tightening...

"It wasn't your fault," Blake repeats. "He made his own choice."

"She didn't tell me. She knew he was dead when she walked down the aisle, but she didn't tell me until the reception was over. I'll never forgive her for that."

"You don't have to. Forgiveness is overrated."

That almost makes me smile, but I can still see the water soaking into the carpet.

"I need to clean up that mess." I cover my face, nails digging in. "I can't fucking believe I did that."

The panic is still there, and now that I know that it's panic, that only makes it worse. A heart attack would be less emasculating.

"I'm cleaning it up," Blake says, no room for argument. "In a minute."

"I can't believe I did that. I don't know why I'm so FUCKING upset by it, I can get new shit..."

My hands are shaking.

Blake says, "You're upset because you hate being out of control."

I turn to look at her.

"That's why the drawers are upsetting you so much," she repeats. "You can get new shit, you can buy new drawers, but you made a mistake. Your discipline is what makes you powerful. When you're distracted and you make mistakes, you think you're less in control, and you feel less powerful. And then you feel...," her eyes drop, and her voice, too, "...fucking terrified."

Slowly, I nod.

"That's exactly right."

Blake understands because she's felt this, too.

Nothing has changed, but everything has changed.

Warmth floods my chest, the iron bands relaxing.

Blake kisses me on the mouth, then on the cheek, and lightest of all on the edge of my eyebrow.

"Get in the shower," she says. "I'll clean up the drawers—no, don't argue, I can do it fast. We're not going out, we're staying right here."

I smile, enjoying the sternness of her face when she takes charge. "Will you put some music on for us?"

"I will." She bounces up, pleased that I've given her the go-ahead to set the mood.

As I step under the shower spray, a familiar song comes through the speakers, the one I played the first time I touched Blake in the cat suit. My cock, disturbingly dead up until this moment, finally comes alive.

I grip it in my hand, feeling it respond, sensitive, warm, and swollen instead of hatefully numb. That alone puts a lump in my throat. I fucking loathe when my cock doesn't feel right.

I turn the water up hot. Steam fills the glass box. I can hear Blake moving around but can't see her anymore. I soap my body, stroking my cock, thinking of the moment I ripped open that suit and saw her bare pussy for the first time...

The next song she plays was on the radio the night we drove to April's house. The next is one we listened to on the way to the Hamptons. As I'm rinsing off, a song we sang together at a Yankee's game plays. Blake made a whole playlist of music we've heard on our dates.

Each snatch of chorus reminds me of some joke between us, some taste of Cherry Coke on her lips. Each bright moment is linked forever to these songs, strung through my brain, glinting like holiday lights.

I towel off, spraying on the cologne Blake seems to like best, the one that makes her cling to me most. She slipped out of the bathroom without me noticing; I don't know where she went.

I set the bottle down, realizing Blake managed to clear the water out of the drawers, mop up the counters and floor, and dry off my toiletries. Anything still soggy, like my shaving brush, has been propped up neatly to air dry. A pile of sodden towels sits draining in the bathtub.

I stare at the miraculously restored bathroom then pull on some soft, comfy clothes in a kind of daze.

Blake waits for me in the den, looking bright-eyed and disheveled like she only just beat me here. She's wearing her ears and collar and a fresh cat suit.

She looks so fucking tempting I want to sprint to her side. But I hesitate in the doorway, painfully aware that my cock still isn't quite responding like it should. If she touches me and I'm not fully hard...

I push that thought away, striding to the couch. I don't have a problem performing.

I sit down and pull my little Minx onto my lap, running my hands over her body. The sleek feel of the suit under my palms makes my heart jump, and my cock too, though not as quick as

I'd like. The delay causes a hot, prickling sensation on the back of my neck.

Minx can feel the tension in my hands. She turns in my lap, looking up into my face. I try to smile, but I'm stiff; I'm fucking this up. She smiles back at me anyway.

Delicately, she puts out a hand in its black glove. She touches her curled fingers to the empty water glass resting on a coaster on the coffee table, slowly pushing until the glass reaches the edge. She pauses then pushes a little more until the glass topples, falling dully to the thick carpet below.

A smile tugs my lips. "Oh, is that how you're gonna be?"

Eyes wide and unblinking, Minx holds my gaze while she slowly pushes a small stack of books off the table. They cascade to the floor in quick succession, *thud, thud, thud.*

"That's adorable," I say. "You're an adorable asshole."

She touches her hand to the full water glass close where the empty one used to sit.

"Don't even think about it," I growl.

She pauses in her pushing. Waits two seconds. Then shoves it right off the edge.

I leap on her, snarling and kissing her everywhere, making her scream. She's giggling, and I forget to worry about my cock. Until she takes it out of my pants and tries to put it in her mouth, and I realize that even though her tongue feels fucking phenomenal and I want to be inside her like I want to breathe, I'm still only sixty percent hard.

"Sorry," I mutter. "It's not you, I—"

She kisses me, her tongue wet and ravenous in my mouth.

"You're perfect," she says. "Fucking perfect."

It's the first time she's talked during a Minx scene—usually we wait until after.

I'm glad she's talking now. It feels exactly right in the moment. Rules are only rules until you make better ones.

"*You're* perfect," I say, kissing her everywhere I can reach. "I don't want you to think I don't want you, because I'm fucking dying for you. My body's fucked up because I'm fucked in the head."

"You want me?" Minx says, kissing me the way I love.

"*Yes.*"

"What turns you on the most?"

"Your scent." I don't even have to think about it. "The way you smell here..." I put my face against her neck, under her hair, and breathe in deeply. Her scent floods my nose, filling every cell in my body. "And here..." I press my nose into the patch of skin between her breasts, inhaling until my eyes roll back. "Here..." I lift her arm, breathing in the fine spice of her sweat. She shrieks and tries to pull away, but I make her let me. Now my cock is all the way hard, pointing straight at the ceiling. Now it's fucking raging.

"And *here*..." I rip open the crotch of her suit, butterflying her thighs and nuzzling my face into her sweet, soaking pussy. I fill my lungs with her scent, again and again until her thighs shiver around my ears. "*That's* my favorite."

I take a long swipe with my tongue between her pussy lips. She's drenched and slippery. I lap while her legs shake around me.

This is the taste I love. This is the feeling I love, those velvety folds melting on my tongue, warm and sweet and satisfying. I close my eyes and drown in it.

She mounts my face, her bent knees resting partly on my shoulders and partly on the backrest of the couch. I cup her ass in my hands, eating her pussy like a watermelon. She rolls her hips, her hands thrust into my hair, her nails scratching my scalp.

Her spread thighs let my tongue delve deep. I lap at her like an animal, dipping my tongue into her warmth, scooping out her wetness.

Her hands grip my head as she fucks my face. I never did end up shaving. The friction of my stubble against her slippery cunt only amps her up, making her crazy. She bucks her hips faster, her thighs flushing red.

She starts to come. I drop her down on my cock, shoving inside her so her first cry goes from high and clear to deep and wrenching, "Oh my god—oh, JESUS!" I grip her hips and drive up into her, watching her tits bounce.

She pogos on my cock faster, harder. Each hit pounds a little more of the orgasm out of her, "*Ah! Ah! Ah! Ah!*". Muscle stands out on my chest and arms, sweat running down my face. I bounce her full weight on my cock, watching the ripples of impact through her luscious curves.

I rip open the front of the cat suit, her tits spilling out. I cup them in my hands, squeezing nipples as thick and hard as pencil erasers. I milk her breasts in time to the thrusts of my cock until her eyes go glazed and her mouth hangs open. As she comes one last time, her back arches and her nipples turn to diamond, each shuddering wave of pleasure seeming to flow down to their very tips, her pussy squeezing around my cock in much the same motion as my hands.

It's the hottest thing I've ever experienced, and I thought I came at the same time.

But when Blake climbs off of me, she shakes her head.

"You didn't come all the way."

I laugh. "What does that mean?"

"It means there's still more."

She reaches down and grips my cock.

"*Whoa,*" I say as it jolts in her hand.

"See?" She grins, her hand slowly stroking.

My cock has gone back to that hateful level of hardness, thick and throbbing but flexible in her hand. She's right, I can feel that anxious pulse like there's more to unleash, but I don't think I'm going to be able to clear my mind and let go. Not tonight.

"I don't think—"

"Do you trust me?" Blake says.

She can't keep that naughty look off her face even to ask the question.

"Yes...though I shouldn't."

Blake smiles. "Trust me to take care of you."

My body goes warm and heavy because that's exactly what I trust her to do.

I sit back on the couch. Blake runs into the bedroom. Her ass flexes in the transparent suit, the bare soles of her feet flashing. She's back in a moment with the bottle of lube that sits next to the bed and a pair of scissors.

"Relax," she says. "Get comfy. Don't try to come. Just let me enjoy the feel of your cock in my mouth."

She kneels in front of me on the thick rug, holding out the scissors so I can cut the gloves off her suit.

Just the reveal of her naked hands makes my cock twitch. Her skin is smooth and clear, the color of ash wood, glowing with that faint interior light that's a part of Blake, like her dimple, like her voice.

This is a girl who's meant to shine in the dark like a silvery star.

I found her. I brought her here. Now she's lighting up my night.

"Thank you for being here with me," I say. "If I didn't have you tonight..."

Blake grins. Her tongue darts out, dancing around the head of my cock. "Then you'd have to do this yourself. When I'm so much better at it..."

We both know that if Blake weren't here, I'd still be crying in the closet. My dick would be dead, and I'd be wondering why the fuck I do anything in my life.

But she *is* here. She's looking up at me with those eyes that make the rest of the world fade away. She's smiling around my cock, rubbing the head across those lush lips, forcing it into her mouth then sighing with pleasure when it hits her tongue.

"I love it like this, when I can fit more in my mouth. I love feeling it twitch on my tongue..."

She rolls her tongue across the underside, flicking, teasing, giving a pleased little groan when she feels my cock leap in response.

"*Mmm....like that...*"

The music switches to a song I know very well because Blake plays it all the time while she dances around my apartment, shaking her ass at me.

♪♫ *Turn Up— S3nsi Molly*

She strokes my balls with her hand, cupping, tugging, making a game of how she plays with my cock, how she teases out sensation. She creates combinations with her mouth and her hands, not like she's trying to make me come, just trying to make me feel good.

Each time my cock pulses in her mouth, she moans with satisfaction. She chases whatever seems to be working like a fox after a rabbit. When I don't respond the way she wants, she switches to something else until she has me flexing and groaning with each flick of her tongue, a marionette on her strings. All without her making me feel like she even wanted me to get hard.

She squeezes under the head with one hand, massaging my balls with the other. Meanwhile, she's got her mouth clamped on the underside of my cock, sucking at the base like she's trying to give me a monstrous hickey where only the two of us can see it.

"Fucking *JESUS!*" I cry as she drags me closer and closer to the edge.

The way she builds her pace is devilishly tricky—pure fucking torture but powerful, a storm under her tight control.

She builds and builds and builds, then right when I think she's going to let me loose, she captures the sensation, corrals it, and starts building all over again.

She strokes light and fast on the shaft, faster, faster, faster, her arm a blur, until my balls are boiling like a champagne bottle shaken hard. Then she switches to warm, sliding motions, her bare palms caressing the head, milking my cock while I melt, melt, melt....

By the second or third time through, I realize she's playing with me, a cat with a mouse. Making me think I'm running free into pure pleasure until she captures me and starts torturing me all over again.

"You little monster..." I breathe, my eyes rolling back.

Blake only grins, squirting lube into her hands, rubbing it all over like lotion.

When her fingers are coated, she starts stroking under my balls.

"Don't worry," she purrs. "I'm gonna make you feel so good..."

"You're gonna kill me."

"You can't be mad if you're dead," Blake says, closing her mouth firmly around the head of my cock.

Her logic is impeccable.

I'm starting to hope this is the way I go. I can't think of a better send-off...

Her mouth is pure nirvana. It's like she knows exactly how this feels to me, like she's reading each shiver and twitch with her tongue, her hands on my body, her eyes watching my face.

Her fingers slide lower, massaging around my ass. I feel the impulse to tell her no, to move her hand, but that impulse is rooted in discomfort, not in what I actually want. Her hands feel good like they always do—no, even better, because her warm, slippery fingers are pressing and playing in a space I've never tried to eroticize before.

Curiosity is stronger than taboo. And pleasure rules them all.

Her fingers stroke and massage, patient, confident, firm, showing me that this part of my body has just as many nerve endings as my cock, and every one of them feels about Blake like the rest of me does...

Her mouth envelopes the head of my cock, warm and wet. Her sensitive finger presses against my ass. With each push, she drops her mouth lower around my throbbing cock.

The sensation is uncomfortably intense and desperately filthy.

I can't believe one small finger could make me feel like this—turned inside out. Women are fucking insane to let a cock inside them.

That's the last conscious thought in my head. Blake's middle finger makes contact with my prostate, and I'm no longer in charge. That little button is the key to the kingdom—I give it all to her, and my brain goes blank.

Her finger works inside me, pressing against that delicate, crucial place. My cock has become a new kind of substance, molten, pumping magma, rammed deep in her throat. Blake grips the base of my cock, her other hand slotted inside me, working my body like a master.

I'm good at sex, but this is her *job*.

And Blake is not a nine to five, show up and punch a card kinda gal. She's more like a "if they gave Nobel prizes for this, I'd have five" kind of person. She's invented something spectacular, and I wish I could invest all my money in it, 'cause this stock is going to the *moon*.

Her mouth bobs on my cock, her finger pressing deep.

"You like that?" she murmurs, her eyes locked on mine. "That's how it feels when you're inside me."

In a burst of brain-bending clarity, I finally understand the female orgasm—the interior stimulation and helpless clenching, combined with the sucking on the outside of what feels like one huge, swollen clit.

I'm not in control, not even a little bit.

As she drives her finger deeper, harder, in time with her mouth, she forces the orgasm out of me like she has me pinned to a wall.

It's fucking terrifying, a pleasure so huge, so overwhelming, it tears me apart.

I don't want to give in, but I don't have a choice. This is what it means to be penetrated, impaled, your most powerful and vulnerable inside places at the mercy of someone determined to exploit them for all they're worth.

Her left hand squeezes my balls like she's juicing fruit. Her right hand fucks me, slow, steady, and deep. Her mouth is a warm, wet black hole from which nothing can escape.

I'm rushing down a tunnel of light and sound, coming while I'm still building, my body shaking, hips lifting, back bent like a bow. Someone bellows, *"Ohmyfuckinggodjesusfuck!"*

Then I'm lying in panting, throbbing blackness on the couch while Blake cleans me with a warm cloth.

"Now you're done."

23

RAMSES

When we're finished fucking, neither of us has any interest in sleep. Blake shimmies out of the ruined cat suit, pulling on one of my baseball shirts instead.

I take out the panini press and make us two perfectly toasted grilled cheese, which Blake and I have agreed is the only dish I cook better than she does.

I'm aware that it's a stretch to call this "cooking," but I'm pretty fucking proud of my personal innovation of cutting the sandwiches diagonally with the spatula midway through pressing so the cheese melts out and gets all chewy and crispy on the edges of the bread.

That and a fuck ton of butter on both sides has resulted in a grilled cheese that even Blake hasn't tried to improve. She sits patiently on the other side of the island, pouncing on her food the moment I pass her the plate.

I give her the top half of the sandwich while keeping the bottom portion warm on the press. Blake likes to eat her food at the temperature of lava.

"Ah! Fuck!" she cries, biting into the crispiest, gooiest part, burning her fingers, dropping her grilled cheese, and snatching it up so she can do it all over again. "God, that's good."

I watch her eat, feeling ten times the satisfaction I'd feel eating the food myself.

"Aren't you hungry?" she says.

"Yeah." I pick up my sandwich and chew, though really, I'm just watching her.

She's absorbed in her food, delighted as a kid.

I say, "You want some chocky milk?"

Blake grins. "You're goddamn right I do."

I head to the fridge to take out the whole milk and Hershey's syrup. Blake told me that was her favorite food as a child, the first thing she learned to ask for by name. *Chocky milk*...I think of her, tiny and determined, and I smile while my chest aches.

My fridge used to look like a bodybuilder lives here—stacks of ready-prepped meals left by my chef in clear glass boxes. Now it's full of all the ridiculous foods I think Blake might want to eat when she's happy, when she's vegging out—Candy Hearts grapes and pickled artichokes, wedges of fancy cheeses, the last of the peaches from the farmer's market, shaved ham from her favorite deli...

I mix up the chocolate milk and pass it to her. She takes a deep draught, licking the mustache from her lips.

"You take such good care of me."

My chest feels soft and bruised. Her words burrow in and make a home there.

"That's what I want. I want to take care of you."

Blake looks at me, setting down her glass.

The silence between us is full of so many things. I know what I want to say to her. I wish I knew what she wants to say to me.

Blake chews the edge of her lip, her eyes searching my face.

Is she hopeful? Nervous?

Fuck, I can't tell.

At last, she says, abruptly and perhaps like this was a different idea, "Would you look over my plan for the week? Or maybe you don't feel like working—"

"I'd love to. Grab your laptop."

♪ *Like Real People Do — Hozier*

She brings it to the kitchen island, slipping back onto her stool. I take the one next to hers, reading the screen over her shoulder. She shows me the investments she has going and her strategies for the upcoming week.

Maybe she really does want my help. Or maybe she knows this is another way to make me happy, to take my mind off my problems by focusing on her.

Blake's investments are clever and much more fun than mine. She gets to zip around like a hornet, stinging here and there, too small for anyone to swat.

I like seeing how her tricky mind works. When I can help her, I feel a satisfaction that has begun to eclipse the pleasure of my own deals.

Blake is sucked into the numbers on the screen, her eyes bright, her hands rapid on the keys. As she shows me the details of her play, her hand swings wide and knocks the chocolate milk all over the keyboard.

"Fuck!" she cries in real frustration. She grabs a wad of paper towel and mops at the keyboard, red-faced.

I set the glass in the sink and wipe the counter.

Blake's lips press together, all the excitement vanished from her face. The chocolate milk has dripped down through the keyboard, ruining any chance of further work and probably bricking the laptop.

"Don't stress," I say. "I'll get you a new one. That one was getting old anyway."

Blake stares down at the keys, at the wad of brown, sodden towel in her hand.

"It's not the laptop. I wish I wasn't like this."

Her head hangs down, her bangs covering her eyes.

I know she's not talking about a single glass of milk. Blake knows that no matter how careful she tries to be, she'll always spill drinks, or drop food, or break plates, or walk into door-frames, or confuse people's names.

I was upset earlier because I almost never make mistakes. Discipline and precision got me where I am.

Blake makes errors all the time in small ways because that's how *her* mind works—in creative leaps and incredibly rapid recognition of patterns.

I close the laptop, putting my arms around her.

"Don't apologize. Don't feel bad. You make mistakes some-times because you're focused so hard on the thing you're focused on. And that's your gift, that's your power, that's what lets you do so many incredible things. Don't ever be sad about what makes you *you*—that's what I love."

We both realize in the same moment what I just said.

Blake blinks and a tear tumbles down.

When I kiss her, I taste it on her lips.

"I love you." I say it again, clearly and distinctly. "I love you *exactly* how you are."

Emotion battles on her face. This time I see it for what it is—hope and fear in equal measure.

I cup her cheek.

"It's not a game. I love you, and it's real, and if I would've known what it's like, I wouldn't have spent one minute of my life chasing anything else."

She's shaking. I know, I know she wants to say it back to me, but my baby girl has been hurt and life has been cruel to her. She's not a giant like me, she has to be careful.

"I'm afraid," Blake says, barely more than a whisper. "I don't want to fuck up again..."

I scoop her into my arms and carry her back to the bedroom, to the warm nest of the bed where I know she'll feel safe. I hold her in my arms and kiss her and touch her in the ways I know make her feel calm, make her feel soothed and protected...

In the darkest hours of the night, we tell each other everything.

Blake tells me how awful it was at Crossroads, locked up with only an hour a day in the sun. She tells me how she wasn't allowed to see Sadie, not even after she was released and put in a new foster home to finish her last six months of high school. She won the stock-picking competition and earned her ride to Columbia, but that's when it all went to shit.

"I don't know why it happened..." she says from the shelter of my arms. "I was finally free. I had a full scholarship, all I had to pay for was food and books. I liked the school, I liked the classes. But right when it was all there waiting for me...I fell apart."

She tells me how the food stopped tasting good, how the words stopped making sense on the page. She slept late in the mornings, then huddled for hours in the shower, missing her classes.

"It was like I'd been climbing all my life, trying to get out of the pit. But when I finally stood on solid ground, all my problems had come with me. And now they were tearing me apart."

Blake falls silent. Though the lights are off, I can see that blank look on her face—the look when she's lost in the darkness of her head.

I take her face in my hands and kiss her to bring her back to me.

"I wish I could have been there for you."

Blake smiles a little. "Me too."

"Was that when you dropped out of school?"

She nods. "I was failing anyway. I thought I'd take a semester off and go back. But once I was alone all day long, no job, no classes...it just got worse."

Dread presses down as I sense what she's about to say next.

"I went to a dark place. I started to think...that pain and ugliness were more than the good parts of life. I started to think there was something wrong with me, deeply wrong. Not imperfections like everyone has, but something truly fucked up. Enough that my mother couldn't wait to get rid of me and Davis zeroed in like he could see inside my head, like he already knew what I'd be willing to do."

"That's not true."

I don't want to argue, I don't want to interrupt, but I can't let that pass.

"The first part is. The world is tragic and painful, and it hurts." Blake smiles slightly. "Even when you're a billionaire."

She trails her fingers down my arm, creating a sensation like sparks. "But it's also too beautiful to miss."

She looks up into my face, hers naked and lovely. She closes her eyes and kisses me, a kiss that feels like a blessing, like the worship of everything sensual and spiritual between us.

When she opens her eyes, I say, "Do you think I know what I'm doing?"

Blake smiles all the way, her dimple winking into view. "Definitely."

"Nobody spots an opportunity faster than I do. The *moment* I saw you at the Belmont, I told Briggs, I want to know everything about that creature. And I haven't stopped pursuing you since."

Blake glows with pleasure, her body tight like she's hugging herself.

"There's nothing wrong with you," I repeat. "Except how long you're taking to tell me this story."

Blake laughs, low and rich. "We're basically at the end—I ran out of money, had to get a roommate. That roommate was Magda. I was a fucking mess, barely leaving my room, late on rent. I got fired from a coffee shop, that's how fucking pathetic I was."

She pauses. Though she's trying to keep the same amusement in her voice, it wavers when she says, "I was trying to make it through Christmas because—because I wanted Sadie to have that at least."

My stomach is a boiling knot, all the sickening fear of never having met Blake rushing past my face like a bus. I take her hands in mine and hold them tight.

"Magda said if I wanted to get something for Sadie, she could help me make some cash. Probably she was hoping I'd pay the fucking rent, too." Blake gives a short laugh. "But mostly, she could see I was drowning. And she threw me a line."

Blake tells me how she got ready for that first date, nervous, shaking, wondering if she was going to end up in a dumpster.

"It was a disaster. The guy was awkward, I was worse, there was zero attraction from my end, it all felt so mechanical and fake. I cried when I got home. But he tipped me five hundred bucks, which let me pay Magda half of what I owed her and buy Sadie this gorgeous watercolor set for Christmas. For the first time in months, I felt like I'd accomplished something. The next date was a little better, and by the one after that...I realized I could be good at this."

I can only imagine how quickly Blake must have spotted the patterns of what men want and how easily they can be manipulated. I know her determination. In a strange way, I envy Tabitha this young, hungry version of Blake, rough and unformed but a ravenous student.

Blake tells me how she joined Tabitha's agency, how she built her book of clients and eventually struck out on her own.

In return, I share the details of how Briggs and I turned our hustles into actual office space. I tell her the highs and lows, the worst things I've done and the things that make me proudest.

We talk for hours, pausing only to raid the fridge for grapes and cheese and a bottle of champagne.

We toast each other, drinking straight from the bottle, grinning like idiots and saying nothing aloud.

We both know it's a cheers to being in love.

24

BLAKE

Ramses and I spend the most incredible weekend together, even better than the Hamptons.

I've never felt connected to someone like this. I'm telling Ramses things I've never told a living soul—all my secrets, my insecurities, my passions, my plans.

Honesty is like taking off a piece of clothing—you're watching the other person's face to see how they respond.

When I tell Ramses these intimate, sometimes embarrassing things, if he made fun of me, if I saw judgement on his face, I'd snap shut like a clam. But every time I crack my shell for him, he responds with warmth and understanding.

I love the way we work together.

When we pull up our laptops and run through our numbers side-by-side, it's like we're a pair of skaters whipping across the ice, sometimes spinning together, sometimes splitting off to accomplish our own neat little trick before floating back in tandem.

We replace my fucked-up laptop first thing Saturday morning, and then Ramses spends most of the day formatting the new machine. He copies over all my files, restores my software, and even makes sure my passwords have been saved.

I could have done those things myself, but I would have been miserable the whole time, pissed at myself for creating such an immense amount of work by such a stupid mistake.

Visiting the Apple store with Ramses is fun. Picking a new desktop photo together is hilarious. He pretends to approve my selection of a starry desertscape, but when I open the screen later, I'm greeted by a shirtless photo of Tom Selleck, complete with '70s chest hair.

I retaliate by making Ramses' screen-saver an embarrassing photo of him and Briggs, provided by Briggs himself, who keeps a whole selection of pics of Skinny Ramses with acne, braces, and Brillo-pad hair "for the days when he forgets I've got three decades of dirt on him."

The next time I open my laptop, I see a giant ball of yarn, and after that, a pic of the little girl from the Ring crawling through the screen that makes me shriek. Ramses gets a screenshot of his own desktop, then a close-up of Biden's bare feet.

He knows my passcode and I know his. That alone is the most intimate thing I've ever shared with someone.

Besides laptop shopping, we visit the flower markets by my house and pick out a gorgeous fiddle-leaf fig tree for Ramses' place to soothe his jealousy of my flourishing jungle wall. Then we swing by the farmers market so we can try making gazpacho together for dinner.

All day long, through all the silly errands and games, I'm dancing in my skin because this song is playing in my head: *He loves me, he loves me, he loves me...*

Sunday, we go to a baseball game. The Yankees are making a championship run, so I'm surprised Briggs isn't taking advantage of his season tickets right next to Ramses'.

"I don't know where he is." Ramses glances at the empty seats with annoyance. "Something's up—he left work early twice this week."

"Wow," I say. "I hope it's not serious."

Ramses knows I'm teasing him, but he won't be baited. "It's bad fucking timing, dealing with this Reeves shit."

"He's still coming after you?"

"Worse than ever."

Needless to say, Ramses did *not* attend his mother's party. I wonder if she knows how mercilessly her lover is hammering her son? Or is she telling him to do it?

"What's your plan?"

"I don't know," Ramses says, and I can tell that's what irritates him most of all.

When Ramses has an unsolved problem, he obsesses and obsesses until he knows what to do. I've watched the cycle several times already. When he figures it out in a couple of days, it's not a big deal, but when the problem drags on, Ramses is like an engine running too hot until he starts to shake himself apart.

We sit quietly for a few minutes, watching the players on the field, but each of us thinking of Halston Reeves and his huge, untouchable hedge fund.

"He knows I want to hit him back," Ramses mutters. "He's hunkered down..."

I slip my hand into Ramses', linking our fingers.

"We'll figure it out."

MONDAY, it's back to work. I've got a couple of options strategies running, but instead of focusing on my own shit, I spend the entire day doing a deep dive on Reeves' fund. Tuesday, I crawl through his PF filings, and by Wednesday, I've found something useful. I call Magda to request one very large favor.

Ramses is waiting for me at his place. He's roped me into working out with him even though that's the type of sweating and panting I do *not* enjoy.

I'm already late, but when my phone rings and I see Sadie's name on the screen, I pick up at once. If she's calling instead of texting, she probably needs something.

"What's going on?"

"Nothing," Sadie replies a little too quickly. "I was wondering if you wanted to grab lunch this week."

"How about Friday?"

"How about tomorrow?" she says.

"Tomorrow's great."

I haven't actually checked my calendar, but I can make it work. Something in Sadie's tone is making me nervous.

"Are you okay? You sound a bit—"

"No, no, I'm good." She's slightly out of breath like she might be walking. "I'll see you tomorrow at noon. Frankie's?"

That's where we usually meet. The food is shit, but their strawberry shake is Sadie's most passionate long-term relationship.

"Yeah, that's perfect."

"Great," Sadie says. "Love you, sis."

My eyes go hot. I'm pinched between my deep affection for Sadie and the nagging fear that something is wrong.

That's what it means to care about somebody else—it means you'll never be free of fear and worry and responsibility. But you'll also have joy at the sound of their voice and warmth in your chest when you picture their smile.

Once more, I ask, "You sure you're okay?"

"I'm great," Sadie firmly says. "I promise."

This time, I believe her.

RAMSES WAITS in the gym on the lowest level of his penthouse. He's wearing a pair of loose cotton pants and a tank top, all in black like a ninja. His chest and shoulders look outrageously strong. The idea of picking up a weight next to him feels like an exercise in humiliation.

He's smiling but his eyes are tired. As many times as I cheer him up, he won't be happy until this Reeves problem is solved.

"So..." I pretend to stretch so Ramses can admire me in my workout shorts. "Are you my new personal trainer?"

Ramses grins. "Here to whip you into shape."

"Where's your whip?"

"Right here." Ramses brandishes his heavy hand to remind me what a smack on the ass feels like.

"Where do we start?" I say, looking around at the cardio equipment, the barbells, the cable machine.

Ramses' private gym is closer to an Equinox than the usual basement set-up. All the walls are mirrors, and the floor is made of spongy, rubbery material. His dumbbell selection would make Schwarzenegger weep with pride.

"Take off your clothes," Ramses says with stern professionalism. "I need to see what I'm working with."

Ramses has, of course, seen me naked nearly as many times as he's seen me clothed, but I play along, pretending to be shy as I slowly strip.

I take off my top and shorts first so I'm standing in a sports bra, thong, and sneakers.

"Underwear, too."

I drop my bra and panties on top of the rest of the clothes but keep the sneakers on.

Ramses walks around me in a slow circle, his eyes crawling over my naked flesh. He stands behind me so we're both looking at my body in the mirror.

I could examine all my flaws—and there are many—but what

I'm actually looking at is Ramses' face. His eyes burn and his tongue wets his lips.

"Incredible..." He reaches around to cup my breasts, lifting them and letting them drop. "Gorgeous lines..." He slides his hands down my sides.

My nipples are stiff, goosebumps breaking out on my skin.

There's something insanely erotic about being examined by Ramses. The closer he looks, the more docile I become, like a patient at a doctor's office.

He cups my asscheek in his hand then gives it a smack. "We're gonna tighten that up."

I laugh at his rudeness.

Ramses spanks me harder on the other side. "You better be ready to work."

I love when he plays like this, fierce and intense. I want it to feel real.

"Start on the AMT," he orders.

I have no idea what an AMT is, so Ramses has to show me the cardio machine that looks like a cross between an elliptical and a stair-stepper. I climb on it naked in my sneakers, enjoying the amusing sight of myself in the mirrors all around.

He sets the level, and I churn the footrests of the machine, breasts bouncing and ass flexing in the mirror. I'm no athlete, but the look of my naked body in motion is kind of fucking cool. I've never seen myself quite like this—skin dewy with sweat, flushed in all kinds of interesting places.

Ramses watches from behind, just as tall as me even when I'm standing on the machine.

"That's right...work that ass."

I glance over my shoulder to see the tent in his pants. Grinning, I lean forward and drive my heels down harder, making long lines of my legs.

Ramses puts his hand on my asscheek, feeling the muscle work.

"Good girl," he growls.

After the only ten minutes I've ever enjoyed on a cardio machine, I hop down and await Ramses' next set of instructions.

He takes me over to the bench where he's set up an Olympic bar. He shows me the basics of a proper bench press, which I thought were self-explanatory but apparently not. Turns out, there's a lot of technique to shoving a bar straight up in the air.

Ramses puts his big, warm hands on my body, showing me how to arch my back, how to put the weight over my chest in the right place. As he takes me through the motion, it actually feels pretty good. Maybe it's because I'm horny as fuck, but each contraction of muscle is strangely pleasurable. My nipples are hard as rock.

It's kinky as fuck working out naked, seeing how my pussy looks with my legs spread around the bench. I keep imagining what it would be like to do this with other people around, if Ramses took me to a Gold's gym and put me through this exact workout in nothing but sneakers.

Ramses can't take his eyes off me, which is precisely what I like best. Nothing makes me feel safer than knowing he's watching my every move.

On my second set, he slips a finger inside me.

I gasp, the bar trembling in my hands.

"Do your reps," Ramses growls. "Lower the bar down slow and explode up."

Slow and controlled, I lower the bar to my chest. When I push it up again, my pussy clenches around his finger and pleasure jolts all the way down to my toes.

"*Fuck!*" I gasp.

"Keep going," Ramses says.

I press out my reps, two, three, four, five, each contraction sending a pulse of pleasure down my legs. My breasts are throbbing, the muscle beneath pumping hot.

Ramses slides his finger out of my pussy and sucks it clean before helping me re-rack the bar.

"Two more sets."

"Two more sets!" I cry.

"Of this exercise," Ramses gives a wicked grin. "Then we move on to shoulders."

I groan.

"Aw." Ramses pretends to pout. "You need a break?"

"Yes," I say, grabbing his cock through his pants.

He adds two fifty-pound plates to either side of the bar. "Suck my cock while you take a break."

He pulls out his cock, thick and heavy and hanging, and lies down on the bench. I kneel between his knees, taking his cock in my mouth while he unracks the bar and starts his set.

Every time he pushes up the weight, the force moves through his frame and his cock surges against my tongue. I feel his shocking strength, how easily he lifts a bar that weighs twice what I do. His body is a furnace, his thighs burning beneath my palms.

Watching him lift is turning me the fuck on. His chest swells, his shoulders and arms become monstrous. I never cared much for muscles before I met Ramses, but once you go jacked, you can't ever go back. Any other man would look tiny by comparison.

I wait for Ramses to start his second set, then I climb on his cock. He looks like a stallion, and I want to fuck him like one.

His cock leaps inside of me with each push. His strength flows into me and I'm drunk off the power.

When he racks the bar, the ground shakes.

I ride him on the bench, holding the bar to steady myself.

Ramses is enormous beneath me, reflected in the mirror. We don't even look like the same species.

He grabs my hips and fucks me harder, his face flushed, his muscles swollen. We were sweating before we started, breathing hard. Now my heart is galloping, droplets of sweat pattering down on Ramses' chest.

He bounces me on his cock, and I hold tight to the bar, my toes barely brushing the floor. The orgasm that's been building in a low-level way battles against my trembling muscles and aching lungs.

Ramses waits until I'm looking down in his face. Then he says, "Come for me, good girl."

I come like I'm sprinting across a finish line, chest burning, pussy pulsing, every muscle on fire. I come like a motherfucking champion, then I collapse on Ramses' chest.

LATER THAT NIGHT, I get a message from Magda:

Tell him to check his email.

Trying to hide my excitement, I say to Ramses, "I did something you're going to like."

Ramses smiles. "You did a lot of things I liked today."

"Well, this one's the cherry on the sundae."

We're lying on the couch in the den, sort of watching a movie but mostly just chatting while Ramses rubs my feet. We showered post-gym, and his hair is still slightly damp, his face freshly shaven.

Ramses presses his thumb into the arch of my foot, making me groan. "What have you been up to?"

"Well, I was digging into Reeve's fund..."

Ramses nods, his hands on my feet but his eyes on my face.

"And I realized something. Did you know that a big chunk of Oakmont's revenue comes from their aeronautics division?"

"How big a chunk?" Ramses says. His voice is calm, but the angle of his head changes, a dog catching a scent.

"Enough that this is really gonna hurt."

Hedge funds aren't just companies that buy stock. A hedge fund is a black box that can include almost anything. Berkshire Hathaway, for instance, owns GEICO, a non-publicly traded company worth thirty-two billion all on its own.

When I dug through Reeve's shit, I found a glaring vulnerability. Thirty-six percent of his hedge fund's revenue comes from one single government contract for aeronautics. And the government official in charge of assigning that contract...happens to be Magda's favorite client. The very same senator who took her for dinner at Harry's Steakhouse.

"Pull up your email," I say.

Ramses' thumb moves across his phone screen. Stillness falls across his face as he reads, followed by wicked amusement. His eyes flick up to mine.

"You *are* a little Minx. How did you do this?"

I explain, saying, "Magda asked him to BCC you on the email so you could read how nicely he tells Reeves that the United States government will be moving in a new direction. *It's not you, it's us...*"

Ramses roars with laughter. "It's not every day you get to read a break-up email to your enemy. *After careful consideration...*god, I wish I could see his face. Reeves is gonna have a bad day tomorrow."

I grin. "Nobody fucks with my man."

Ramses sweeps me into his arms, kissing me wildly. "That's right, you rowdy bitch; we'll fuck 'em up together, anybody who so much as steps in our direction."

He sets me down again, his expression suddenly serious.

"You solved a problem for me, Blake. There's only a couple of people in this world who have ever solved a problem for me."

"Just me and Briggs."

Ramses shakes his head. "Even Briggs can't take care of me like you do."

"Of course not." I smile. "I'm the only one who fits in the kitty suit."

25

RAMSES

Briggs comes into my office while I'm leaned back in my chair, staring up at the ceiling with my hands clasped behind my head.

"Busy?" he says, half joking but ready to leave if I don't want to be interrupted.

I was trying to figure out what I could do to thank Blake for hitting Reeves for me. And not just a punch—a fucking machete-chop of thirty-six percent off his top line. It was so goddamn beautiful, flowers won't suffice.

And it's not just Reeves. It's the way she comforted me the night I flooded the drawers. I would have been so fucking embarrassed for anyone to see me like that—anyone but her.

"What's up?" I say to Briggs. He's got a weird look on his face like something awful happened out on the floor.

He closes the door behind him, which is even worse.

"I've got to talk to you about something."

He takes his usual position in the overstuffed chair across from my desk but then immediately jumps up and switches to the window, where he can't seem to decide between looking out and looking at me.

"Spit it out," I say. "You're making me nervous."

"Yeah, of course."

Briggs takes a breath, runs both hands through his hair, puts his hands on his hips, then drops them.

"Sadie's pregnant," he says all in a rush.

That's so far from what I was expecting that I have to repeat the sentence in my head a couple of times before it makes sense.

"Blake's sister?"

"Yeah, that one." Briggs looks extremely foolish.

"With your baby?"

"*Yes,*" he hisses, getting annoyed.

"I thought you hated her!"

"I didn't hate her. I thought she was loud and annoying and unattractive and had terrible style."

"Don't write that in her Mother's Day card."

Briggs gives me a long, silent look.

"Sorry," I say. "Please continue because I have to know how this happened."

"We hooked up the night of the party, and it was...kind of fucking incredible. She was *insane,* she fucked me raw down on the beach, then we went to this shitty motel. She pinned me down on the bed and whipped me with her riding crop while she rode me like a horse..."

Briggs eyes go misty like he's recounting a cherished memory.

I'm wondering how in the hell I'm going to explain any of this to Blake.

"We've kind of been seeing each other since then—"

"Wait, what? You've been dating Blake's sister?"

I'm surprised he didn't tell me and annoyed at myself for not noticing. Makes sense why he's been fucking off work early so often.

"Not exactly dating," Briggs says uncomfortably. "It was more like weird, kinky sex that turned into having a couple beers, and now...I dunno, I kinda like her. She's funny and she's a fucking badass. I watched her race last weekend; she was fearless, just like at the Belmont. She bought that horse, can you believe it? The big bay, the one we saw win."

"Blake told me," I say distractedly.

I *can't* believe it, actually. Briggs has been dating Sadie. And knocked her up!

That thought is strangely colored by jealousy.

I imagine nutting raw inside Blake, my swimmers surging deep into her body, a part of me taking root inside of her...The two of us tied together forever...

"What are you going to do?" I ask Briggs.

"Sadie wants to keep it. And actually...I'm kind of excited. Is that crazy?"

"No, it's not crazy at all." I slap Briggs on the shoulder and pull him into a hug. "Congratulations, man. You're gonna have a kid!"

He lets out a huff of air like he's really taking that in for the first time.

"Yeah," he says. "Yeah!" And then, his face turning strangely vulnerable, "You think...you think I'll be okay as a dad?"

Briggs' father has been in prison most of his life, which is actually an upgrade on how he behaved when he was at home.

"You're gonna be the best fucking dad," I say. "Look how well you take care of Chumley."

Chumley is Briggs' British Bulldog, who lives the most pampered existence imaginable. He has his own swimming pool, a legless bed complete with sheets, blankets, and pillows, and closet full of sweaters.

"That's true!" Briggs brightens. "Chumley's spoiled as fuck!"

He tells me how Sadie's planning to move into his apartment for the duration of the pregnancy.

"Her place has mold, and this way I can take her to doctor's appointments and stuff."

"You're moving in together?" The hammer blows keep coming. I don't know why this is all making me feel so agitated. I'm happy for Briggs, but, fuck, it's a lot out of nowhere.

"Yeah. And if we can do all that without killing each other...I think I'm gonna ask her to marry me before the baby comes."

"Jesus, Briggs! You just met each other."

"I don't care." He shakes his head, jaw set so he looks a lot like Chumley. "I don't want this kid to grow up like I did. I'm gonna do whatever I can to make sure he's got every chance. All kinds of people make it work, why not Sadie and me?"

"I'm happy for you," I say, and I really mean it.

But inside, my guts are slowly sinking because I know how much things are about to change. "Briggs, the husband and father" is not going to be like "Briggs, my right-hand man and best friend". The person he'll become is probably even better, but the person I've had by my side all my life is going away forever.

Everything changes, nothing stays the same.

I think of the moment on the bed when I panicked, when the room swelled and dropped, and the only things that remained were Blake's arms wrapped tightly around me.

When Briggs is gone, I sit for a long time gazing out the windows at the cloudless sky.

He's taking this wild leap with Sadie with no plan, no surety it will work. But nothing will stop him snatching his chance for happiness.

I'm jealous.

Jealous that a momentary accident has linked him to Sadie with a bond brighter than fate.

And even more jealous that he's not afraid.

That's what decides it for me.

I'm no fucking coward.

If there's something I want—and there *is*, I know that now for a certainty—then I'm just as ready as Briggs to risk everything to get it.

I SPEND the whole next day preparing for what I hope is going to be the perfect night with Blake. By the time I pick her up, I'm spotlessly groomed, fresh as a rainforest, with a huge bouquet of orchids in hand. I hold it up in front of the fisheye lens so when Blake peeks out she'll see nothing but a sea of purple.

She laughs, sweeping the flowers into her arms and burying her face in the blooms. "You spoil me."

She puts her mouth up to mine, kisses me, then moves like she'll take the flowers into the kitchen and put them in water.

"Don't you dare kiss me just once," I growl, pulling her back again.

She kisses me longer and deeper, her body tucked obediently against mine. "Is that better?"

"Yes," I say, giving her a little smack on the ass as she carries the flowers away.

"Oh my god," she calls, running water into a vase. "Did Briggs tell you the news?"

"I hope they're planning to name the baby after us."

Blake grins. "It's only fitting."

"They could call it Bramses."

"Or Rake!" She's laughing, but I see that little line of concern between her eyebrows. "Briggs will take care of Sadie, won't he?"

"There's *nobody* more loyal than Briggs."

"Good," Blake says. "Then I don't have to kill him for knocking her up."

"I don't know if you can blame Briggs. From what I heard, he was the victim..."

Blake snickers, arranging the orchids in the vase. "God, I wish I'd known what was going on when he was limping down the beach looking like he stole his grandma's pie off the sill."

"You sister's a sadist. And she seems so sweet..."

"She's like a murderous little squirrel, isn't she?" Blake smiles fondly then sighs. "Sadie's over the moon; she always wanted kids."

"You're gonna be an aunt."

Blake looks startled then pleased. "Yeah, that's true. I'll have a sister and a niece. And a boyfriend."

Our eyes meet with sudden heat.

"I wanted to talk to you about that, actually..."

I had a whole thing planned—dinner, a helicopter ride over the city—but I don't want to wait another minute.

I take Blake's hands in mine and pull her over to the couch. She sinks down next to me, turning expectantly, eyes bright and curious, dimple flirting at the edge of her mouth.

I say, "When I called you my girlfriend in front of my mom, and again with Desmond, you didn't stop me. Of all the things I've pushed you into doing, that gave me the biggest thrill because it's what I want the most. You're so good at making my fantasies come true...but the part where you make my life sing is when it's real. I *want* it to be real."

Blake's cheeks are full of color, her lips trembling. She's gripping my hand just as tightly as I'm holding hers.

"Open up your phone," I say.

She blinks, confused. "Okay..."

"Pull up your account."

I watch her face, thinking I'm about to see a rush of joy and excitement.

Instead, darkness falls like a veil. Blake goes still, her breathing fading away.

"Why did you do this?"

It's not the response I was expecting. The mood has shifted, clouds over the sun, chill in the air.

I just deposited $37M in Blake's account. Yet she's staring at her phone screen with pale lips and white knuckles. Almost like she's furious.

"I thought you'd be happy."

Her head whips up, acid in her eyes.

"You thought I'd be *happy* that you hit my number for me?"

I hold up my hands. "Look, I was fucked up and you helped me. It made me realize that I want us to start a new chapter together—"

Blake cries, "Is this about Lukas?"

"What? No, I—"

"Because I cut him loose a month ago!" Blake jumps up from the couch, her phone tumbling to the floor. "I thought you knew that."

I *didn't* know that, but I also hadn't thought about it. I'm way past giving a fuck about some old client.

I stand up, meaning to calm her. The second I'm towering over her, I realize that's wrong, too—she shrinks back in my shadow, her breathing rapid, face red and eyes too bright.

Carefully, I say, "Hitting a hundred million was your old goal. I want us to make new goals together."

She shakes her head, hair flying. "How benevolent of you to decide that for both of us, Ramses. But that's not how you start a partnership with someone. You're *still* trying to buy me."

"I just wanted to help you."

"Yeah. It's what *you* wanted. What *I* wanted was to earn it just like your fucking watch, and you took that from me."

Tears spill down her cheeks.

Quietly, she says, "You'll never see me as an equal."

That makes me *really* fucking angry. No one has ever taken better care of Blake, no one's treasured her like I have.

Furious, I say, "When have I ever treated you as less? I've respected you from the moment you opened your mouth. Even before that—from the moment I watched you work a room. Fuck's sake, Blake, I told you how highly I valued you the first time we talked—three million for one fucking date!"

"Yes, three million," she says. "It's a lot, I was flattered. But let me ask you something, Ramses...could I buy you for three million?"

"That's not—"

"Come on," she snaps. "How much would I need to buy you? What value do you put on yourself?

When I don't immediately answer, she says it for me:

"*Billions*. Well, guess what, me too. I'm just as smart as you are, I'm just as capable."

"I know that! I opened my books to you!" I don't want to shout, but it's fucking outrageous that she doesn't understand this. "I've never shared with anyone like I have with you."

Blake trembles, color flushing through her face before she goes dull and still.

"I loved that day," she whispers. "I felt like a partner that day. I *don't* feel like a partner today. I feel like you stole my accomplishment and you're about to tell me what my new one is. Let me ask you something—when was the last time Briggs decided the direction of Obelisk? Ramses, you don't have partners. You want the world to yourself, and you just share pieces of it."

That fucking slaps me.

My control slips. I bite her back.

"Every day since I met you, I've shared more and more of myself. *You're* the one who pulls away, afraid. You're telling me I need to treat you like an equal? Blake, we're not equals. The reason I'm a billionaire is because I *do* make all the decisions. And every time you want to act like you know better than me, why don't you check the scoreboard."

Blake's face goes blank. That's how I know I hurt her because she can't even pretend.

"Red," she says.

Then she walks over to her front door and opens it, waiting for me to leave.

"Blake—"

She whirls on me, furious as I've ever seen her.

"You say I'm not your equal today? Well, I goddamn will be tomorrow. But I'll never be your equal in our relationship if you don't treat me like one."

"Blake—"

"Get out."

When I'm standing in the hall, she says, "You don't want a partner—you want a pet."

And she closes the door in my face.

26

BLAKE

Hours after Ramses leaves, I'm still running through the same cycle of thoughts over and over.

It's not that I'm angry, though I *was* angry in that first violating moment of pulling up my account and seeing that he'd fucked with my balance again.

What I really am is so fucking disappointed.

I thought he understood me.

And maybe I'm just an asshole who's mad at someone for giving them thirty-seven million. That's a distinct possibility.

But I'm still disappointed.

I made the cardinal mistake.

I believed the dream. I spun the fantasy and lost myself inside it, as if I could actually find connection, as if I could actually find love.

Men who buy women don't give away their hearts.

Women who sell their bodies have already lost everything else.

That's what I tell myself, lying alone in the dark.

All the old, ugly thoughts have returned, more powerful than ever.

It's better to feel nothing than to feel this kind of pain.

The only way to protect yourself is to be alone.

And worst of all:

No one actually loves you once they get to know you.

That's the knife in the ribs that twists and twists.

My mother gave me away. I couldn't make Ingrid and her husband happy. Desmond was embarrassed of me. And Ramses...

I can't even picture his face without another round of messy, gulping tears.

Does he love me? Or does he only love owning me?

I'm not sure which is worse.

Because if Ramses really does love me...then I fucked it all up.

Every day since I met you, I've shared more and more of myself. You're the one who pulls away, afraid...

I have been afraid.

That's the problem with caring, that's the problem with giving a shit—the stakes go way up.

Liking someone is handing them a bat, saying, "This is how much I care what you think of me. Hit me with it any time you want."

I made myself vulnerable to Ramses. Then the moment he blundered, I slammed the door in his face. Literally.

I knew this would happen—the higher we flew, the more I knew it would hurt when it all came crashing down.

But I kept flapping my wings because every minute with him felt so fucking worth it. Every time he looked at me or touched me or made me laugh, I flew straight into the sun. Now my wings have melted and I'm plunging down.

I think of the moment I pulled up my account, that spike of red-hot fury followed by a cringing feeling of cheapness...

He put a number on you. It's a little higher now, but he still thinks he can write a check for your soul.

Then I remember the outrage on Ramses' face, how his voice shook when he said, *I opened my books to you...I've never shared with anyone like I have with you...*and I'm washed in misery and regret.

I think of his eyes locked on mine, pleading:

You're the one who pulls away...

But then the flash of teeth and the words I can't forgive or forget:

We're not equals, Blake.

And I burn with rage and bitterness, and the cycle starts again.

Think what he's done for you...

Only what he wanted to do for himself.

He's proud of you...

He likes to show me off.

The sex...

Is a trap.

But the sex...

Tricks me into making terrible decisions.

He means well...

He wants to control me.

He said he loves you...

He also said we weren't equals.

He was angry...

He let the truth slip.

Around and around I go, over and over in the pitch-black bedroom until I've cried myself stuffy.

I fall asleep tangled in the sweaty sheets only to be jolted awake by a call. I scramble for the phone, hoping it's Ramses.

When I see Magda's number instead, my sleep-addled brain decides she must have gotten stranded on a date or else her mom's taken a turn for the worse.

"Hey," I croak. "D'you need a ride to your—um—mom?"

"What?" Magda sounds as stuffy-nosed as I am.

My contacts are glued to my eyeballs. I blink until I'm pretty sure the time on my phone reads 2:23 a.m.

"Sorry, I was half-asleep."

"You were all the way asleep," Magda says. "I should have waited—"

"Don't be silly."

We're both talking in this strangely polite way, the tension in our voices cranked all the way up because any second Magda is going to tell me why she called at 2:23 in the morning. And even though the lump in my chest means my body already knows, I'm dragging out the seconds, a tiny, ugly part of me still hoping the problem is Magda's mom...

"It's Tabitha."

That's all Magda has to say.

We both knew it was coming. And yet we're bawling on either side of the line.

You can't prepare for pain.

All you can do is share it.

TABITHA'S FUNERAL is on a gray, blustery day where the streets are still wet with rain and the clouds are one solid blanket. Bright leaves stick like band-aids to the damp sidewalk, sending up a peppery scent when I tread them underfoot.

I spent the morning at her apartment, packing up the last of her things. What she had left, she gave to Magda and me with a request to take care of her finches.

Magda took the birds and anything else she wanted. All I asked for was Tabitha's favorite coat. I'm wearing it now as I walk the winding pathways of the cemetery.

When the wind gusts, showers of rusty leaves rain down. The

long brocade coat swishes against my legs, still smelling faintly of smoke and violets.

The smoke is from the fire in her old mansion, not from cigarettes. Tabitha tried to save as much as she could. She kept some beautiful ornate mirrors, their wooden frames singed and cracked. Some of her books were salvaged, the covers blackened. Saddest of all were the photographs in their frames—a teenaged Tabitha, lithe and lovely in her tutu, Tabitha and her first American lover standing outside the Majestic in evening clothes, Tabitha at a gala, Tabitha on a yacht outside Monaco...

No one was touching her in any of those photos—no arm around her shoulders, no hand linked with hers.

And when I reach the open lawn where the service will be held, not a single person from those photographs is waiting in the chairs.

Only a few girls from the old agency have come. There are no former clients and very few people who look like friends.

"Allie had to work, but I thought Kirsten would come," Magda frets, distressed by the thin turnout.

I tell her, "You did an incredible job."

Magda handled all the arrangements while I did the packing. Tabitha, as efficient as ever, had already bought her plot twenty years before.

I stare at the closed casket, wondering if she's really in there. Is any part of her somewhere else?

I imagine her watching me, though I don't really believe in that.

Crying at funerals is maudlin.

I don't think she'd like the flowers, either, though I'd never tell Magda.

Only men are stupid enough to pay money for something that dies.

She definitely wouldn't like my dress.

Is this a funeral or a seance?

I smile a little, though it doesn't last. My insides are quicksand. Any spark of happiness is sucked back down.

I've never felt lower than this, even in the darkest days after I dropped out of college. Back then, I hadn't tasted something better.

Now I have, and whether it was real or it wasn't real, I can't go back to how I was before.

I feel my own loneliness now. I feel it like cold, like hunger. A constant ache that steals the life and color from everything else.

As I packed up the few surviving beautiful things that Tabitha managed to cling to until the end of her life, I thought how pointless it all was. You can't take it with you, and even if you can keep it until the end, it just becomes a pile of shit somebody else has to sort through.

Of all the gifts I've ever received, what shines brightest in my mind are the times Ramses made me laugh. I'd return every dollar, every piece of jewelry, but I hoard those memories like dragon's gold.

Tabitha was my mentor. More mother to me than my actual mother. Yet sitting here today...I don't want to end up like her.

The last years of her life were spent smoking into an alleyway. She died alone in her apartment, and her birds sang as merrily as ever when Magda picked up their cage.

I was so fucking angry at Ramses for hitting my number for me. But why did I pick that number in the first place? Why did I pick any of my goals?

I think of the castle of my dreams.

Castles are fortresses of solitude. When I pictured myself there, I was always alone. Reading, cooking, gardening...alone, alone, alone.

Ramses wanted us to make new goals, goals we'd achieve together.

I screamed at him and pushed him away.

You'll never see me as an equal...

Was I shouting at him or at myself?

Is Ramses holding me back?

Or am I the one who pretends to be confident, while deep down I can't see myself as anything but malformed...

The service commences. A cellist plays a selection from *Giselle*, Tabitha's favorite ballet. The director placed us in a secluded corner of the cemetery, silver maples and willow trees all around. Still, it's painfully apparent how few people have gathered. Out of a dozen chairs, several are still empty.

Magda gets up to speak. She asked me if I wanted to, but I fucking hate crying in public and haven't been able to stop. Even now, tears run down both sides of my face, cooling as they fall. I squeeze my eyes shut, but they still flow down.

The wind picks up, sending leaves skidding across the polished lid of the casket. Petals tear off the floral arrangements and whirl through the air like bruised snow. I'm cold even in Tabitha's coat. The sky is the color of slate. The chill of unshed rain sinks into my bones.

A heavy arm drops around my shoulders. Ramses sinks into the chair next to mine, pulling me into his warmth.

I turn my face against his chest and sob. He cradles my head, shielding me with his coat so no one will see.

"How did you know?"

Ramses kisses the top of my head. "Just because you're mad at me doesn't mean I stopped paying attention."

"I don't think I'm mad at you anymore," I whisper. "Actually, I kind of feel like a dick."

Ramses chuckles. "I was gonna give you another day to cool off, but when I heard—"

"Thank you." I sob. "I needed you today."

He pulls me close, murmuring, "I'm always going to take care of you, Blake."

He holds me while Magda tells us everything she loved about the woman who whipped us into shape like a ballerina corps and sent us out into the world to entice, beguile, and entertain.

When the funeral is over and the coffin has been lowered into the ground, Ramses and I stay awhile longer. I'm not cold anymore with his arm wrapped around me. However, I do notice a certain squirming in his left breast pocket.

"Ramses...I think your coat is moving."

He delves his hand into the woolen pocket, scooping out what looks like a ball of soot.

A kitten sits up on his palm, tail curled around its toes. Every inch of it is black as night, even the tip of its nose, except for the wide blue eyes blinking up at me.

"You replaced me already?"

Ramses grins. "I already have a kitten. But I couldn't stand the thought of you going home alone tonight."

I cradle the little soot-spot, feeling its fragile heartbeat. My own heart is burning, burning, burning in my chest.

"What's its name?"

"I was thinking Ramses the Second. But unfortunately, she's a girl."

"Then I know exactly what to call her." I hold her up so I can plant a kiss on her tiny nose. "This is Bastet."

"You're making me jealous," Ramses growls.

I tuck the kitten in the crook of my arm so I can kiss him, too. The taste of his mouth is so much even better than I remembered.

"Nice coat, by the way," he says.

"It was Tabitha's." I look at the hole in the ground, an emptiness where something ought to be, like the socket of a tooth. "This is what she bought with her first paycheck from the Bolshoi Ballet. It was all the money she had, but she told me, *the way you treat yourself tells everyone else how to treat you.*"

Ramses' palm makes long, slow strokes down my back. "I wish I could have met her."

"She would have liked you." I smile to myself. "Even if she didn't want to."

"What did you love about her the most?"

I think of all the things that were impressive about Tabitha. And at last, I say, "She never pitied herself. And she sure as shit wouldn't let *us* make excuses. Perpetual victimhood can be just as dangerous as the thing that hurt you—you can't escape the prison of your past until you let go of that crutch."

Ramses says, "I'm so sorry."

He's talking about Tabitha. But I throw my arms around him anyway, careful not to crush Bastet, and I say, "I'm sorry, too."

We walk through the headstones arm-in-arm, the kitten in my coat pocket now instead of Ramses'.

He regards the battered tombstones, leaning against each other as if in exhaustion.

"My father's buried here."

"Where?"

"Somewhere that direction." He angles his head.

"Should we go see?"

There's a long pause where Ramses holds my hand tight, his thumb stroking against the back of my hand.

"Yes," he says at last. "If you'll come with me."

We wind through the trees to a heavily shaded area, the ground spongy and thick with leaves.

Ramses walks unerringly to the right place and stands looking at a plain gray stone. His father's name and the brief span of his life are the only ornament.

"I didn't know what to write. But I never felt good about leaving it blank."

Emotions pass over his face in painful spasms. Abruptly,

Ramses drops to his knees and clears the leaves off his father's grave.

I say, "I'll be right back."

Holding my hand against my pocket so I don't jostle Bastet, I run to Tabitha's plot, returning with an armful of white roses. I lay them across his father's grave, the blooms ghostly in the shadows.

"There," I say. "Tabitha won't mind."

"Thank you," Ramses says.

His hands are muddy, but I link our fingers together anyway, my other palm cradling the sleeping kitten.

27

RAMSES

♪♪ *Love — Kendrick Lamar*

B lake comes home with me, carrying Bastet, who woke for
a moment, but fell asleep again as soon as I started the
car engine.

Blake makes a nest of blankets for her new kitten while I start
dinner. I set the pasta water boiling, then pour two glasses of
wine, filling Blake's almost to the rim because it looks like she
needs it.

She sinks down on a padded stool across the kitchen island,
gratefully gulping her wine. Then she sets down her glass, taking
a deep breath.

"Ramses, I'm really sorry about the other night. I was upset
that you did that without asking me, but I shouldn't have
assigned malintent. I know you want good things for me."

"I do, but I still fucked up."

Blake looks surprised that I'd admit it so readily.

I haven't been upset with her the last couple of days. I've been obsessing over this problem, trying to figure out where I went wrong. And I think I finally understand.

I skirt the island, sitting down next to Blake and taking her hand in mine.

"I'm so sorry for losing my temper. You're the most precious thing in the world to me, and you've put up with so much of my outrageous personality. And even though I meant it to be a celebration, I never should have been angry with you. And I *never* should have said what I said."

Blake takes a shaking breath, her shoulders rising up to her ears and then her whole body going limp, head hanging, tears flowing down her cheeks though I hardly know how she has any left.

I bit her and I'm so fucking ashamed of that.

She seems so resilient, so indestructible. But I already knew she could be hurt, and I should have known she'd be the *most* hurt by me.

I put my arms around her, pulling her onto my lap, our faces inches apart.

"I've *never* had someone stand up to me like that. Not even Briggs. Honestly, it kind of turned me on. I left your apartment angry, but by the time I'd gotten to the stairs, it had turned to melancholy because I already missed you. And even though the point was to do something special for you, you were right that I was doing what *I* wanted."

Blake turns all the way around, straddling me. She takes my face in her hands and kisses me softly on the mouth. She's crying, but she's smiling now, too.

I tell her, "I've never had anyone call me out like that, and it took a two-hour walk home for me to realize something about myself that I never knew. My entire life, I've masked my inadequacies with my accomplishments. And when I was the most upset, and the most immature, I learned that about myself when I told you to check the scoreboard. Because yes, I'm at the top. But you know what it says? Ramses. Ramses the Conqueror. And when I was walking home alone, I didn't feel like a conqueror. I was fucking miserable. Because I was worried I'd lost you forever."

Blake sighs, her forehead pressed against mine. "I was so depressed. I couldn't believe I'd fucked it all up."

"You didn't," I tell her. "You can't. Up until I met you, winning was all that mattered. But now that I have you, *none* of it seems to matter if I can't share it with you."

I put my hands around her waist and lift her up onto the kitchen counter so she's still facing me, but I can look at her clearly.

"The other night, you asked me how much would it cost to buy me. And I had nothing to say because I knew you were right. So, I'm hoping I can make you a final offer…"

I put her cellphone in her hands.

"Pull up your account."

Blake gives me a look like she can't believe I'm about to fuck this up all over again.

"Are you serious right now?"

"Don't worry, I don't make mistakes." I wink at her. "Twice."

Blake's thumb moves across the screen, her shoulders stiff and her expression anxious.

When she sees the balance, she goes completely still. Her eyes rise slowly to mine.

I say, "I know you can't be bought. But here's everything I have."

She looks down at the screen again. Then back up at me.

"What is this?"

I push back my chair and drop to my knees in front of her.

"Blake, I only want you. I want to grow with you, I want to become better with you, I want to laugh and love with you. And most of all, I want to share in our accomplishments together. I knew that's what I wanted when you took care of me when I was spiraling about my dad. No one's ever helped me like that. I know it's not enough, but here's every dollar I have."

I put it all in her account, $7.2B, my entire war chest. Every penny I have liquid.

She can't stop looking at the number.

"I can't make a move without it," I tell her, smiling. "So I guess *you'll* have final say."

Blake sets her phone down. She slides off the kitchen counter and I stand to meet her, sweeping her into my arms.

When we kiss, I know this is what I've been longing for all my life. Because I finally feel like I made it.

"You make me so fucking happy," Blake says, kissing me again and again.

When I set her down, I say, "Now that you're in charge, what should we do? You want to buy your castle? I could learn to ride a horse."

Blake laughs. "You'd crush a horse."

"Then what should we do? Where should we go?"

The whole world seems open to us. I want to make a thousand plans. But I'm waiting to see what my little Minx thinks— Blake is my partner, and I won't fuck that up again.

I kiss her, then I hold her hands in mine, looking into her eyes.

"So, what do you want to do?"

Blake grins.

"Let's go hunting."

EPILOGUE
BLAKE

I t's moving day.

I'm moving into Ramses' place because it's way bigger than mine and Bastet prefers it—the little traitor.

I haven't actually been staying at my apartment, or Ramses', because we've been in Sydney watching Sadie race in the Everest. It's the world's richest race on turf, with a $15M purse. Ramses paid to stake Sadie, which made both Briggs and me want to murder him.

Sadie hasn't started to show, and apparently vomiting five minutes before she hopped on her horse didn't bother her either because she still took second place. Briggs leaped right over the barriers and reached her before the officials did. I think he was mostly just relieved, but I've never seen Sadie happier than when she jumped off Flightline and into Briggs' arms.

She's been trying to convince Ramses that he should finally pull the trigger on buying a horse of his own. Ramses says he will if I'll lend him the money.

That's his favorite joke now. He won't pay when we go out to eat and makes me swipe my black card, which is actually *our* black card, linked to our shared account. Never in my wildest dreams did I think I'd have a shared bank account with someone.

This is so much more intimate than marriage. This is partnership, real and whole. There's no *my deals* and *his deals* anymore—just what we're working on together.

The day Ramses sat beside me and opened his books to me was the best day of my life. Now every day is like that. It's connection, it's challenging each other, it's all the stimulation and escape I used to get out of my work infinitely increased because I'm sharing it with someone else.

That's what I was missing, though I never knew it at the time.

Ramses was the same. He thought he was pointed exactly where he wanted to go...until we created Minx together.

The game was our deepest desires breaking free—the subconscious part of my mind trying to tell me what I needed to be happy. That buried part of me was crying out, showing me the pleasure, the peace I could feel if I only changed what I was chasing.

I knew what I needed before I knew what I needed.

So did Ramses.

He thought Minx was about control, about connecting me to him. What he actually needed was someone to take care of, and I needed someone to force me to accept that care. Neither of us expected the catharsis and healing that followed.

Sex isn't just sex. It's where all the barriers dissolve. It's fantasy and the realest real. It's where we're the most human *and* the most animal.

I'm waiting in the elevator with about a hundred plants. I've got my entire jungle wall plus some extras I thought Ramses would like. I'm high on oxygen and the thrill of knowing I'm sleeping here tonight, in *our* apartment...

The doors open. Ramses jumps inside, making me shriek and laugh as he lifts me into his arms.

"I missed you!" he says, kissing me again and again.

It's been about three hours since we saw each other. We slept at my place last night, crashing hard after our flight home. Jet lag is still a thing, even when you fly on a private plane.

But that's what love is—it's how excited you are to see each other, every single time. Because everything is better when I share it with him.

Waking up here will be better. Making breakfast together will be better. Working together will be better.

And some days, he might really piss me off. But we'll figure that out, too. Ramses isn't perfect...but he fills me with happiness. He makes my world grow and bloom.

Most of all, he makes me want to change whatever I have to change to be a good partner to him. And that's the hardest thing to find—someone worth the painful and difficult work of trying to be better.

"I have a surprise for you," Ramses says.

"That's great. Because your surprise percentage is...almost eighty percent positive."

Ramses grins. "I deserve that. But this time, I'm extra confident..."

He steps aside so I can see inside his place. Inside *our* place, I mean.

I follow the trail of plaster dust to what used to be Ramses' office.

Two chairs share one massive desk with twin computers and our own Bloomberg terminals. Ramses has taken down his Wall Street Journal headlines.

"I thought we could put up some of your prints...definitely the *Bocca Baciata*."

My chest is hurting so hard that I have to kiss him until that feeling bursts into warmth that flows down to my toes.

Maybe I'm crying, I don't know. I let myself cry now.

Ramses knows he did well. He's radiating satisfaction, which makes even his hardest edges look warm and inviting. I want to touch that jaw, I want to drape myself over his chest...I want to live on top of him and make him my home.

Ramses is my castle. I've never felt safer than when I sleep in his arms. And best of all, I can take him anywhere I go.

I can't stop kissing him. I'm not going to try.

"But what about your building?"

"I'll still go there sometimes. When you want to come with me, I cleared out the office next to mine. Not Penn's, don't worry —this one smells great." Ramses nuzzles his nose against my neck. "It'll smell better once you've been in there..."

I nip at the rim of his ear. "Why are you so amazing?"

He shrugs and pretends to be modest. "I dunno. Comes naturally."

Ramses grabs my hand, pulling me along. "That's not the only thing..."

"What else?"

I'm feeling slightly dazed. Too many good things at once make me nervous.

He takes me into what used to be a spare bedroom—the one where I changed clothes the very first time I put on the Minx suit.

Ramses has ripped out everything that was here before and filled the space with bookshelves. All the shelves are empty except for one.

I lift a lovely little leather-bound copy of *How To Win Friends And Influence People*.

"A seed for your library," Ramses says. "If it gets big enough, we can knock down another wall."

The fact that he didn't fill the shelves himself means everything to me.

I clutch the book against my chest and now I'm definitely crying.

Happiness is scary. But I'm not going to let it scare me away.

"Thank you," I say, and I let the tears fall down.

Ramses' eyes are shiny, too.

"I love you. And I'm so fucking glad you're here."

AFTER WE'VE SPENT hours unpacking my shit and shared take-out and a bottle of wine, Ramses rubs the knots out of my shoulders.

It takes strong fucking thumbs on the best of days, let alone when I've been lugging boxes.

"Jesus, baby..." He works the muscles all around then firmly presses the source of the trouble until it releases. "I think I got 'em all."

I say something that sounds like, "*Ah, fuck, oooooooo, okay, okay, okay, ahhhhh, god, okay...*" and then finally a fervent, "Thank you."

I'm feeling extremely grateful and a little bit filthy.

Ramses reads the look on my face.

"What do you want to do now?"

His slow smile spreads.

I say, "I have a few ideas..."

What I'm about to do is a little bit twisted, but I think Ramses will be into it.

I found his ex-girlfriend on Facebook. I wanted her Facebook and not her Instagram because what I really needed were pictures from her first year of college.

Ramses waits in the den while I change into what might be the most specific "sexy outfit" ever created.

♪♫ *Woman—Emmit Fenn*

I walk out wearing what Ashely would have worn in 2004:

flared jeans, Converse, and a Lacoste polo. I've even styled my hair like her old photos, bangs swept to the side.

Ramses' mouth falls open.

"Oh my god."

It takes everything I have not to laugh.

"How'd I do?"

He can't stop staring, eyes bright and face flushed with much more than wine.

"If I told you that's almost exactly what she was wearing..."

I pump a fist. "Fuckin' *nailed* it."

Then it's back into character.

I raise the pitch of my voice a little, making it softer, sweeter...

"Ramses, I miss you...I'm so sorry, I know I messed up...what will it take to get you to forgive me?"

Ramses puts both hands over his face then slowly drags his fingers back through his hair while he looks at me sideways. "This is so fucked up."

Maybe it is, but I want to shake this idea out of his head that both his mother and his first girlfriend were lured away by a "better man."

I want to give Ramses what he never allowed himself to have.

So I pout.

"Please, please forgive me. I'm so sorry, I never should have left. I'll do anything to have you back..."

I drop to my knees at Ramses' feet.

All the conflict vanishes from his face. His eyes darken while everything else relaxes.

"Stand up." His voice is low and deep and commanding.

I'm already standing. It's Pavlovian—I have to obey when Ramses takes control.

"Take off your clothes. Slowly."

My hands find the button of my jeans. I'm moving, dreamlike, while my eyes stay locked in Ramses' gaze.

I'm wearing the kind of underwear a college girl would wear —pastel lace from Victoria's Secret. The kind of lingerie a good girl thinks is bad.

The truth is, I feel sorry for Ashley. She made a teenager mistake. She didn't know Ramses was exceptional—how could she? She'd barely dated anyone else.

By the time I met Ramses, I'd probably fucked three hundred men. *He* was the one who made me laugh. He was the one who looked in my eyes and praised me for all the things I wish people saw about me.

Ashley's married now and has a baby and lives a thousand miles away, but I'm still going to slip inside her freshman skin to give my lover the sexual catharsis he needs.

I pretend to be nervous while I take off my clothes.

"Underwear too," Ramses says mercilessly.

I flinch but don't argue. My head is full of how desperately I want Ramses back.

This is the fun of role-play—it's all the highest and lowest moments of life made filthy and fantastical.

I look at Ramses' lean face, his stern eyes, and the body he definitely didn't have his first year of college filling out that baseball shirt with the thickness of a man fully grown.

All I want is for him to smile at me again. To feel those hands on my body...

I unclasp my bra, briefly covering my breasts with my hands before letting them drop. Then I take off my panties, too.

It's like I've never been naked in front of another person before. Every inch of my skin feels the air and his eyes.

"Dance for me," Ramses says.

I dance, shy and awkward at first, then slow and sensual as the wine loosens my muscles and my inhibitions. Ramses stays seated, fully dressed, his face unsmiling but his eyes roaming rabid over my flesh.

My body is throbbing. I've never been more wet.

"Turn around," Ramses barks. "Put your palms on the floor."

I turn and slowly bend until I'm touching the carpet. I'm not flexible enough to be completely obedient.

I hear him move behind me, swift and terrifying. I yelp when his hands grip my thighs.

He parts my pussy with his thumbs, peeling the lips open, exposing everything to his view.

My pussy quivers. That raw, open flesh feels everything—cold air, his hot gaze, and those thick, rough fingers....

I start to twitch and clench around nothing, thighs shaking... just the stretching sensation is making me come...

Ramses touches my wetness. It's so slippery, it's like he's rubbing against raw nerve. If I wasn't already hands-to-the-floor, I'd fall over.

"You're soaking," he says. "Look at yourself."

He knows I like to be degraded, but he can't keep the delight off his face.

I'm half-laughing, half-swooning. Standing like this with my head hanging down is making me dizzy in the best kind of way.

What follows is some of the darkest, roughest sex we've ever had. Ramses is testing what I'll do for him, but really, we're proving it to *me*. Every time my body gladly performs some fucked-up act, it tells my brain how much I respect him and sets my arousal on fire.

We're way past the original scenario—this is about my longing for him, what I'd do for his attention, his touch...and the pleasure I get fulfilling his darkest desires...

We progress from the den to the bedroom and back to the den again. Sex toys are strewn everywhere, and we might have ruined another couch.

I'm thinking how incredible it is that I don't have to start gathering up my stuff to go home. I'm already there.

Ramses sprawls across the cushions, sweating and limp.

"I must have thought about that situation thousands of times..."

He's gazing up at the ceiling, eyes unfocused.

"The 'one that got away' is a situation that can't be fixed. It's a permanent wound in your history. She's married with a kid, we're completely different people, I wouldn't want to be with her anyway...but the pain she caused me is something I've never entirely healed from until today."

He rolls over on his side, looking at me.

I'm sitting on the rug, trying to comb the rat's nest out of my hair with my fingers.

"It's like when we went to Desmond's and we realized we'd grown past him—I could finally let go of all the stupid shit that was still bothering me."

"Exactly," Ramses nods. "You set me free."

"I'm just glad it worked out. This one was a bit of a flier."

Ramses shakes his head. "We're so far past you just making a fantasy come true. Being with you is changing me because I feel motivated to be the person I think you deserve. And meanwhile, you're helping me clear the cobwebs in my head. It's just...it's everything, Blake. You've given me everything. What can I do for you?"

The question surprises me. I meant to pay Ramses back for all the things he's done for *me*.

But there is something I've been wanting to try for quite some time now.

"You'll do anything?"

"Yes..." Ramses replies with a little more caution.

"No questions asked?"

"Uh—"

"Perfect. Because I have a surprise for you."

Now Ramses looks distinctly nervous. "That doesn't sound good."

"I thought you loved surprises?"

"Only when I'm dropping them on you."

He's even less pleased when he sees what I've brought for him.

I hold up the collar, nearly as wide as my hand, with flat metal studs. This isn't just any collar...it's one made for a giant.

"No way," Ramses says.

"Tough shit," I grin. "You already promised."

This is something I know about Ramses—he won't go back on his word. Even a promise made flippantly.

But he's looking at the collar with real discomfort.

I'm wondering if I should push this.

"I'll do it," Ramses says as if he's assuring himself. Then he looks at me, exposed and unguarded. "I'm worried you won't be attracted to me."

Now that I understand the problem, I almost want to laugh.

"Ramses, I promise you...That's the one thing you never have to worry about."

When he still looks apprehensive, I say, "I could go get Sadie's riding crop instead?"

Ramses laughs. "Alright, fair's fair."

That's what's so funny—he thinks I'm getting even for Minx. But this isn't for me at all.

I'm not doing this so Ramses can experience the degradation of being a pet. I'm doing it so he can experience the joy of being a good boy.

♪♪ *Kream—Iggy Azalea*

"Down on all fours."

Ramses takes his position on the carpet. I buckle the collar around his throat.

It's amazing how one single strap of leather can change everything.

The collar covers Ramses' neck, making his shoulders look broader and bulkier than ever. Naked on his knees, his body is beastly and powerful.

I run my hand down his back, feeling the thick slabs of muscle.

"Look at that body...You're so strong..."

Ramses tightens his frame, lifting his chin.

I run my hands down his arms, squeezing his shoulders, his biceps. "Your shoulders are like granite..." I run my palm down his flank, slapping him hard on the ass. "I bet you can't even feel that, can you?" I slap him again. "Can you?" He stays solid as stone, chin lifted, not even a wince. "No, not my Brutus..."

Ramses holds his position, but there's a change in his breathing.

I thought long and hard about what nickname would suit my lover best. I wanted to capture what's essential and animalistic in Ramses, just like he did for me.

"My Brutus is strong and powerful," I croon in his ear as I run my hands over his body, "Every room you enter, everyone's afraid of you..."

Brutus can't hold back. He turns his head against my neck, nuzzling, snarling, licking. His cock hangs down, heavy and full. I grab his head and rub my hands in his hair, rough and messy.

"Yes, you're my good boy...you're my best good boy..."

He's kissing me like an animal, licking with wild tongue. I've never seen him like this. He's feral, and it's awakening something truly depraved inside of me.

Domming Ramses isn't like domming anyone else. I've got a monster under my control.

I grab the ring on his collar and tug, leading him back toward the bedroom.

Brutus leaps on top of me on the mattress, smothering me with his mass. His mouth attacks my neck, hot and wet, while his cock jabs against my thigh. Sometimes, despite all the evidence right in my face, I forget how much stronger he is, how helpless I'd be if he really wouldn't stop.

"Alright, that's enough. That's enough!"

Obediently, he sits back on his heels and fists, awaiting instructions.

The sight sends heat raging through my brain. To have a creature like this—as devious, as determined, as powerful as him—at my beck and call is a rush like I've never experienced.

I could tell him to do anything.

"Lie back on the bed."

Brutus lies in the center of the mattress, no pillow under his head. I've taken all the pillows and chucked them overboard.

I can't get over how good he looks in that collar. Being honest, I was two percent worried this might be emasculating. Ramses and I have never switched roles like this—he's always been firmly in the dominant position, and I've never been the dom for my own pleasure, only as a job.

But he has *never* looked more powerful than he looks in that collar. His body is brutish and enormous, his face lean and ferocious.

I'm not just attracted to him. I'm fucking ravenous for this feeling of ownership and possession, for the all-consuming thrill of knowing I can do whatever I want with him and take my time...

Submission is a gift. The more powerful the person, the greater the gift.

Putting a collar on the man I admire most is setting my brain and my body on fire.

As I straddle Brutus' face, he looks up at me, pressing his nose into my pussy, inhaling deeply. He growls low in his throat.

I stroke my fingers through his hair, looking down at him.

"Put out your tongue."

He opens his mouth and puts out his tongue.

"Now hold it there while I ride."

Gripping the top of the headboard, I rock my hips, sliding my clit across the flat of his tongue. Each stroke is wet and warm and melting. I sink down on his mouth, pressing harder, grinding deeper.

I ride his face like a saddle, holding the top of the headboard, body moving like a wave. Pleasure rolls over me, along with something much darker—the desire to dominate.

I stare down into his eyes, the only thing visible as I smother him in pussy.

"Grab that thick cock," I say. "Stroke it in your hand."

He grunts his assent and grips his cock.

"Now match my pace."

Each roll of my hips is matched by the motion of his hand. I start slow at first, letting him build. Then I let go of the headboard and grasp his head between my palms while I fuck his face in earnest.

I've never ridden a face as hard as this, but Brutus can take it.

His fist hits his body with meaty slaps as he pumps his cock in time with my hips.

"You're waiting for me, aren't you, good boy? You're so controlled...you're the smartest, the best good boy....God, I fucking love you...No one could ever love me like you do. No one could ever take care of me like you do...I've never been spoiled like this. Your thoughtfulness, your surprise, your work, your intuition, your perception of everything I need...I *need* you to take care of me and protect me. Look how you spoil me, look at the life you built for me..."

I'm pouring praise on my Brutus, and I can see how his pupils expand, how his whole face flushes. His body shakes beneath me with each mighty stroke of his arm.

"And even when I was a bad master and I was scared, and yelling, and upset, didn't you come right back to me? Didn't you love me? Who's always been there for me?"

Brutus makes a smothered sound like a groan of pain and a sigh of deepest longing. Our eyes are locked, everything I feel and everything he feels flowing together.

Gripping the headboard with my right hand, I reach behind me with my left, taking that thick cock from Brutus and stroking it myself. His tongue pushes inside me while my hand slides up and down.

"Now, if you want to be the best good boy, I'm building up the biggest orgasm and I want you to come with me...but don't blow until I'm ready..."

I'm already ready, but I'm taking him right to the edge. I can't close my hand around his shaft, he's too swollen. His flesh is hot and pumping, just slippery enough for me to run my palm up and down.

"You're incredible," I say, looking down into his eyes. "I've never been so attracted, I've never felt pleasure like this...Are you ready?"

He makes a strangled, desperate sound.

"Then come for me."

His cock explodes in my hand. I stroke all the way over the head, using each fresh burst to create the hottest, wettest climax. Brutus shakes beneath me, his animal sounds smothered by my pussy.

I'm coming with him, as loud as I can, because that's what he needs to know he did a good job. It's not difficult—all I have to do is open my mouth and I'm speaking in tongues.

He grabs my hips with both hands, his chest heaving beneath

my ass, each jerk of his body sending a fresh pulse into mine. I'm clinging to the headboard for dear life as I milk the last drops from his cock.

When it's over, I take the collar off his sweat-drenched neck and I stroke the hair back from his face, kissing his messy mouth.

"How was that?"

Ramses looks like he got run over by a cement truck. He's sprawled out on the bed, his chest the color of brick, his expression dazed and glazed.

"Oh my god..."

It takes several more minutes before he's breathing steady.

"That was...fucking spectacular."

I've got an afterglow like Bikini Atoll. Every bit of me is radiant.

"I wasn't riding your face too hard?"

"*Never*. Literally kill me, that's how I want to go."

I'm so proud of myself for pulling that off, I feel like I just dunked on Jordan.

"You really liked it?"

Ramses shakes his head in amazement. "Men don't get praised by their dads, let alone their lovers. The way I felt with you looking down at me...I finally get it."

"Great," I tease, touching his limp, soaked cock. "You want to go again?"

"I can't," Ramses groans, lolling his head like he'll never walk again. "You finally did it. I'm spent."

He's truly distressed—he's never been outlasted before.

"I win." I'm gloating shamelessly. "But you can try again tomorrow."

EACH MENTOR TEACHES us something different.

Tabitha taught me how to use my gifts and how to take control of my life.

But the last lesson she taught me was the one that mattered most of all.

Tabitha did everything she could to protect herself from pain. But nothing stopped that fire raging through her mansion.

She didn't avoid all pain, she just avoided most of it. But to do it, she had to be muted. She lived a life of less emotion. Of treasures kept under glass.

Life will throw tragedy at you no matter what you do. So the question is, do you want someone with you when you go through it?

The benefit is that you have someone to share the positives. The downside is that you expose yourself to vulnerabilities. The other person can and *will* sometimes hurt you.

So, you'll have more pleasure, more pain, and you'll share it all with someone else.

Is that a good deal?

No.

It's the best deal you'll ever make.

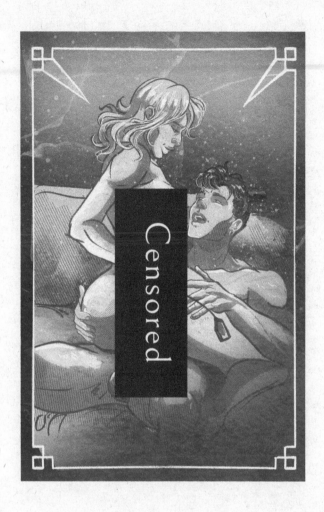

WONDERING WHAT HAPPENED ON BRIGGS & SADIE'S WILD NIGHT?

BRUTAL PRINCE

SOPHIE LARK

★★★★★ "By far the best hate to love/arranged marriage I've read." – Sylvie R. (Goodreads)

AUTHOR'S NOTE

This book includes the use of sexual slurs. I have the greatest respect for the erotic industries (selling sex is part of my job). The words used in Minx were chosen for realism and to illustrate how derogatory sexual terms are used to tear down women and diminish their accomplishments.

The depictions of Blake's autism are drawn from personal experience and my experiences with other woman on the spectrum, including my daughter, who is non-verbal but is one of the most brilliant little humans I've ever known. They are not meant to be descriptive of anyone but Blake.

ACKNOWLEDGMENTS

I have to thank Ry first and foremost. He contributes heavily to all my books, but as someone who started his career in finance, I particularly needed his help with Ramses' voice (not to mention the rest of the Minx "research").

I also want to thank our team, Arin, Brittany, and Maya, for all their incredible hard work, creative ideas, and emotional support when this business is trying to kill us.

For my assistant Kamrah, who saved me so many hours this year and helped me to not crash and burn as a mom, thank you for taking care of us.

Thank you to Emily Wittig as always for her gorgeous cover design!

And of course, infinite thanks to Line Eriksen, who brings so much inspiration and depth to the story with her incredible illustrations. She is my muse and a crucial part of the process from the very beginning of character design.

And finally, thank you to Dave Chapelle for spotlighting the book *Pimp* by Iceberg Slim in one of his specials, which provided fascinating, though often upsetting, psychological insight into sex work. It's not the only book I read for Minx, but it's the one that stuck in my head the hardest.

I started writing to create the kind of intelligent and powerful female characters I wanted to read about myself. When I moved into romance, my goal became to write relationships that are true partnerships between equals. My couples love each other because they're better and stronger together. Each of my books is different, but one theme remains: a life centered on self can never match the power of a life lived for love.

MERCH & SIGNED BOOKS → SOPHIELARK.COM

Instagram | TikTok
@SOPHIE_LARK_AUTHOR | @SOPHIELARKAUTHOR